# the Chinese Jars

a novel

by William C. Gordon

Bay Tree Publishing, LLC
Point Richmond, California

—

Calligraphy by Ward Schumaker
Cover design by Lori Barra and Sarah Kessler
Interior design by mltrees

Library of Congress Cataloging-in-Publication Data

Gordon, William C. (William Charles), 1937-
   The Chinese jars : a novel / by William C. Gordon.
      p. cm.
   Includes bibliographical references and index.
   ISBN 978-0-9819577-8-4 (alk. paper)
   1.  Deception--Fiction. 2.  Smuggling--Fiction. 3. Homicide--Fiction. 4.  Chinatown (San Francisco, Calif.)--Fiction. 5.  San Francisco (Calif.)--Fiction. I. Title.
   PS3607.O5947C55 2011
   813'.6--dc22
                                        2011032003

**This book is dedicated to
San Francisco's Chinatown.**

# Table of Contents

1    Reginald Rockwood III   8

2    Camelot   25

3    Virginia Dimitri Entertains Xsing Ching   35

4    Rafael Garcia   44

5    Blanche   53

6    Samuel Starts Digging   60

7    Rafael in a Muddle   86

8    Xsing Ching Surrenders   93

9    The Missing Page   100

10    The King of Wands   115

11    Rafael's Luck Runs Out   125

12    Something's Cooking   138

13    Chinatown Mourns   159

14    Mathew Tries to Deal   182

15    Everybody's Two Cents   188

16    Rafael and Mathew   208

17    Samuel Takes Charge   220

18    Samuel Holds Court   250

# 1

## Reginald Rockwood III

Reginald Rockwood III died today at the age of 35. He was an heir to the fortune of one of California's wealthiest families. Born in San Francisco in 1925, he attended the Cate Preparatory School and the University of California, Berkeley, where he graduated with honors. He served with distinction in the armed forces of the United States, and was decorated for bravery during the Korean War. His parents and a sister, Mrs. Eugene Haskell of Palo Alto, survive him. Services will be held at Grace Cathedral this coming Tuesday.

IT WAS A CRISP autumn day in San Francisco in 1960, and John F. Kennedy had just been elected president. Samuel Hamilton was sitting at the large round table at the front of Camelot, his favorite bar. Little did the public know the bar's name would soon be co-opted by pundits to describe Kennedy's short reign. It was the table he had shared with Reginald almost every night for the last two years.

Samuel, a transplant from Nebraska, was a mix of Scottish and German ancestry. He had dropped out of Stanford at the end of his second year after his parents were mugged and murdered by unknown assailants. That, however, was not his only woe. While in mourning, he had gotten drunk and driven head-on into another car, badly injuring a young woman. He would have gone to jail had it not been for the maneuverings of a young San Francisco lawyer. As a result of the accident, Samuel had lost his driving privileges for three years, which further plunged him into a darkness that he was still unable to exit.

He read with sadness the words in the obit column of the local newspaper, where he worked selling classified ads. Rockwell's death did not help his state of mind. Unable to shake his parents' demise or the accident, he had been wandering aimlessly for the past six years, nursing the depression that seemed to follow him and that served as an excuse for his lack of purpose. And now this!

With Reginald's death, Samuel had lost his drinking buddy and the person he'd gotten used to commiserating with. Samuel had listened with admiration and a certain envy to Reginald's stories of world travel and his conquest of exotic females in every corner of the globe. They'd even talked about the possibility of taking an adventurous trip together. For someone in Samuel's condition, Reginald was a life raft.

He scratched his head of fast-receding red hair in puzzlement, drawing deeply on his unfiltered cigarette. His baggy sports coat, its sleeves freckled with burn holes, hung limply from his shoulders, which were flaked with dandruff. Everything about him stood in sharp contrast to the dapper Rockwood, who'd been a handsome and charming man in spite of the disdainful smile that often twisted his expression.

Samuel recalled the deep lines around the corners of Reginald's mouth and eyes—eyes that had begun to protrude slightly, probably because of the fast life he led. Not that the lines had detracted at all from his distinctive looks: he was slim and long-boned, with heavy eyelids, well-defined eyebrows, and a full head of black hair that was always slicked back. He looked like an Italian movie actor, and in Samuel's estimation he was an immaculate dresser. In fact, he never saw Reginald wearing anything other than a tux. Sometimes he even wondered if Reginald's dress wasn't out of place, but he never dared mention it. Who was he to have an opinion about fashion? His friend was a nocturnal creature and Samuel assumed he circulated in high society, where a tuxedo, perhaps, was appropriate. He flicked the ashes of his cigarette toward the ashtray but missed. A few spilled onto the table while the rest floated gently to the floor.

It was eleven o'clock on Saturday morning. Outside the bar, one could gaze at the San Francisco Bay and watch the cable cars as they turned and made their way down Nob Hill toward the other side of the busy city, their bells clanging. On cold and windy days like this one, the conductors provided blankets for passengers who wanted to cover their exposed legs.

Samuel was the only one at the table that morning. He called to Melba, one of Camelot's owners. She was a woman in her early fifties, but she looked older; smoking, drinking and hard work had worn her out. She had the coarse voice of a sailor, and her only sign of vanity was the blue tint in her gray hair. In the bar's dim light her coif looked like a wig.

"Did you know that Reginald Rockwood died?"

"Yeah, I read the obituary in the paper," she said. "What happened to him?"

"I don't know."

"He was an asshole when he was alive, so he's an asshole when he's dead," she muttered.

"What?" exclaimed Samuel. "I thought he was well-liked and

respected here. He certainly had an air of success about him."

"Bullshit. The guy was always wandering around in that fucking tux like he was on the way to some debutante party. But let's face it, if he was really successful, he wouldn't have spent his time here."

Samuel was perturbed but chose to ignore the obvious slap at regulars like him. "You're just mad because Reginald owed you $200, and now you probably won't get your money." He eyed her thoughtfully. "Or do you know something about him that I don't?"

"Just a feeling," replied Melba. "Just a feeling."

"Based on what?" asked Samuel.

"That the guy was a prick and tighter than a mule's ass. He was here every night of the week and he never bought anybody a drink, not even himself. He was a loser."

"You're just pissed because he never gave you a tip."

"It's more than that. I bet you didn't ever see him eat, other than at the hors d'oeuvre table in the back there."

"That's true. But he was always on his way to some big party. He'd have the invitation in his jacket pocket, and he'd drop in here for a nibble and a drink beforehand."

"Okay, I'll make you a bet," said Melba. "Ten bucks says you can't find one person this guy ever spent a dime on."

"What d'ya mean? He was going to take me to Morocco. He'd already bought the plane tickets. At least that's what he told me on more than one occasion."

"Yeah, sure," laughed Melba. "Show 'em to me."

"Okay, I'll take your bet," said Samuel. He gave her one of his infectious smiles that shone from his face when he was happy or when he thought he'd won a significant coup, such as his bet with Melba. He had no idea how he could prove that Reginald actually had those tickets.

Samuel settled down and returned to his reverie. He lit another cigarette and sipped his Scotch—which he always drank on the rocks—and reflected on the fact that he'd spent a lot of time talking with Reginald and had thought he knew him. He'd found him to be a sensitive and intelligent person who had some insight into the world and its complex problems. He certainly didn't see him as a cheapskate or a loser, as Melba suggested, or he wouldn't have hung around him. Even she must have trusted Reginald a little, since she'd loaned him what Samuel considered a lot of money. And he would have stuck to that opinion and gone on with his mediocre life had he not gone to the service for Reginald at Grace Cathedral the following Tuesday.

\* \* \*

Samuel arrived early, assuming it would be crowded, but he found the church deserted. He waited for the appointed hour, and still there was no service and no sign of anyone even interested in one. He went to the front of the church and checked the log of activities for the day, but nothing was listed for Reginald Rockwood. Figuring he had gotten the date wrong, he asked an avuncular priest he found wandering around if he knew anything about the deceased. The clergyman searched the church record; he showed Samuel that no service was scheduled for Mr. Rockwood that day or at any time in the past or the future.

Samuel went back to Camelot. Melba was just coming on shift. He explained to her what he had just been through.

"Reginald probably planted that obit himself and then skipped town because he owed so much money." Samuel thought she was thinking of the $200 she'd lost.

"What about the body?" asked Samuel.

"That's the thing. Are you sure the cadaver is Rockwood? He's not the only guy in the city who dresses in a tuxedo.

"Someone must have identified him," said Samuel.

"Maybe he was involved in an accident," said Melba.

Samuel didn't know what to make of it. He downed two double Scotches on the rocks and made his way uneasily back to his den on the edge of Chinatown, at the corner of Powell and Pacific. It was a small place with only enough space for a pull-down bed, a sofa, and a table, and it was badly in need of a cleaning. He hung his laundry on a wire strung across the room. There was also a little kitchen, which he never used, and a bathroom with rusty faucets. It wasn't a palace but there was no reason to complain. A whole family of Chinese could live in an apartment this size.

He staggered up the stairs, went to bed, and didn't wake up until the next morning.

\* \* \*

After finishing his ablutions he went for a cup of weak coffee and a pastry at Chop Suey Louie's, the local Chinese bargain café near his flat. He said hello to his friend, the proprietor, and received a broad smile in return. Louie's mother was there, as usual, sitting at a table near the door keeping an eye on the clients. The little old lady had been in San Francisco for thirty years, but she thought she was still in Canton. She didn't speak a word of English, and she never ventured outside of Chinatown. Louie, on the other hand, spoke English without an accent and was so proud of being an American that his restaurant was decorated with American flags and photographs of him and soldiers he'd served with in the army in the Second World War and Korea. He was about Samuel's height and had black bushy hair; a round, kind, acne-scarred face; and an amiable personality that gained him more clientele than his kitchen merited.

The twelve tables of his small restaurant were all draped with blue oilcloth coverings. On each was a bottle of soy sauce, a saltshaker, a pepper container, and a chrome paper napkin holder. The counter where Samuel usually sat had six seats that faced a large aquarium covering almost the entire back wall in front of the kitchen. The tropical fish that swam among the carefully tended tank flora had a hypnotic effect on him. Sometimes he would come in just to watch them.

After his morning infusion, he caught the Hyde Street cable car to its terminus at the end of Powell Street and walked the few blocks to his job at the newspaper located at Third and Market, setting his watch to the clock in the tower of the Ferry Building at the foot of Market. His office, which he shared with five other ad salesmen, was in the basement of the twenty-story building that housed the giant journal. He walked down two flights of dimly lit stairs and when he finally reached the hallway, he felt grateful that the ceiling fan was working that day. It took away some of the musty smell that usually lingered there. He opened the opaque glass door with black bold letters that spelled "Advertising Department". He flicked on the fluorescent light, which gave a greenish hue to the windowless room. Five desks were crammed into a space that should have accommodated two; each one was piled high with telephone directories and stacks of papers. Some had been there for a long time. He looked through his messages, all of which were pretty mundane: mostly promises to buy an ad at some undetermined future date. He tried to focus, but Reginald Rockwood's ghost haunted him. Why wouldn't a dead guy show up for his own funeral? He started thinking about what Melba had said about Rockwood planning his own disappearance. He went down to talk to the clerk in the obit department. He had the clipping in hand. "Do you remember anything about this?" he asked, showing it to the clerk.

The clerk absentmindedly took the clipping and disappeared into the back room. While he was waiting, Samuel tried to smooth the wrinkles out of his white shirt and the sleeves of his beige sport coat. The ashes of his cigarette fell on the floor, and the overhead fan scattered them into the corners of the small stuffy office.

The clerk came back with the file. "I remember the guy who brought this in: impossible to forget him. He was dressed to kill, in a tux, no less. He said his brother died, and he wanted to make sure we ran it on Saturday. The only thing that ticked me off was that he wanted to be served like a prince, but the SOB didn't even give me a tip."

"A tux, huh?" repeated Samuel, taking another drag on his cigarette. "Can you describe him? What color was his hair?"

"Real black, slicked back, brown eyes. Very handsome man."

"How tall?"

"Tall, and well-built."

"Did he leave an address?"

"Sure did. A fancy one, way down on Broadway in Pacific Heights."

Samuel wrote it down. When he left, he was puzzled. He began to think Reginald really had come in with his own obituary.

He shot up the stairs and went out onto the street. It had started to drizzle, and he didn't have a raincoat. He caught the Third Street trolley bus, which took him across Market and up Kearney, where he transferred to a Pacific Avenue bus right at the foot of Chinatown. Here even the smell was different. The sterile scent of the financial district was replaced by soy and ginger, and he could almost taste the noodles he knew were steaming in the Chinese kitchens that now surrounded him.

The bus lifted over the hill and across Van Ness into the neighborhood where he thought Reginald lived. He rang the doorbell of the stately mansion with Greek columns on the front porch. When the large, ornately carved mahogany door stained a deep dark walnut opened slowly, he found himself staring down at a pleasant-looking Chinese maid in a black dress covered by a starched white apron, who stared back at him through wire-frame glasses.

"Yes, sir. Help you?" she asked.

"My name is Hamilton. I'm from the local newspaper. I'm trying to run down a story on Reginald Rockwood III. Our records indicate he lived here."

"No, no. That man no live here," she responded.

"Did you know him, at least?" he asked, sounding relieved.

"That man came to party here. Vely hungry. Eat lots of free food and free drink from the trays, and then leave."

"When was this?"

"Three months ago."

"How is it you remember him?"

"I remember everybody that come here, including name. He tall, handsome, for white devil. Black hair. Vely hungry. Eat everything, then go."

"Do you know where he lives or where he came from?"

"No, no. Just come to party. Never saw him before. He had invitation."

"Can I talk to the lady of the house?" he asked.

"Not here. Leave card, maybe she calls you."

Samuel gave her his card.

"Welcome, sir," and she closed the big door.

\* \* \*

Samuel had time to think on his bus ride back downtown. It was becoming clear that his friend had written his own obituary. He realized that it was probably all lies but he couldn't figure out why Reginald would do such a thing. Melba's doubts rang in his ears. He certainly wouldn't do it to get out of repaying $200. Surely he owed more than that or had other serious problems. What did he know about the guy? Not much, really.

He got off the bus when it stopped in front of the newspaper office, went downstairs, and sought out a friend of his who was a reporter on the police beat. He found him pounding away on his typewriter, his fingers smudged with black ink from the carbon paper. He explained to him what he'd found out.

"Try the medical examiner. They investigate deaths," the reporter said.

Twenty minutes later, Samuel was at the medical examiner's office right behind the new Hall of Justice, where all the criminal courts were located.

"Is the boss in?" he asked the clerk, an emaciated young man with yellow teeth.

"He's with someone right now. It'll be about fifteen minutes. Who should I say is calling?"

"Samuel Hamilton. I was sent over here by the reporter on the police beat; I work for the newspaper."

"Maybe I can help you?"

"We're looking into the death of Reginald Rockwood III. Does the name ring a bell?"

"Yeah, it sure does. I was fussing around with that one for a while, but the boss took it over personally. They say the guy was a socialite."

"What d'ya mean, 'they say'?" asked Samuel.

"Take it up with the boss," said the clerk. "He's free now."

Samuel walked into the medical examiner's office. He was a tall, shabby-appearing man, with the melancholy air of a turtle, dressed in a white medical jacket with a nameplate. There were anatomy charts displaying different parts of the human body, and in one of the corners stood a real skeleton, on which he'd placed a French beret.

"The clerk tells me you're inquiring about Reginald

Rockwood," the examiner said.

"He's the one. Some things about this guy just don't make sense," Samuel confessed. "You know, he planted his own obituary a few days before he died."

"Well, the body we've got here is him, all right. The fingerprints check out."

"What was the cause of death?" asked Samuel.

"Suicide. He jumped in front of a trolley bus. But he needn't have bothered; he was a pretty sick young man. The autopsy showed that he had a liver the size of a football. I guess he knew what was coming and took a shortcut."

Samuel shook his head in disbelief. "I went to the address he left as his own, but the maid said he never lived there."

"Really? We haven't found a home address yet. Did they know who he was?"

"Only that he went to a party there three months ago," answered Samuel.

"We called the Haskell woman, the one he claimed was his sister, but she never heard of him," said the examiner.

"I'll cross her off my list," said Samuel. "Do you know if and where he worked?"

"Not a clue," said the examiner. "He was admitted to San Francisco General on Friday night, but he was in a coma, according to the records. He died on Saturday morning without regaining consciousness. No one's claimed the body yet. And from what I gather, no one will."

"You have his body here?" asked Samuel, surprised.

"This is the morgue. Where else would it be?"

"Can I see it? He was a special friend of mine, and it would mean a lot to me."

The turtle face expressed doubt for a moment. "This is a little out of the ordinary, but I suppose we could use a physical ID for the record. Follow me."

Together they walked down the hall, through some

swinging double doors, and entered the morgue. They went through another door on the right side of the hallway into a room full of what looked like stainless steel boxes stacked four high along three of the walls. Each was eighteen inches square and had a number on it. On a desk right next to the entrance door was a ledger book and a notepad. The examiner looked up the name Rockwell and wrote a number on the pad, then ripped it off and walked down the row of squares until he reached number twenty-five. He rechecked the number.

"You're not suffering from heart trouble or anything like that, are you?" he asked Samuel.

"No, sir. I admit, though, I haven't seen a dead person since my parents died a few years ago."

"You're sure you want to see it."

"Yes, sir. It's important to me."

"Okay, you asked for it," and he opened the drawer.

Samuel saw a white sheet covering the outline of a body on a metal tray. He felt the cold air from the open box. The examiner stopped pulling when the drawer was about three feet out, then slowly peeled back the sheet to expose the head and shoulders to just below the nipples.

"That's him," said Samuel, when he was able to speak after a long pause. He expected to see Reginald's smiling face as he remembered it, but the violent death had smashed that face to bits. Samuel supposed that he'd fallen in front of the trolley bus and been dragged along the asphalt. His nose was flattened and one of his cheekbones was caved in; but it was his friend: the same black hair, well-defined eyebrows, and refined lips. He saw the autopsy stitches on his torso in between his breasts.

"That's awful," he murmured.

"What did I tell you?"

"What do these bruises on his arms mean? They look like someone had a pretty strong grip on him."

# The Chinese Jars

"I wouldn't put too much emphasis on those," said the examiner. "He was in a coma for several hours before he died. Obviously, the nursing staff was moving him around." He waited a few seconds then asked, "Seen enough?"

"Yeah, thanks. You understand, don't you? He was a good friend of mine."

"I understand," said the examiner, covering the body and pushing it back into its place.

On the way back to the office, Samuel asked, "What'll happen to the body?"

"We'll hold it for a month or so; if it's not claimed or there's no other problems, we donate it to science. They always need cadavers at the University of California Medical School.

"I have one more favor to ask," said Samuel. "Can I go through his belongings?"

"That's sort of against the rules, too; but what the hell. We'll say you're helping to solve the mystery."

He picked up the phone and told the clerk to let Samuel see the property file. In a few minutes the clerk entered with a garment bag containing a tuxedo, a shirt, socks, and underwear; and a plastic bag with a wallet, watch, cuff links and studs for a dress shirt, an almost empty pack of cigarettes, a Zippo lighter, and seventeen dollars in cash.

"Help yourself. You can use the evidence room right through there. Make yourself at home."

"Thanks. I'll report back if I find anything that might help," said Samuel.

When he looked at the pile of stuff in front of him, tears welled up in his eyes. He didn't cry easily, but it made him sad to think that this was all that was left of the poor bastard. He wiped his eyes with his sleeve, realizing he just couldn't turn and leave, as he had wanted to.

Instead, he started methodically going through the wallet. There was no driver's license, only a social security card and a photo of a younger Reginald in an army uniform. He had lieutenant's bars on his shoulders, but Samuel couldn't tell if they were silver or gold. Next, he searched the pockets of his tuxedo and found an invitation to a party for the night Reginald had apparently jumped in front of the trolley bus. It was to an exclusive cocktail bash in Pacific Heights at the home of a wealthy industrialist. The invitation was engraved at Engel's of San Francisco, an upscale printing establishment on Sacramento Street in the financial district. There was an RSVP number on it, so Samuel interrupted his search and called the number. They'd never heard of Reginald Rockwood III, and they had no idea why he would have an invitation. He certainly wasn't invited.

In the autopsy folder, in addition to the examiner's findings, was a one-page police report that indicated Rockwood had suddenly appeared in front of a trolley bus right by General Hospital, and the driver couldn't stop.

He went back into the medical examiner's office and told him what he had learned. "I'll go over to the printers and let you know if I find out anything new. Thanks for sharing," said Samuel, as he left.

\* \* \*

Engel's was on Sacramento Street a few blocks east of Montgomery, close to the Embarcadero, which ran next to the bay. Samuel pushed open the door and found himself in a nicely furnished waiting room with Piranesi engravings of old Rome on all the walls. There was no one at the reception desk, so he rang the bell. Almost immediately an attractive young woman dressed in a severe two-piece suit appeared and asked if she could be of service.

"My name is Samuel Hamilton. I work for the local newspaper," he said, surprised at his own audacity. "We're doing a story on a young man by the name of Reginald Rockwood. Do you know who I'm talking about?"

"You'd better talk to Mr. Engel." She dialed the phone. "Someone's here inquiring about Mr. Rockwood." Then she turned back to Samuel. "He'll be right with you."

A distinguished elderly man soon appeared, elegantly dressed in a dark three-piece suit but with a wide and bright tie. He greeted Samuel with professional courtesy. "You're inquiring about Reginald Rockwood? He worked here, but we haven't seen him in several days."

"You apparently haven't heard the news," responded Samuel.

"What news?" inquired the old man.

"He died on Saturday."

"Oh, my goodness. How unexpected. He was young and apparently healthy," Engel commented.

"Can I talk with you in private?" asked Samuel.

He was ushered down an endless hallway to an office decorated with photographs of Engel alongside prominent social and political figures. The man offered him a seat. He seemed upset by the bad news.

"I didn't want to discuss the details of his death in front of your employee."

"How did he die?"

"Looks like he committed suicide on Friday."

"Good Heavens! Why would he do that?" he asked searchingly. "You know, he was here on Friday as usual, and then didn't show up again. We were wondering what'd become of him."

"What did he do for you?" asked Samuel.

"He was our night janitor."

"Janitor?" Samuel asked, in disbelief. "I always saw him dressed in a tuxedo."

"A tuxedo? That explains it," said Engel. "Here he mopped

the floors and took out the trash for almost four years." He was about to continue but Samuel interrupted him.

"Do you have an address for him or his kin?" asked Samuel.

"We did have an address and a phone number, but when he didn't show up on Monday, we called the number and it was out of service. We sent a man out to the address. It turned out nobody lived there; it was a vacant lot. Then we started to worry because we thought that he'd left town for some mysterious reason, so we changed the locks on all the doors.

"That's when we had a big surprise. We opened the broom closet where all the supplies are kept, and we found four tuxedos, a mini dresser full of his undergarments, and a shaving kit. There was even a sleeping bag tucked in one corner. He must have been sleeping in there."

"Did you have any idea this was going on?" asked Samuel.

"None whatsoever."

"If I understand your business, Mr. Engel, you do a lot of engraving for the socially prominent in the city?"

"That's correct. For four generations we've taken care of the upper crust, and we do so with pride," he answered.

"Is it possible that Mr. Rockwood was taking an invitation from each of the engravings your company made and attending the corresponding social events, pretending to be an invited guest?"

"Well, anything's possible," said Engel. Samuel could see that he was disturbed by the possibility that if this were made public, it would damage the prestige of his firm.

"Let me show you what I mean," said Samuel, taking out the obituary clipping and handing it to him. Engel read it quickly and turned even paler.

"It's beginning to make sense now. In the closet we also found a box of invitations from the past four years. They were filed in alphabetical order and had notes and phone numbers on them. It was as if he were making some kind of a record for reference purposes."

"So the guy was actually living in your broom closet and feeding himself at your clients' parties? No wonder his liver was shot," said Samuel. "Did you find any plane tickets to Morocco, by any chance?" he asked.

"Nothing like that in his belongings. I would have noticed."

"You've been a big help, Mr. Engel. Would you like me to let you know if I find out anything?"

"It would be greatly appreciated, young man. Mr. Rockwell was a pleasant employee. We'd like to know what happened to him."

Samuel walked out of the engraving shop and confronted the afternoon traffic. The man was a cheapskate and probably a phony, he mumbled. His own dream of going to Morocco had gone to hell, and he'd lost the bet to Melba. He got on a bus, rode it up to Nob Hill, and walked to Camelot. He entered with his head hung low and took a seat at the bar in front of Melba.

"How did you know that Reginald was an imposter?" he asked.

"Did you ever look at his hands? They didn't go with tuxedos and that air of grandeur. They were the hands of a working man."

Samuel took a ten-dollar bill out of his wallet; he slapped it on the bar and walked out.

The sound of Melba's laugh followed him.

# 2

## Camelot

IF YOU LIVED in San Francisco, you knew the place. Unlike any other neighborhood bar you've ever been in, it was right next to the cable car tracks on a corner that overlooked San Francisco Bay. With its steel colored waters, its slick sailboats, the sinister profile of Alcatraz prison on its lonely island, and one of its famous bridges, the view of the bay through the window from the front of the bar was breathtaking. When the sun was shining, the park's green lawns directly across the street glimmered softly and in contrast with the reflection of the water and the color of the sky. In summer the sun disappeared behind blankets of fog that rolled over the hills from the Pacific Ocean and engulfed the city and the Golden Gate. In winter there were days when the view looked like it was painted in gray watercolors.

Evening was the busiest time at Camelot. It filled up with locals and tourists alike. People had their own reasons for coming there, but it usually wasn't for the glamour of the place or the spectacular view. There was a mysterious bond that held a handful of the regular patrons together, and an unexpected kindness in the ambiance that excited those outsiders who decided to drop in, and motivated them to return.

Inside the front door was a round table that seated twelve

comfortably. Further in, a semicircular bar fit another twelve, and the rest of the clientele could sit at the smaller tables. Behind the bar was a large mirror that went all the way up to the fifteen-foot ceiling and let one see the whole bar from any angle. Glass shelves going part way up contained exotic liquors, some with such suspicious colors that no one dared try them. Below them, and accessible to the locals, was the usual well stock, which Melba, one of the owner's, called the "rotgut trough."

Standing in the middle of the semicircle was Mathew O'Hara, a silent partner in the establishment. He was making his nightly appearance. Melba guessed that he was coming direct from London and some big business meeting, dressed in a dark blue suit, a white linen shirt, and a silk tie with matching handkerchief in the upper left pocket. His full head of brown hair was closely cropped, which gave him a military air. His shaggy eyebrows accentuated his hazel eyes. Even though he could gain a stranger's confidence with his easy smile, he projected authority. He looked like the epitome of success. He was born into it. For him it was easy—all the money one could ask for, the best prep schools, association with the highest social class, and all the connections a good family could buy in California. He took his position in society for granted. He had a wife of equal pedigree, and three spoiled daughters in the best Catholic school in San Francisco. He appeared to be one of the pillars of the city's elite, at least on the surface; only a few suspected the dark side of his character.

He bragged of his good luck and skill in making money, which allowed him to increase what he had inherited. His great-grandfather had started the trend during the gold rush. Toiling in the streams of the foothills, he was different from the others and soon saw that it was more lucrative to supply the miners than to be one of them. His grandfather speculated in sugar and his father in petroleum exploration. All the men in the family had in common the talent to make money fast, the ruthlessness required for that pursuit, and a total lack of scruples about to how to spend it.

Matt, as he preferred to be called, had an additional quality, which his forbearers lacked and that gained him respect from his peers, even the shady ones. He was a man of his word. With him there was no need to sign papers: a handshake was enough; but anyone who crossed him would pay a huge price. He won fame for his honesty, thanks to gestures that didn't cost him much but left a good impression. When he ended up with more money than was his due on small deals, he sent his loyal chauffer back with the unearned extra and a word of apology. That kind of honesty was almost unheard of in those sub-worlds; it was appreciated though seldom imitated. As he saw it, it was good business. But for the big business deals that he carried out in other circles, he was pitiless.

O'Hara felt strong and healthy. He was in the prime of his life. His businesses were booming and his family wasn't causing him any problems. He and his wife led independent lives, each concentrating on their own interests, but he couldn't complain because she handled the domestic part with efficiency; she was a good social companion and she didn't ask questions. But he didn't, either. He could have been a contented man, but his greed got in the way.

On this particular day, Mathew was in deep conversation with Maestro Bob, a part-time magician, part-time notary seated next to him at the bar. Maestro was an old-fashioned gentleman. He had absurdly named himself Roberto, and given himself the title Count Maestro de Guinesso Bacigalupi, Slotnik de Transylvania, to further his career as a magician, even though only he could pronounce it. His real name was Robert Murphy. He was a black Irishman from County Cork. No one could remember his title or even wanted to, so everyone called him Maestro Bob. He spoke in a fake Slavic accent and wore dark pinstripe suits, which would have been considered stylish at one time but were now passé and a little tattered at the edges.

He was just over five feet tall, had unruly black hair and the waxed mustache of a lion tamer from the circus. His fingernails were professionally done and were so highly polished that the lights of the bar reflected off them.

Maestro had tried in the past to make a living as a magician and clairvoyant, but he failed due to his drinking. The adults in the Pacific Heights party world got fed up with him, so he was relegated to doing children's birthday parties on the weekends, where the grownups made sure there was no booze. He found his niche with the children and became a favorite on the kid's birthday-party circuit. They were attracted to his fantastic stories about witches and magic spells. However, he couldn't get by just doing that. Needing to make additional money, he studied for his notary license and opened a small office in the Flood Building at 870 Market. It was home to most of the foreign consulates in the city, and many patrons visited his small office to have official papers notarized to send to their home countries. But that never became his calling; he was interested only in exploring the frontiers of psychic phenomenon.

After five o'clock every evening, he frequented the bars of San Francisco, trying to fool loneliness. He had established himself as a favorite at Camelot, where his talents were fully appreciated. There, he would hold court, telling fortunes for a drink or two or, if the traffic would bear it, a ten-spot. But his instincts were good, especially regarding money, and the patrons returned with regularity when they had a pressing problem, especially concerning money.

So it was no surprise that Mathew O'Hara bought Maestro a drink and then another while describing to him in very general terms a deal he was working on. When he thought that Maestro had heard enough, he popped the question.

"What's your hunch, Maestro?"

"I need to see more of the picture before I can give you an answer," responded Maestro.

"What else do you need to know?" Mathew didn't want to give too many details away. He liked to keep his cards pretty close to the vest.

"That's not up to me. You give me the information you want me to have, then I have a vision based on what you tell me. Sometimes I have the vision based on what you don't tell me," he laughed. "So, for now, I see nothing and I hear nothing."

"There's a lot of money involved in this, and the merchandise comes from outside the country. I want to know whether or not I should do it."

"I think I see a lot of zeros."

"How many?"

"Divining is an art, not an exact science, but I see between five and six zeros," said the magician with great hesitation because he wasn't capable of imagining that much money. "But I can't tell if you're paying it or receiving it."

"Thanks. I'll stew on that," said Mathew.

Although he wasn't superstitious, he'd gotten the answer he wanted. He thought the maximum he could make on the deal was a million, and that was the figure that he was hoping would pop out of Maestro Bob's mouth. The strange little magician had a reputation for never being wrong; if he was right, Mathew was going to make a big profit. He gave Maestro a five-dollar tip and signaled Melba to serve the little man another drink. He said good night and walked out.

At the bar, Maestro savored his drink until he realized that he couldn't mooch another free one there. So he moved to the round table near the entrance, ready to keep company with Samuel Hamilton, the sloppy ad salesman from the morning paper, who was also a regular.

"Still grieving over Reginald?" Maestro inquired, eyeing the rumpled pack of Philip Morris Samuel had on the table.

"Yeah, it's taking me some time to get over it. Did you see that coming, Maestro?"

"I only saw the darkness; I couldn't see the end. But I suppose with all those negative forces at work, he was predestined to die in a bad way. Are you taking care of yourself, young man?" he asked.

"That's not my style," answered Samuel.

"Cheer up. I'll see you tomorrow, when I hope you'll be feeling better." Maestro was through for the night. Samuel offered him a cigarette; Maestro took three, then left.

\* \* \*

Melba Sundling, the official owner of Camelot, was a piece of work. Mathew had chosen her carefully because she had experience, good references, and he'd been told she could keep her mouth shut. She came from a tough Irish neighborhood in the Mission and grew up in a poor immigrant family with bad luck. They were hard-working, hard-drinking, blue-collar people. She now lived on upper Castro Street, where the gay population would thrive in the coming years.

She was married briefly to a journeyman marine engineer, who died of alcoholism within three years, but not before giving her a daughter whom they named Blanche. She remembered him with gratitude because he left her with her child, whom she adored. She'd held every kind of job imaginable in her youth, from factory worker to waitress, and she'd even had a short stint as a prostitute. No job was unbearable if it helped her support her daughter. Eventually, she left that profession because she decided she wanted to choose the people she slept with. She didn't want to charge for something she would give away under the right circumstances. Then she opened a bar in the Mission.

Mathew got her name from one of his attorneys. At their first meeting he was blunt, thereby establishing the tone of their future relationship. He invited her to his luxurious office in downtown San Francisco. Melba, who was getting on in years, was still an attractive woman, but it was obvious that her dress was secondhand and too small for her. She made an effort to put on an ugly hat and matching gloves, but her shoes didn't fit right and she had runs in her stockings. Her first physical impression wasn't good, but O'Hara knew immediately he was with a person of great character.

"I'm looking for someone to be a partner in a bar on Nob Hill. I just received as payment for a debt. I took the place because I realized I'd never get my money back if I didn't. But I don't know anything about the bar business. It's also not a good idea for people to know that I own such a place. So I prefer that someone else manage it. This someone else has to be a person in whom I have absolute confidence.

"What's in it for me?" asked Melba.

"I'll make you a fifty percent partner."

"Fifty percent? That's unheard of. There's something fishy here, buster. You gotta be hiding something illegal. I ain't no saint, but up 'til now I ain't had no problems with the cops," she said, as her face reddened and she got up to leave.

"Hold it! I'm serious. There's nothing illegal, but there is one condition," he said.

"Yeah, nothing's cheap or free," she chuckled, sitting down.

"Here's what I propose. I want the bar to be in your name only, and the same for the liquor license. Our arrangement is on a handshake. My lawyer says I can count on you that way."

"What do I have to do for this little gift?"

"I want $500 a month from you, in cash. That's all."

# The Chinese Jars

"That's it? That's not such a little bit considering the bar business is tough. How do you know I know how to run a bar?"

"You've done all right with your place in the Mission, haven't you?"

She laughed. "It's a hell of a lot different running a dive for a bunch of neighborhood drunks in the Mission, and running a joint on Nob Hill for the rich."

"Don't worry. I'll give you access to a bookkeeper and whatever legal and management expertise you need."

"I have my own bookkeeper," said Melba, "and I trust her. She's my daughter."

"Fine with me. How the bar is run is of no interest to me. The only thing that concerns me is that I get the $500."

So the deal was made on a handshake. She closed her place in the Mission and moved uptown.

Melba was a natural. Once she was installed as the proprietor of Camelot, which had been as somber as a funeral parlor, it didn't take long before the place was doing well. She had a warm and engaging personality, in spite of her rough exterior and gravelly voice. Her cordiality allowed people to forget her defects, which were many.

She came with her pathetic dog, an Airedale mutt with a missing ear and tail. For reasons unknown, most of the patrons adopted him as a mascot and some of them even ventured in just to say hello or give the scrawny animal a bone. Once inside, they would, of course, buy a drink. In keeping with her new venture at Camelot, she renamed him Excalibur—his original name was Alfred—and threw a party for his baptism on a Friday night. Drinks were on the house for fifteen minutes, but the crowd stayed for hours and the cash registers filled to overflowing. One of the reasons was that Melba showed Excalibur off. It seems that he had a super snout. Melba would make a patron hide a dollar somewhere in the bar, then let the dog smell the person's hand. She would release the dog, and he would pick up the scent and find the money, without fail.

Besides her daughter as her bookkeeper, she brought Rafael Garcia with her as her janitor and sometimes bouncer. Her biggest fear was that her bartenders would steal money and liquor. Rafael, whom she totally trusted, would help her prevent that by counting the take and the bottles at the end of the night and comparing one with the other. He was Mexican with Indian features, almost six feet tall, well-built, just muscles and sinew, without an ounce of fat on his wiry frame. He inspired fear in others, but at his core he was very sentimental. He had a private vice: he loved romance novels. They were sent to him from Mexico and he read them in secret. Melba loved him like a son and scolded him like one, too.

\* \* \*

"Why would Reginald commit suicide? It wasn't like him," Samuel asked Melba.

"Maybe it wasn't suicide." She was scratching the dog where he lacked an ear. "Why do you always growl at Samuel?"

"Are you sure you have a good hold of that dog, Melba? If that fucking lame pooch of yours bites me, I'll sue you."

"Just ignore him. He'll get used to you and you'll like him. You notice he also growls at Mathew O'Hara. You should be grateful I have such a good watchdog."

Samuel shook his head. "Why do you think that Reginald didn't commit suicide?"

"I didn't say that. I said maybe it wasn't suicide. I think Reginald was in over his head, playing out of his league, if you know what I mean."

"I don't have the slightest idea what you're talking about," said Samuel.

"You lack imagination. You're stuck in the ad department

of that rag you work for, but I know that you want to be a reporter. Why on earth, I don't know. But here's your chance. Just start digging, and you may be surprised by what you find."

Samuel's adrenaline started pumping. What if he could prove that Reginald had, in fact, met with foul play? That would be a scoop. Nothing better than solving a crime to get into what he considered big-time reporting.

"Are you holding back something from me, Melba?"

"Whatever gave you that idea, buster?"

"Out of the blue, you just drop this on me."

"These last few days I've seen you moping around as if your head was in the clouds. You told me that the guy lived in a broom closet but he sponged off the rich in their homes. He had expensive tastes; he didn't act like a bum. He got money from somewhere other than just his work as a janitor."

"Why do you think that?" asked Samuel.

"Because it showed. That's why I loaned him money, because I thought he could pay me back. Besides, you told me yourself that he had four tuxedos in the closet where he lived, plus the one he was wearing when he died. Do you know what they cost? A tuxedo isn't cheap. Doesn't that make you suspicious?"

"I hadn't thought about it."

"Did you search for his bank accounts? I bet you he had a lot of money hidden away. Of course, if you find it, you'll have to figure out where he got it," said Melba.

Samuel walked to the door with his head spinning and the dog growling at his heels. He tried to kick at him, but the dog easily got out of the way.

# 3

## Virginia Dimitri Entertains Xsing Ching

GRANT AVENUE was the main thoroughfare for Chinatown's tourist business. It was crammed with shops and restaurants. Large brightly colored signs in Chinese script announced Asian delights. They fascinated tourists and warned the locals prices were elevated. All sorts of lit lanterns were draped from one side of the street to the other. It was totally different than Stockton Street one block above it to the west, where the Chinese did their own serious shopping in no-frills storefronts piled high with merchandise or meats, fish or produce, including the famous roasted Peking ducks hanging in the windows of local restaurants.

When Mathew O'Hara left the bar, he didn't go home to his residence in Pacific Heights. Instead, he went to one of his many apartments spread all around San Francisco. This one was in Chinatown on the fifth floor of a very ordinary-looking building on Grant Avenue. From the outside one could be fooled, but once inside it was clear that it was one of the best buildings in Chinatown. O'Hara owned the penthouse, tastefully decorated with priceless antiques from ancient China, including a couple of porcelain vases from the Ming

## The Chinese Jars

Dynasty the size of an adult, and a collection of jade carvings from the fifteenth century. From the apartment windows there was a panoramic view of the bay, the Bay Bridge, and Treasure Island.

Once he was inside, a sultry voice greeted him.

"Hello, Matt. I wasn't expecting you this evening," it said.

Virginia Dimitri stood five feet ten inches in her stylish high heels. She was expensively dressed in the style of Jacqueline Kennedy. This evening she had on a black silk dress from San Francisco's most sought-after fashion designer. Around her neck hung two strands of perfectly formed Japanese pearls. Her black hair fell to her shoulders. She had modest but well-formed breasts, and long memorable legs that she knew how to display.

They had known each other since college. She had come to Berkeley from the East Coast to get away from her abusive father. She and Matt had been lovers in their university days, off and on since then, and had stayed in touch. Now, she worked for him on important projects in which her beauty and cunning could be put to use. He liked the way she feigned vulnerability, which fooled others, but not him, because he knew her well and was sure she was made of steel. She was always in charge.

"I forgot to give you some details about tonight," said Mathew. "So I'm glad I caught you before your appointment, Virginia."

"I'm all ears. I already have a pretty good idea of what you want from Mr. Ching. It's not going to be easy to get, because he's no dummy."

"You look elegant this evening. I've every confidence in your powers of persuasion, but you should change a small detail of your attire. Remember, this guy isn't very tall. Take off your high heels so there's not so much of a difference in height. That way he'll be more comfortable."

"Okay, but I don't think that just putting on flats is going to solve the problem."

"It may take some time, but you'll get what we want from Mr. Ching. Just make sure he likes what you have to offer. One never knows with these rich Chinese men," said Mathew.

"He's just as aware as you are that it's illegal to bring art objects from Communist China into the U. S. He won't take more risks than are absolutely necessary."

"Yeah, but he also knows we can both make a fortune off the items, if they are handled properly. As it stands right now, he has the shipment divided into five parts, and I'm scheduled to get only one part of it. I want the whole thing! That's where you come into the game."

"I understand. Ching isn't the kind of man who loses his head over a woman. He certainly didn't let down his guard that night at the cocktail party you threw for him in June," she said.

"Find his weak point," said Mathew.

"That goes without saying," said Virginia.

Then Mathew delved into the details of the dinner that would be served, and went into the kitchen to talk to the cook.

"Hello, how are tricks?" Mathew asked.

"Vely fine, Misser O'Hara, vely fine," the cook responded in his Cantonese accent, not interrupting the chopping of vegetables.

"Did you get me the shark fin soup, as I asked?"

"Yes, sir; yes, sir. This will make you guest vely happy and full of power," he laughed.

"I hope so. I'm counting on you to give this guy lots of power so he thinks he's a lion," said Mathew, also laughing.

He wandered into the dining room and made sure the silverware was positioned exactly where he wanted it and that the ivory chopsticks were placed in front of the exquisite porcelain place settings on top of the embroidered tablecloth. He then turned the overhead light off and lit several candles, placing them in different parts of the room. He called Virginia over and sat her down where he wanted her, then continued to position the candles until he had just the right light to soften her features.

"The light should be suggestive. Ching is a very refined man, and he'll appreciate the details. Good luck," he said, as he kissed her on the cheek before leaving.

\* \* \*

Xsing Ching arrived promptly at nine-thirty. He was smartly dressed in a suit from the best Hong Kong tailor. He had an ageless face with high cheekbones and languid eyes. Virginia couldn't help but again notice his strong, trim figure she remembered from their previous encounter. She watched him stroll across the foyer with confidence and ease after being let in by Fu Fung Fat, the manservant. The contrast between the two was striking. Fu had been a ferocious guerilla fighter for the resistance against the Japanese, where he lost an arm and was honored by Chiang Kai-shek, who personally bestowed the rank of colonel on him. He escaped with Chiang to Taiwan when the Communists took over and, because of his war record, was allowed to immigrate to the States. The only things left of his military service were his medals and his memories. He had been Virginia's servant and confidant for years.

Virginia ushered Xsing Ching into the living room and resumed her seat at a right angle from where she seated him on the sofa so he could have the view of the bay and her crossed legs.

"May I offer you a drink, Mr. Ching?"

"A martini, if you please," he answered in perfect English

with a British accent.

Virginia was relieved. She wouldn't have to talk in sign language.

"Would you like something to nibble on as well? We have raw oysters with a spicy sauce."

"Of course," he accepted.

She rang a little jade bell she had beside her. "I don't remember you speaking such fluent English when I last met you."

"We really didn't get much of a chance to talk then," he said. "Too many people."

The cook walked in from the kitchen, and she ordered the oysters.

"Where did you learn to speak it so well, Mr. Ching?" she asked.

"You may call me Xsing. I suppose I may call you Virginia? I learned it in London."

"I see. I understand that you don't live here."

"I just arrived from New York, where I now have my main office for my export company. I travel a lot, including coming and going from Hong Kong," he said, sipping slowly on his martini.

"Nice time of year in New York," she commented.

"Autumn is always nice on the East Coast. Fortunately, I spend enough time in San Francisco so that during the winter I don't get what you Americans call cabin fever," he responded.

Xsing savored the oysters slowly. He watched Virginia, discreetly admiring the graceful and professional way she handled herself. They made small talk for fifteen or twenty minutes; then she directed the conversation toward dinner.

"Would you like to go to the dining room?" she asked. "I was told you are a big fan of shark fin soup, so I thought we'd start with that."

# The Chinese Jars

"That was thoughtful of you," he said, smiling for the first time.

They moved to the table that Mathew had arranged and were soon enjoying the meal that he had also engineered.

"Would you like some wine, Xsing?" she asked.

"Chablis will be fine," he answered.

She was prepared, and the chef brought a bottle of French Chablis and another of California Fume Blanc, Virginia's favorite. He poured the wine into the crystal goblets.

"I commend you on the shark fin soup; it is some of the best I have ever tasted," said Xsing for the benefit of Virginia, and he repeated it in Cantonese.

The cook smiled. He knew that Mr. Ching was a real connoisseur. He then went back to the kitchen and returned with a delicately prepared whole fish, several plates of vegetables, and two bowls of steamed rice, which he placed to the left of each plate. He scraped the skin off the fish, boned it in front of them, and served each a discreet portion, then retired.

"How long will you be in San Francisco?" she asked.

"It depends. There's a business deal pending that may take a few weeks."

"Your family will miss you."

"Yes, but unfortunately that cannot be avoided."

"Where is your family?"

"Normally in Hong Kong, but for the last several months they've been in New York."

Is this because of your business?"

"For personal reasons. One of my children requires medical treatment."

"Oh, what a shame. I hope it's nothing serious."

Xsing nodded but said nothing.

After a light dessert of lychee fruit, they moved to the sofa that overlooked the city. They watched the lights of San Francisco shimmer as the moon, which was almost full that night, made a golden path on the bay. Virginia snuggled in next to Xsing Ching.

"Mathew speaks highly of you, Xsing."

"That is kind of him. I hope we can complete our transaction in a satisfactory manner," he responded without emotion.

She put her hand on his thigh and moved closer. He accommodated her, so she put her arm around his shoulder and kissed him gently on the neck. He knew Virginia's role in his deal with O'Hara, and why she had invited him to her apartment, so he didn't resist what would have been an overly aggressive move by a woman in his culture. He loosened his tie and was soon kissing her strongly and fondling her breasts. She noted he was a passionate man, and she liked the way he forced his tongue into her mouth, searching for hers.

"May I suggest we retire to the bedroom?" she said.

He stood up and put his arm around her waist with the palm resting casually on her buttock, guiding her in the direction she pointed. The bedroom had golden wallpaper, and the ceiling was dimly lit by recessed lamps that shone softly on an elaborate comforter, neatly folded at the foot of the bed. There were a few decorated pillows near the ornately carved rosewood headboard. The radio was playing soft jazz.

Xsing let her down gently on the bed and lay down beside her, kicking off his shoes. Normally he took his time, but tonight he felt on the verge of losing control. He pulled her dress up above her panty line and kissed her and brushed her moist sex with his fingers. She responded by unbuckling his belt and taking his penis, hard like a young man's, in her hand. She then pushed him away and motioned that he should finish disrobing as she slipped out of her dress, letting it fall to the floor. She removed her bra slowly and threw it across the room, watching it land on an armchair in the corner. She then lay down on the bed dressed only in her laced garter belt and black stockings, and waited in the soft light for him to come to her. She watched his wiry frame as he took off the rest of his clothes. She liked his maleness. In other circumstances, perhaps it would have excited her, but she wasn't there for that; she needed to keep a clear head.

He lay down beside her, naked, and his lips sought the curve in her neck right next to her ear. He removed her stockings with skill, admiring her firm legs and refined ankles. With the finger of one hand he massaged her clitoris while he fondled one of her breasts with the other. Her nipples were now erect, and she pulled Xsing over on top of her. He began kissing her again as he penetrated her. She acted as though she was trembling with delight. They started moving together slowly toward what Xsing hoped would be the inevitable crescendo.

Every time she had sex with a man, she thought of the way her father fondled and used her when she was a teenager. She hated him to this day for doing what he did to her. She learned then to fake orgasm to get her father off her quickly, just as she was on the verge of doing now. She felt Xsing's broad back and whispered a string of obscenities in his ear while writhing like a snake with her legs elevated to her waist. He thought her sex was pulsating with the rhythm they made together and in spite of his experience and cynicism, he believed her when she moaned and told him not to stop. Deep inside her, he started to reach a climax, which surprised him, and he couldn't resist. He liked to prolong sex and prided himself on his self-control, but it was too late.

Afterwards he lay on top of her and fell asleep for a minute or two. He woke up confused, and it took him a second to remember who he was with. He first recognized the smell of her perfume, and he murmured her name before sliding off to her side.

"You're a good lover, Xsing," she whispered in his ear.

He said nothing. She noted he took it for granted, which

was very convenient for her. As Xsing lay beside her in a vulnerable position, she started the most difficult part of her job.

"Tell me about your family," she asked.

"I have four children, a boy and three girls," he answered.

"Which one needs medical attention?"

"The boy. He's thirteen; he's the oldest and the brightest. Of course, he's my favorite," said Xsing, but his voice broke in the middle of the sentence.

"What's wrong?"

"He has leukemia, which makes his life difficult," said Xsing Ching, surprised he was divulging such intimate information to someone who was almost a stranger. He seldom spoke about his family.

"My goodness. What a shame. Have you sought treatment for him? It is treatable, isn't it?"

"I have sent him to many specialists, but have been advised that with his condition the only treatment is a bone marrow transplant, which is risky."

"I've heard of that. There are doctors who are experimenting in that field at the University of California Medical Center. Do you want me to make some inquires?"

"Thank you," he said, moved by her concern.

# 4

## Rafael Garcia

THE MISSION District was the home of Mission Dolores, which catered to the religious needs of the Catholic community. It was the nineteenth of twenty-one missions founded by the Spanish as they conquered California. El Camino Real, or the Royal Highway, connected these Missions. Each was one day's ride from the next.

It was here Melba had grown up, and it was here Rafael Garcia lived. In its past it was home to Irish, Italian, and Scandinavian blue-collar immigrants. Now it housed a large Latin population, mostly Mexican but increasingly Central American. Part of it housed San Francisco's heavy industry, which meant the inhabitants didn't have to travel far to get to work. It was also home to Seals Stadium, the baseball park made famous by the likes of the DiMaggio brothers before big-league baseball came to Candlestick Park. There were plenty of good cheap restaurants and drinking establishments, including Melba's, until she moved uptown to Nob Hill.

Rafael Garcia stopped at the mailbox, took out his mother's welfare check, and bounded to the top of the rickety stairs to his family's third-floor apartment. The paint on the walls was flaking, there were puddles of water on the floor, and there were bags of garbage in the hallways waiting for Thursday, when the renters brought them down for collection. He entered the cold-water flat he shared with his mother and three siblings.

Inside, the smell of the beans cooking on the hot plate infused his nostrils. He made his way through the confusion of objects that blocked his way so he could embrace his mother, who came to meet him, dragging a leg and supporting herself on the secondhand furniture and piles of boxes. He saw her crutch standing in a corner. She always greeted him with disproportionate enthusiasm, as if she hadn't seen him for months or had feared that he would never return. Rafael was the oldest, the main support of the family, and was like a father to the other children. Rafael thought his mother was getting shorter by the minute; he now had to bend over to kiss her forehead.

"Bless me, Mama," he repeated, as usual.

"God bless you, m'ijo. How are you?" She set a place at the small kitchen table, aware that he had arrived late and would have just a moment to eat something before he rushed off to his evening's work at Camelot.

"Muy bien, Mama, muy ocupado. Very busy."

"What are you up to?" She served him beans and a couple of tortillas and sat down heavily on a stool next to him.

" Nothing," he answered. "How's your leg, Mama?"

"The same. You know there's no cure for this, m'ijo."

"When's your doctor's appointment?"

"Why waste money on doctors? We have more important expenses. It's better to entrust it to God."

Rafael thought otherwise. It'd been five years since his drunken father had attacked her with a baseball bat, thinking she was a demon. He'd been carted off to jail for what turned out to be the last time; he died in the detox ward of San Francisco

# The Chinese Jars

General Hospital. Rafael hoped that modern medicine could help his mother. Every day there were new advances and new techniques, but money was needed to take advantage of them. Just then his two sisters, who looked alike, came in dressed in school blouses and blue skirts.

"Have you girls done your homework?" Rafael asked.

"Yes," answered one of them.

"I can hear the radio," said Rafael.

"We're finished, hermano."

"Sí, m'ijo. They did their homework and sewed the blouses. With this lot we got thirty dollars. The sewing machine you bought for us is much faster than the old one. It was expensive, wasn't it?"

"You don't have to worry about that, Mama."

"I worry about it because I don't know how you support us, son. You can't do it on your earnings."

"I have other jobs."

"What kind of jobs are those?"

"That's my business, old thing. I'll take the blouses. Are they in boxes?"

"Yes, they're ready."

"Are there any more beans?"

"Serve you brother more beans," the mother ordered one of the girls. "How's Sofia?"

"Beautiful as ever," said Rafael as his eyes lit up. "We saw the priest yesterday at Mission Dolores. He said he would marry us for free because I have helped so much at the church."

"I suppose it's finally time, m'ijo. How long have you been going together?" asked his mother, hiding the anxiety the subject produced. If Rafael married, he'd have his own family. What would happen to her and the children?

"Three years, two months, and twenty-two days," laughed Rafael. "I'm tired of begging her."

"Don't say that, son. Sofia has loved you since she was a child."

"Three years holding her hand secretly at the movies. I can hardly wait until she's my woman," said Rafael.

Neither of the two families knew that Sofia was three months pregnant.

"Melba says that we can have the reception at the bar. We're going to close for a day so we can have the party. We can invite our families and friends and it won't cost much, only for the food, because Melba will provide the drinks and I've got the music."

"At the bar? That's fantastic! What are we going to wear, Mama?" asked one of the sisters.

"We'll see. Don't you think we'll be out place, son? Nob Hill is for the rich, not for people like us."

"We poor people can't choose, Mama."

"Around here there are others who are poorer than we are. Thanks to you, m'ijo, we have all we need."

Rafael knew what she was thinking. He squeezed her hand to reassure her. "That's the way it will always be, old thing."

"Are you going to Sofia's uncle's house in Mexico for your honeymoon?" asked one of the girls.

"No. We're going to get married without asking for a dime from anybody. And since right now we don't have a dime, I'm afraid we won't have a honeymoon." Rafael finished his beans and wiped the plate clean with a piece of tortilla.

"Where's Juan? Is he out on the street again?"

"Don't pick on him, son. Juan is devilish like all boys his age. I can't have him sewing with the girls. And when he's here, he bothers us, so it's better if he's playing out there with his friends."

"Lupe, go and find Juan and drag him here by his ear if you have to."

The girl ran out, followed by the laughter of her sister,

who ran to the window to see the show. Rafael was upset as he drank a cup of black coffee, and he checked the clock every so often. Twenty minutes later, when he was supposed to leave, Lupe came in crying, with a defiant Juan right behind her. The boy was dressed in bulky pants with a chain hanging from his waist halfway down his thigh, boots with metal tips and elevated heels, and he had sideburns and a mop of black hair plastered down with pomade. He had a tattoo on one of his arms, and and he said his fondest wish was to save enough money to have a gold tooth. Rafael grabbed him by the shirt collar and lifted him off the ground until they were face-to-face.

"You smell like perfume and cigarettes, you little shit. Where did you get that cholo look? Take down the boxes of blouses and put them in my truck. And while you're at it, take down the garbage, and then you come back here and do your homework. You can't go out until I say so. You understand?"

"You're not my boss. I'm almost fifteen years old. I don't have to take orders from anyone."

With one slap Rafael sent Juan's hair flying and with the next he left finger marks on his cheek. The boy lost all dignity and started crying, wiping his nose on his sleeve like a child.

"As long as I'm supporting you, you do as I say. You're wasting time, you jerk. I'm going to send you to the army so you can learn to be a man."

"Ay, Rafael, no diga eso!" said his mother. "Don't you know that President Kennedy is going to send troops to Vietnam? You don't want your brother killed in a war, verdad?"

"He can't send me to the army, Mama. I'm not old enough yet," interrupted Juan.

"Then you'll go to work so that you aren't just bumming around getting in trouble. Are you trying to kill your mother with worry?"

"Pero, m'ijo, Juanito has to go to school. How can he go to

work?" interceded his mother.

"The same way his sisters work," concluded Rafael with authority. "Okay, now that you finished sewing, it's time to open the fold down beds, so you can rest. Tomorrow I want to see your report cards, especially yours, Juan. And watch out if your grades are down."

He put on his jacket, kissed his mother and sisters, and left, slamming the door. Juan gave him the finger.

"I'm going to tell," threatened Lupe, and Juan lifted his arm as if he was going to hit her but restrained himself. He had enough problems for the time being.

\* \* \*

Melba arrived late at Camelot. She saw Rafael's truck in the back alley, and she came into the storeroom just as he was taking off his old leather jacket and hanging it on a peg in the liquor closet. He had on the same blue jeans he always wore and a clean white T-shirt.

"Take that goddamned net off your head, Rafael. I keep telling you if you walk around this part of town looking like a cholo, you're asking for trouble. Why won't you listen to me?"

Rafael blushed and removed it, smoothing out the black knitted squares that had kept his medium-length black hair in place, and stuffed it in one of the pockets of his jacket.

"No, no!" said Melba. "Give me that piece of crap. I want it in the trash."

Rafael reluctantly handed it to her. "That's no fair, Melba. Maybe it's not cool up here, but I need to be one of the vatos to survive. That's part of the code where I come from."

"Maybe, but it gets you into more trouble than it's worth. How many times have you been stopped by the cops wearing that thing on your head?"

"Two or three times a week. They already know me,"

he laughed.

"Two or three times a week? And what do they do when they stop you?"

"They search me and my truck, but they never find anything. I'm not that stupid, Melba."

"You've been lucky. I hope you don't have to learn the hard way."

Excalibur wandered in, happy to see Rafael. With his rear end wagging, he sauntered up and licked Rafael's hands. After Melba, Rafael was his favorite human.

Rafael began his work shift carrying bottles of liquor to the bar and removing the empty ones, putting them in boxes so Melba could keep track and figure out which bartenders were stealing from her. She and Rafael always met before the end of the evening to analyze the drinking habits of the patrons and compare them with the bar receipts. It was usually Rafael who noticed that there were too many empty bottles and not enough cash.

About one in the morning Melba approached Rafael. "There're a couple of guys at the back door asking for you, and they don't look like altar boys. I already told you what I think about the way you dress. I also think you should do something about the company you keep."

"Thanks, Melba. I'm real sorry they came during working hours. It won't happen again."

He went out the back door and closed it tightly behind him, making sure no one from the bar followed him. The only light in the alley was a single sixty-watt bulb surrounded by a cone-shaped protector, which pushed the light down and out, giving some illumination to the otherwise dark passageway.

Two Mexican men got out of a black '55 Chevrolet sedan with tinted windows. The rear end was lowered and there was a single stripe of red painted on both sides of the car. The seats were upholstered with fake tiger skin, and there was a large crucifix hanging from the inside mirror.

"Órale pues," said Rafael, "What are you vatos doing here at the place I work? I told you we do our business down in the Mission."

"Listen man," said the bigger of the two. He had a slight paunch and a black mustache. "We got to unload this piece of shit. It's really hot, and the cops are after us," he said nervously. He pulled a cigarette out of his black leather jacket and lit it by striking a match with his thumbnail and cupping his hands in the shadowy darkness of the alley. Then he looked around furtively to see if he could perceive any movement.

"That's great, pendejo. So you lead them right up here to your old buddy, Rafael. That's real smart. I told you I couldn't get a buyer for that X-ray machine until next week, and I told you not to come up here looking for me. You guys are fucking with my livelihood, man."

"Calm down, ese," said the shorter one. "It was my idea. We can't wait more than a day, and we wanted to give you one last chance."

"I don't know, man," said Rafael, "I'll have to see if they can get the money by then. Like I said, they told me it wouldn't be until next week. That thing is as big as a house. "

"All right," said the big one. "Call me before noon tomorrow or we'll unload it to the next in line."

"You didn't come here because you like me," said Rafael. "You must like the bread my people are willing to pay."

Rafael went back inside as the black car crept down the alley with its lights still out. Those fuckers just don't listen, he told himself, as he walked into the office where Melba was counting the day's take with Excalibur lying at her feet.

"Like I've told you a thousand times, son," Melba blurted out, "you're gonna end up in trouble dealing with people like them."

"Were you spying on me?"

## The Chinese Jars

"I don't like your friends. I don't want to see them around here. Got it?"

Rafael shook his head. He knew she was right, but he also had his own reality to deal with, and the world that he shared with Melba was only a small part of it. Before he left that evening, he went to the wastebasket, retrieved the net, and put it in his jacket pocket.

# 5

## Blanche

WHENEVER he thought of Blanche, Melba's daughter, Samuel felt romantic. In fact, he thought about her all the time but had to make an effort to suppress his sugary sentiments in public so that his knees wouldn't buckle. He was also aware that his obsession was ridiculous: they were totally different. But in his eyes, Blanche wasn't really a head taller than he was; instead, she was a slender reed whose freckles weren't freckles but rather a golden halo. Her eyes, blue like her mother's, were transparent lakes that he didn't dare dive into for fear of drowning. In her presence he became withdrawn and speechless. For her part, Blanche always walked erectly, not at all ashamed of her height, which would have been a defect in another woman. She was a tomboy and a fanatic about sports. An expert skier, she sometimes spent two or three months of the winter at Squaw Valley as a ski instructor. In the spring and summer, she was into swimming and long-distance running, when she wasn't mountain climbing. In the fall, she found other invigorating activities to help her burn energy.

Melba had lost hope that she would marry, like all the other girls her age, and give her grandchildren. Her daughter made fun of those television programs that portrayed perfect families of neatly groomed children, a hard-working father, and a mother who baked cakes and vacuumed wearing high heels and a string of pearls.

In spite of their differences, mother and daughter were very close. Blanche worked for free as Melba's bookkeeper while she was studying to be a certified public accountant. Even in winter, she came down from Tahoe once a month to straighten out the bar's accounts, pay the Board of Equalization and payroll taxes and, of course, make out the employee checks.

If Samuel learned she was going to be at the bar, he made sure to be there, too, even though she didn't pay any attention to him. She was one of those few women who didn't seem to care about the effect she had on men. Her indifference only aroused more passion in Samuel. He would wait patiently, nursing his Scotch on the rocks at the round table or watching her in the mirror behind the bar, while she pondered the business ledgers and chewed on the end of a pencil, periodically brushing aside a tuft of unruly hair. At times he would try to catch her attention with some banality because he could never come up with anything smart or sexy to say.

That day he thought he'd struck it rich. "Hi, Blanche, haven't seen you in awhile. How're things?"

"Hi, Samuel, you've been sitting there for three hours and you didn't see me?"

"I'm thinking. I've got problems."

"Don't tell me about them now, I'm really busy." Then she stopped what she was doing and took a closer look at him. "You're pale. You look like a worm. You need some exercise. How about running with me this weekend?"

Surprised, Samuel weighed the horror of jogging against the possibility that he might never have another opportunity to be alone with her. "I'm not much good at that, but we could take a stroll in Golden Gate Park. How about that?" he stuttered.

"Okay, I'll meet you at the windmill down by the beach at eight this Saturday. I'll run and you can walk. We'll get a bite to eat at Betty's in the Haight. You know, that place right near Kezar Stadium?"

From the round table where she had installed herself with Excalibur, Melba observed the goings-on with curiosity. She had never said a word, but she was clearly amused by the mismatch and her daughter's obliviousness to Samuel's not-so-disguised interest in her. As Blanche was leaving for the evening, Samuel followed her, trying to get another whiff of her pheromones. He'd heard on the radio that pheromones were responsible for sexual attraction, and he concluded, naturally, that Blanche's were very powerful. He sighed, resigned to leave also, at the same time counting the hours before he would see her in the park on Saturday.

When he went past the round table, Melba grabbed him by the arm. "What can I do for you?" he said, acting surprised.

"Relax, Buster. Sit down and talk to us," she said, smiling. "Excalibur was telling me that you two aren't a bad couple," she said as she motioned for Samuel to light her cigarette.

Samuel plopped down in the empty chair next to her with such a sullen expression that Melba started to laugh.

"Why don't you ask her to do something less physically demanding than running?"

"I don't know what you're talking about, Melba," he mumbled, examining his fingernails.

"Knock off the shit, Samuel. You're drooling over her."

Samuel turned red and was silent for a few seconds. "It's that obvious, huh?"

"It's not a bad thing, sweetie. You're just going at it the wrong way."

"What d'ya mean by that?"

"If you want to have anything to do with Blanche, it has to be in an area where you can compete. You're no more fit to run a few yards than I am. In fact, it might kill you," she said laughing, taking a deep drag off her cigarette. By that time, Samuel had also lit up, and he began to laugh, too. Now they both had a case of uncontrollable giggles until all the patrons left in the bar were staring at them.

"Kind of pathetic, isn't it?" said Samuel.

"Yeah, pathetic, but that's life," she said in the middle of a coughing spell.

\* \* \*

Samuel and Blanche met Saturday morning at the western end of Golden Gate Park near the Pacific Ocean at the Murphy windmill, one of the two huge Dutch windmills that looked as if they came right out of a Low Country's picture postcard. They were big, imposing, and in some need of maintenance; their shingles had not been replaced since they started to fall off years before. But they served a purpose. They were used to obtain water for the irrigation of the park and several of its lakes. Quite a chore for the over-a-thousand-acre park, which was designed by the famous William Howard Hall in the 1870s to cover the unruly sand dunes and isolated vegetation, Blanche explained to Samuel.

"It was made into a modern marvel by John McLaren, who was in charge of it and who lived in the McLaren Lodge until his death at the age of ninety-six in 1943," she added for Samuel's benefit.

It was a typical cold day by the beach. The fog hadn't lifted and the wind was blowing in toward the city, but the sand didn't invade the park. It was kept out by the row of Cypress trees between the ocean and the windmills. The trees also told the story of the strength of the wind, as they were all bent heavily toward the east.

Blanche was dressed in sweats and tennis shoes, looking

every inch the athlete, her hair pulled back with a rubber band. Samuel, on the other hand, had on loafers and his usual worn beige sports jacket with the cigarette-burn holes in the sleeves. He'd changed his appearance slightly by donning a Madras shirt, whose brown tones surprisingly blended with his jacket. It was his attempt to be casual.

"I thought it'd be nice to run through the park. There's less traffic. You can trot along if you like; and since I'll get there before you, I'll do some shopping and meet you at Betty's, let's say ten o'clock," Blanche proposed.

"That's two hours from now. You think it will take me that long to get there?" asked Samuel, terrified.

"More or less. It's okay. I'm not in a hurry today, and it'll be nice to talk with you."

Samuel sighed. "What happens if I get there earlier?"

"That would be a stretch! But if you do, you can look for me on Haight. I'll be the girl with the sweats on," she said with a radiant smile. And she was off.

Samuel sat down on a rock by one of the dormant windmills and lit a cigarette while he mulled things over. Things hadn't worked out the way he'd planned. Instead of spending a couple hours in Blanche's sweet company, he would spend them running like an exhausted fugitive, alone. He stood up slowly, put out his cigarette, tried to wrap his thin sports jacket around his exposed torso to protect himself from the wind, and ambled south toward Lincoln Way at the southern edge of the park. He waited for a downtown bus, rubbing his hands together in an attempt to keep warm. When the 72 bus arrived, he hopped on and got off when it got to Stanyan Street, where the park ended. He had ridden east for the entire length of Golden Gate Park. He was now across the street from Kezar Stadium, just at the edge of the panhandle. It was bustling with activity as the groundskeepers prepared it for a Forty-Niners game the next day. He bought a paper, crossed over to the park, and sat down on a bench. The trip had taken twenty minutes. He was surrounded by a myriad of trees, some of which had no leaves, and there were spacious areas of lawn in between them and a children's playground full of toddlers and their mothers, as it was a Saturday. The tots had on their bright jackets of different colors, with caps and mittens to match.

He sat there for more than a half hour before Blanche streaked past him almost in a trance; her blondish brown hair was damp with perspiration, her cheeks flushed, and her nose red, like a clown's. He found her more beautiful than ever. Samuel thought she had the grace of a gazelle loping along on the African plain. Not that he'd ever been to Africa, or ever would be, but he liked the metaphor. He would find an opportunity to say it to Blanche, if he could summon up the courage.

When she reached the corner of Stanyan and Haight, she halted, waiting for the traffic light to change. She kept running in place but stopped long enough to touch her toes. He thought better of running over to greet her, as it would be embarrassing for him to explain his speedy arrival. It was better not to discuss it. When the light changed, Blanche trotted across the street and started to walk cheerfully down Haight Street, the Haight-Ashbury District's main drag. It was then just another San Francisco neighborhood. The Hippies, who would transform it, hadn't yet arrived.

Samuel waited until she passed Betty's Diner. Then he got up and went there and sat in a booth looking out on the street through the plate-glass window. He smoked several cigarettes and was reading the paper, drinking his third cup of coffee, when he was startled by a "Boo!" and the tap on the shoulder. It was Blanche, full of smiles and energy.

"You must be a fast walker," she commented.

"Nothing to it. Would you like something to eat?"

"Thank you. I'll have a carrot and a glass of orange juice."

Samuel called the waitress and gave her the order.

She smiled slightly. "We don't serve carrots here."

"Why not?" asked Blanche.

"Ask the owner."

"Okay, I'll have orange juice."

"Anything else?"

"I'll have another cup of coffee," said Samuel.

They talked about this and that. Samuel felt that something had advanced between them, even though with Blanche he couldn't be sure—she had the innocence and enthusiasm of a golden retriever.

# 6

## Samuel Starts Digging

EVEN THOUGH Melba kept steering him in the right direction, Samuel took his own time to start his investigation into the death of Reginald Rockwood. She was right, he decided. Those tuxes were too expensive. He must have gotten a lot of money from somewhere. But where? As he pondered the problem and weighed his options, he concluded that a broke ad salesman didn't have many.

Then he remembered Charles Perkins. He'd gone to Stanford with him before Samuel dropped out when he parents were murdered. Perkins was a fellow Midwesterner who now worked at the U.S. attorney's office as a lawyer prosecuting federal crimes. Samuel helped him through a couple of very difficult literature courses in their second year, and he was sure Charles would remember the debt even after so many years.

He made an appointment and went to the lawyer's office in the Federal Building on Seventh Street.

Charles met him at the door. He had yellowish skin and a head of limp hair the color of straw. He parted it on one side, but he always had a greasy clump in his eyes. His chiseled face gave the impression of amiability, but Samuel knew him well and knew that he had a petty soul. He was a nervous person with abrupt gestures and was incapable of being still. He had the bad habit of acting like a schoolteacher, pointing his index finger at everything and everybody. This mania always put Samuel on the defensive. Charles was surrounded by paper. Piles of it cluttered all the surfaces in his office, and it was almost impossible to find any vacant space anywhere in the room.

When Samuel saw him, he was reminded of what a critical and boring person he was in college. His immediate sense was that Charles hadn't changed much. He had the same air of being an unkempt, petulant adolescent.

"What's up, Sam? You look like you've had a rough night," Charles commented.

Samuel was surprised. Though he was his sloppy self, wearing his wrinkled outfit, he'd slept well the night before and felt fresh and focused. "I'm investigating the death of a socialite. It's a strange case," he admitted. "The dead guy owned five tuxedos but he lived in a closet at Engel's, the engravers, where he did janitorial work. His death's been called a suicide, but I'm not so sure it was."

"You want the U.S. government to look into this?" asked Charles.

"Yeah. I think he had money hidden away," said Samuel.

"Yeah, sure, that's why he lived in a closet," Charles laughed.

"No, no. Listen, I think he lived that way in an attempt to be inconspicuous," said Samuel, wondering if he really wanted to subject himself to the grilling he was going to get from his pompous friend just to get him to look at some records.

"What kind of proof do you have for that?" asked Charles.

"He had expensive taste. Those tuxes cost a lot of money and his were of the best quality. If he could afford clothes like that, why would he live in a closet?"

## The Chinese Jars

"Maybe he was crazy."

"I knew him well, and I can assure you he wasn't crazy.

"So your idea is he was getting his money illegally? Like he was blackmailing someone? Why would the federal government be interested in that?" asked Charles.

"I don't know yet. But you're the only person I know who has the power to look into this guy's finances. If we find something and the feds aren't involved, you can turn the whole case over to the district attorney, and you'll look like a hero," said Samuel.

"That's a pretty slim thread, ol' buddy. But I tell you what, I'm willing to give two days of my valuable time to this matter. Meet me here tomorrow at ten o'clock. Make sure you have a list of banks or other establishments where you think he could have hidden the money. I'll help you trace it with the subpoena power of the federal government."

\* \* \*

Samuel went to Camelot later that afternoon to consult with Melba. He explained how he was going to meet his friend at the U. S. attorney's the next day and he wanted guidance.

She laughed. "In B movies of the '40s, it was always 'look for the dame'," she said, smiling slightly.

Excalibur trotted up, limping, to investigate, and Samuel made a face of displeasure.

"This dog will end up chasing your clients away."

"On the contrary, they all spoil him. Do you know he has the nose of a bloodhound? He can follow any scent."

"Very useful," said Samuel.

"Of course it's useful. Be patient, he'll get used to you and end up being your best friend. Have you noticed that he doesn't growl at you anymore?"

"Stay alert. That's a sign of interest. Come here, ferocious warrior; sit by Mama," she called softly. Excalibur plopped down beside her chair.

"Have you gone over this guy's possessions, looking for where he could've hid the money?" she asked, taking a sip of her beer.

"What do you mean?" asked Samuel.

"Where's his stuff?" asked Melba.

"So far as I know, it's at the engraving shop. All except the clothes he had on when he died. They're still at the medical examiner's," responded Samuel.

"If he had money hidden away, there has to be some kind of receipt somewhere. It may be unconventional. It could be a checking account, but I doubt it would be in his name. More than likely, he had it stashed away in cash," she said. "If I were you, I'd start in those two places. Look for a clue. It may be something totally innocuous."

Samuel had a couple more drinks while he pondered what she said, exploring with her the details of the avenues she opened for him. There was no trace of Blanche, but he didn't have the courage to ask about her. When he got up to leave, Excalibur followed him with his nose almost stuck to his pant leg.

"He's learning your smell," she said. "Go home, you look tired."

But Samuel went to Chop Suey Louie's, sat in front of the aquarium at the counter, and ordered a bowl of noodles. He watched the colorful tropical fish, especially the gold ones, swim slowly around the large tank. They brought luck to the establishment, according to Louie. His bowl arrived steaming hot. The smell was inviting, and he was suddenly ravenous, remembering that he hadn't eaten in several hours, and his mouth was sour from the Scotch. He dug in, but he couldn't catch a single noodle. Louie approached him with a fork.

"One of these days you'll get it," smiled Louie.

"Yeah, one of these days."

\* \* \*

## The Chinese Jars

The next morning Samuel arrived at the U.S. attorney's office in the Federal Building at Seventh and Mission at ten o'clock. In order to get there, he took the Powell Street cable car from near his flat to Market Street, and walked up to Seventh.

His friend Charles Perkins was dressed in the same suit. Samuel noticed that one sleeve was an inch shorter than the other, so Charles's gold-plated cuff link stuck out against his white shirt.

"Where do you want to start this investigation, Samuel?" he asked.

"We should go to the medical examiner's first, and see if there's anything I missed. Then we should go to Rockwell's employer. I remember seeing a whole box of engraved invitations there, and some of them had notes on 'em," said Samuel.

Charles stuffed a number of blank federal subpoena forms in his tattered brown leather briefcase with the Justice Department insignia on it. He threw on his gray overcoat and wrapped a blue wool scarf around his neck, then motioned with a finger for Samuel to follow him out of the office.

They walked out of the Federal Building and hailed a cab right on Seventh Street. It was a cold, cloudy day in December and the streets were crowded with Christmas shoppers walking toward downtown. That year Jacqueline Kennedy made popular felt hats shaped like candy boxes, but most of the women in San Francisco seemed to be ignoring her fashion tip . Wearing their own fashionable hats and coats, they mixed with the grubby winos coming up from South of Mission and the out-of-towners and weary travelers pouring out of the Greyhound station directly across the street.

Charles told the taxi driver where they wanted to go, and they soon found themselves in front of the office of the medical examiner, a one-story gray stone building. When they arrived,

Samuel said hello to the emaciated clerk who had received him the time before and explained they needed to see his boss, because the feds had a subpoena and wanted to examine their files on Rockwood.

The clerk took the document that the attorney had filled out by hand and disappeared behind a frosted-glass door. Within a minute the door reopened and the examiner appeared in his white coat with the nameplate attached to it. "An investigation, huh? What in particular are you looking for?"

Charles Perkins puffed up. "You know I can't discuss particulars with you, sir. I just need to look at everything you have on Rockwood. Can you hang these somewhere?" he asked, handing him his coat and scarf.

"Be my guest," said the examiner, pointing to the coat rack next to the front entrance. He scratched the thinning gray hair on his head and squinted, curious to know what the attorney was after. "Samuel, can you be of any help?" he asked, directly.

"I'll do the talking. He's with me," Charles interrupted.

Samuel and the examiner exchanged glances. From the looks of it, he thought, he'd have to put up with this peacock.

"Very well," said the examiner, who by now realized he was being left out of whatever was going on.

He gave instructions to the clerk. "Bring out all of Mr. Rockwood's personal belongings and his autopsy file and put them in that room over there. I'll answer any questions these gentlemen have."

"I'm sure you have other things to do," said Charles, who preferred to work without vigilance.

"It's protocol," answered the examiner. "It has to do with the chain of evidence." If he'd wanted to, he could have left them alone with the belongings; but he didn't like Charles, so he wouldn't budge.

"Very well," said Charles. "I assume we can take photos of

anything we want?"

"Yes, of course, as long as no original leaves the premises. You understand, chain of evidence."

"Yeah, yeah, you already told me," murmured Charles.

The examiner accompanied them to the same room where Samuel had been on his first visit. They spread Rockwood's belonging on the wood table and started going through the contents of the dead man's pockets. Samuel wasn't moved this time when he saw the small pile that represented all that was left of Rockwell. He was now convinced that he knew nothing about him, and that he wasn't really his friend. There was a half pack of Philip Morris cigarettes, which yielded nothing, and the Zippo lighter, which Charles stroked with his thumb. It worked. The seventeen dollars cash was still there, as was the engraved invitation. His wallet contained the same social security card and the photograph of Rockwood in army officer's attire. Charles pulled out a flash camera and took pictures of the items, one at a time, throwing the used bulbs into the wastebasket in the corner.

"Is this his social security number?" asked Charles.

"It checked out," said the examiner, "and he really was in the army."

"Interesting, there were no keys on him," said Charles.

"Not necessarily," said the examiner. "This was a suicide. You may find he left his keys at his place of employment, where I understand he lived. If you find out anything new, I know you'll report back to me. Right, Samuel?"

"Yes, sir," replied Samuel, giving him a sly look.

Charles Perkins, ignoring the examiner, and still irked he wouldn't be allowed to borrow any evidence, turned his focus to the invitation. "You say this came from Engel's? How do you know that, Samuel?"

"You see that trademark in the middle of the lower part of the document? If you look real close, you'll see it has their name on it. That's how I knew where to go."

"What about the RSVP number?" asked Charles.

"I called and they never heard of him," answered Samuel.

They searched the tuxedo and at first found nothing. Then Samuel slipped his hand deep into the inside pocket where Rockwood would have kept his wallet. He pulled out what looked like half a claim check with red Chinese characters on it. "Look at this!" he exclaimed. "It looks like a receipt for something." He asked both men searchingly, "Do either of you read Chinese?"

"What do you think, Mac?" said the examiner, laughing. "Does this Irish face look like it speaks Chinese?"

Charles, ignoring their conversation, took a close-up photo of the claim check and tried to duplicate the Chinese characters on a piece of paper. After three attempts he shrugged and said, "This will have to do until we get the pictures back." He and Samuel then put everything back in its place.

"You're acting like you know something you're not telling me," said the examiner. "Do you want me to ask for an inquest?"

"Let's not get ahead of ourselves," said Charles. "We're just starting our investigation. Let's see where it leads, and then you can decide."

On their way out, Charles whispered to Samuel, "We really pissed the old man off," and he smiled with a self-congratulatory smirk. "Now let's see what we can find out from his employer, Mr. Engel."

They walked around to the front of the new Hall of Justice on Bryant Street and got in another cab.

"Engle's on Sacramento Street," said Samuel, "right near Front."

"This is pretty fancy," said Samuel, impressed anew with the elegance of Engel's waiting room. "The owner has good taste. Those are real Piranesi drawings."

## The Chinese Jars

"And who the hell is Piranesi?" asked Charles, examining a couple of them without interest.

The receptionist remembered Samuel. "You're here to see Mr. Engel again about the janitor, aren't you?" she asked. "Just a second." She dialed the phone and called Mr. Engel. He appeared quickly from the hallway by the reception desk.

"Hello again, Mr. Hamilton. I see you didn't waste any time in coming back."

"I'm glad you recognized me," said Samuel. "This is Charles Perkins from the U.S. attorney's office. He'd like to see Mr. Rockwood's stuff and the closet where he lived. He has a subpoena to make it all legal."

"You'll have to give me a few moments. We put everything in boxes. We wanted to get rid of it, but thought someone might claim it."

They followed him to the rear of the building, where he unlocked a storage room. The tuxes were hanging in four plastic bags from an overhead water pipe, and two boxes with the Engel company name on the outside were stacked next to them. They were crammed full and heavy. As Samuel lifted them, Charles talked to the owner.

"Can we use this work table here?" he asked, pointing to one that was directly outside the room.

"Of course," said Mr. Engel. "If you need anything else, let me know." He tipped his hand, as if removing a bowler, and wandered toward the front of his establishment.

Samuel lifted the two boxes onto the table and began to remove several shoeboxes from inside. Charles began taking invitations out of the boxes. They were all in alphabetical order. He examined and looked at the notes on some of them, but he trusted what Samuel had already told him, so he didn't want to waste time on ground his friend had already covered, especially if it didn't produce anything of significance.

"Tell me if you find any plane tickets to Morocco," said Samuel.

"What are you looking for?" asked a surprised Charles.

"Never mind. I'll know if you find 'em."

Samuel searched the pockets of the hanging tuxes, but found nothing. He returned to the boxes they'd started to empty. In the bottom of one he found a set of keys, which he jiggled as he pulled them out to catch Charles's attention.

"Those may be our most important find," said Charles.

"I hope so," said Samuel. He placed them on the table and went on looking for the other piece of the claim check. He found another piece of stiff paper with red Chinese characters tucked in the pocket of a notebook that had "Daily Reminder" written on the front, but was filled with blank pages. Samuel smoothed out the torn piece of paper and placed it right next to the page Perkins had copied at the medical examiner's office. It looked as though they'd found what they were after.

The attorney took photos of the two papers, and then yelled for the owner, "Excuse me, Mr. Engel, can you come back here for a moment?"

Engel didn't respond, so Samuel went to fetch him and brought him to the table.

"Do you know where this piece of claim check is from?" Charles asked the owner.

"I'm afraid I don't. And no one here reads Chinese," he said.

"Did Mr. Rockwood ever mention any Chinese friends?' Samuel asked.

"No, he didn't. I can ask the other employees, but I doubt they know anything," he said. "The janitor was friendly and efficient but he didn't mix with the other employees. I'm afraid he didn't make any friends here."

"Tell us about these keys," said the attorney.

"I recognize this one; it opens the front door. And this one, the back door. The third one, I believe, is the key to the broom closet where we discovered he lived. The one next to that one opens the storeroom. But I've no idea about the other two," said the owner. "They've nothing to do with our business."

Charles separated the two keys from the rest and took photos of them. "Do you know if Mr. Rockwood had a bank account?"

"Yes, at the local Bank of America. At least that's where he deposited his checks. It's right around the corner."

"Can I see his paychecks?" asked Charles. "Frankly, I'm trying to find out where he kept his money, in his own account or in someone else's."

The owner brought the checks pertaining to Rockwood and placed them on the now crowded table. They were typical payroll checks with the name and address of the company in the upper left-hand corner. "I separated all of his checks, thinking someone might make an inquiry," he said, waiting for the next question.

Charles went through them methodically. They were all endorsed the same way, Reginald Rockwood III, all written out legibly, as if the signer took great pride in his name. Underneath the signature was an account number and the words, "For Deposit Only," in the same meticulous handwriting.

Charles took photographs of a few of the checks with Reginald Rockwood's name on the face of them and his signature on the back. He had Samuel write down the account number in his notebook so they wouldn't have to wait for the negatives to be developed. He then picked up the keys. "Can we keep these two?" he asked.

"I'd prefer to make you copies. There's a place right near here. I can have them for you in a few minutes," said Engel. He called an employee and sent him off to get the job done.

"Do you have any information on this guy's private life?" asked Charles.

"None whatsoever. Mr. Hamilton can tell you we were quite surprised to learn he was living in our broom closet."

"Referring to this Chinese claim check, or whatever it is, do you have any idea where this place might be?" asked Charles.

"Absolutely none," said the owner.

"We appreciate the help you've given us today, Mr. Engel. Hopefully, we won't have to bother you again, but we do need to take this claim check with the Chinese writing on it. You understand, don't you? This is official business. I'll send you a photo of it, and here's a receipt." He'd already written it out and handed it to Engel.

"I understand. How long do you want me to keep the rest of this stuff?" he asked.

"Until you hear from me," Charles instructed him.

The employee came back with copies of the two keys. It was now three o'clock. Engle excused himself, and Charles and Samuel put everything back in the boxes, then returned them to the storeroom. They stared at half of the claim check with the red Chinese writing on it.

"Do you think you can find out what this is for and where the place is located?" asked Charles, handing the torn part with the Chinese writing on it to Samuel, together with what he had written at the medical examiner's office. "In any event, come to my office tomorrow at ten o'clock, and we'll at least go to the bank and see what kind of money this guy salted away."

\* \* \*

Samuel knew just where to go. He said goodbye to his friend and thanked Mr. Engel, then he boarded the Sacramento Street bus. He got off at Powell and walked the few blocks to Chop Suey Louie's. His friend Louie motioned for him to sit at his usual counter seat. Samuel shook his head and pointed to one of the tables in a corner, indicating he wanted the smiling man to join him.

## The Chinese Jars

"How's things, Samuel?" asked Louie.

"Good, Louie. We can have one more bet on the Forty-Niners. How much will it be?"

"You're not a good gambler, Samuel. You always lose," said Louie.

Samuel laughed and pulled out the piece of the torn claim check and the characters the attorney had tried to copy on the notebook paper.

"Can you tell me what this says, Louie?" asked Samuel.

The man looked at the two pieces of paper for a long time with a frown on his face, trying to decipher the attorney's attempt to write in Chinese. Finally, he smiled, "This is a receipt for medium-sized jar at a Chinese herb shop," he said.

"What are you talking about?" asked Samuel

"This means you own the contents of an herb jar at a very important Chinese healer's place of business. The problem is you only have one half. You won't get anything without the whole receipt."

"Why do people own herb jars?" asked Samuel.

The proprietor laughed. "Go and find out."

Samuel, puzzled, lit a cigarette and slowly exhaled the smoke into the empty seat across the table as he glanced at Goldie, his favorite fish, darting about the colorful aquarium. He felt tired. He'd eaten badly for days and had slept fitfully the night before. He shifted in his chair, wondering what kind of herbs Rockwood would have in a jar and whatever for.

"Do you know where this place is?" asked Samuel.

"Pacific, between Grant and Kearny. Everyone knows the famous Mr. Song, the owner of the shop. He holds all the secrets of Chinatown."

"Does this place have a name?" asked Samuel.

"Right here." He ran his finger over the red characters, "MR. SONG'S MANY CHINESE HERBS. You have the last part that says CHINESE HERBS in red letters. I've guessed a little about the first part from your friend's writing, but I think it's close enough."

"That was written by a friend of mine who doesn't know Chinese."

"That obvious," he said and laughed.

"I can't thank you enough for your help, Louie," said Samuel. "Say goodbye to your mother for me. Why won't she ever say hello? She at least acknowledges your other customers."

"It's because you have red hair. She thinks you're the devil."

"Shit, you learn something every day. Okay, Louie, don't forget, I'm betting on the Forty-Niners this weekend."

"Goldie brings good luck to my customers, but not to you," said Louie, laughing.

Samuel was too tired to go to Camelot and tell Melba what'd happened. So he went to the corner grocery store and bought a roll and an apple and went home. After he ate, he went to bed and fantasized about having sex with Blanche, until he fell asleep.

* * *

"I know where Reginald stored things away," Samuel informed Charles.

"We'll get to that. Come and look at the photos. I had them developed last night."

He followed Charles over to the small table next to his desk where the photographs were laid out. Samuel took the picture of the first half of the claim check, number 85, and set it alongside the other half they had taken from Engel's. The edges fit exactly.

"I think this will be important today," he said, "and I know where to go. I've found Mr. Song's," he said, smiling, expecting a pat on the back.

"Yeah," was all Perkins said.

"Didn't you hear me? I know the significance of the claim check. It's for a jar."

"Not so fast. I think we should start at the bank, since that's the place where people usually put money," interrupted Charles, pointing his finger in Samuel's face.

"I don't think so," said Samuel, backing up to avoid getting poked in the eye by the finger. "I tell you we should start with Mr. Song's Many Chinese Herbs. Rockwood hid something there. It could be the clue we're looking for. We have the claim check," and he shook half of it in the air.

"You've heard of delayed gratification, haven't you?" asked Charles. "Let's do the perfunctory things first, then we'll go for the goodies."

"Okay," said Samuel, reluctantly. The smile left his face and his shoulders sagged a bit further. Charles was in control; he had the subpoenas.

They again walked out of the Federal Building and this time went up the block to Market, where they hailed a cab. Charles instructed the driver, "Straight down to Front Street." There were decorated Christmas trees in most of the windows; the ubiquitous Salvation Army men—dressed in their dark blue uniforms with the red bands around the caps and their infernal jingling bells stood out in front inviting the public to put some money in their donation pots. The Emporium, at Fifth and Market, had just opened its doors, and people were still filing in.

They exited the cab at Front Street and were directly facing the Ferry Building over the Embarcadero Freeway. They crossed Market Street, walked a couple of blocks to Sacramento, and entered the bank. Just as Engel had said, Rockwood had his account there. Charles served the subpoena and the manager brought them the records. There were weekly deposits of

Rockwood's paychecks, plus a monthly deposit of a check for $150. There were no checks written on the account. Each time it reached $3,000, there was a cash withdrawal and the process would start all over again. They examined the records for the four previous years and the pattern was the same.

"This doesn't help us much," said Charles. "The guy lived a pretty dull life with no surprises."

"What about the $150 a month? What's that all about?"

"I don't know. We'll have the bank check out where it came from, and they'll report back to me."

"I wonder what he did with the cash?" asked Samuel.

"We may never know. How do we find the herb shop?"

"I'll show you. We can walk there," said Samuel. "It's right around the corner. It shouldn't take more than twenty minutes."

Thanks to Samuel's work the previous evening, there was no delay in finding it, and soon they were in front of a shop with a sign that had the same Chinese characters in red that Samuel knew meant Mr. Song's Many Chinese Herbs. Garlands of dried herbs in the windows framed the view of the interior.

As they entered the front door, a small bell attached to the top of it tingled announcing their arrival. In the dimness of the interior were dozens of medium-sized, earth-colored containers eighteen inches high and six inches at their widest point in the middle. They were stacked on shelves from the floor to the top of the eighteen-foot ceiling on two of the four walls. On a six-foot portion of the east wall were shelves of even larger jars, also from floor to ceiling. Each had a top secured by an iron band around it with two padlocks, which Samuel thought must be a precaution against earthquakes and robbers. And each had Chinese characters in black, apparently some kind of number code. On at least twenty wires near the top of the high ceiling hung more bundles of dried herbs of every sort imaginable. Samuel and Charles were almost overcome by the mixture of pungent smells.

About twenty-five feet into the shop, and visible from outside the store, was a shiny black lacquer counter with Chinese scenes painted on the front panels. Behind the counter were hundreds of small boxes, each four inches square, reaching all the way to the ceiling. Every one had a latch that was secured with a padlock, and each had Chinese markings. They saw a ladder pushed up against the boxes in the corner, which was undoubtedly used to access the jars. The lighting was bad so they couldn't tell if the place was dusty or if everything was just in dull earth colors.

From behind a beaded curtain, which separated the front of the store from the living quarters and more storage, stepped such a strange looking man that Samuel and Charles were startled. He was a Chinese albino. He observed the two men with his pink eyes from underneath his bushy eyebrows, while he stroked his wispy white mustache and goatee. His skin was abnormally pale and smooth. His facial features were transparent and looked as though they'd been painted on with a brush. It was impossible to guess his age—he could have been anywhere from fifty to a thousand years old. He was wearing a gray Chinese jacket with an understated design of bamboo in black thread and wide sleeves that covered his hands. He nodded slightly, greeting them.

"We've come to ask you some questions about this," said Charles, when he got over the surprise.

The old man squinted at the photo and the piece of claim check Charles was showing him and then he made a gesture that he couldn't help them because he didn't understand.

"I don't think he speaks English," said Samuel.

A short man, slightly hunched over, wearing blue trousers and a matching blue collarless top, entered the room. He was obviously some kind of assistant to Mr. Song, but it was soon clear that he didn't speak English, either. The albino said a few words in Chinese to the assistant, who then hobbled out the door, leaving the bell tingling in his aftermath.

"Do you recognize the claim in this photo?" asked Charles, pointing to the torn piece of the claim check and the photo of the other half that he'd laid on the counter top.

The albino wouldn't even dignify either of them with a look. He'd already indicated that they should wait, and nothing irked him more than the white man's impatience and lack of courtesy.

"I think...," said Samuel, but he started coughing heavily a few times and took out his handkerchief to clear the phlegm from his throat. Charles gave him a dirty look but the herbalist turned and watched him with interest.

In a few minutes, the bell tingled and a young, fresh-looking Chinese girl entered the herb shop followed by the short old man. She was dressed in a Gordon plaid skirt with the hem just below the knees and a starched white blouse with an emblem on the left pocket. In the center of it was a pagoda. The letters surrounding it read: "Chinese Baptist School, San Francisco, California." Her most notable feature was her buckteeth, which made her look like a beaver. She saluted the albino with great respect and became deeply engaged with him for a while in a language that Samuel, having lived so long in Chinatown, recognized as a Southern Chinese dialect. She then turned to Samuel and Charles. "Mr. Song asked me to come and help him find out what you want."

Charles moved in front of Samuel, who was about to speak, and pointed his finger in an authoritative way. "Tell him I'm an attorney with the federal government. We're investigating the death of Reginald Rockwood. We have reason to believe he has something of value deposited here."

The girl translated for Mr. Song, who didn't seem in the least impressed by Charles's wagging finger.

## The Chinese Jars

"This is an herb shop. We sell herbs to people who are looking for cures for all sorts of ailments," Song answered through her. He spoke in an almost inaudible monotone.

"Can you tell us if this claim check is for something that you hold here for Mr. Rockwood?" asked Charles.

"I only see half a claim check. It is torn in the middle," said the girl for Mr. Song, as he raised a bushy eyebrow.

"Tell him the photo on the counter shows the other half," said Charles.

"He says that is not enough. In Chinatown, there is a famous saying, 'No ticky, no laundry'." The girl couldn't control herself, laughing as if she'd heard the funniest joke in the world. The albino brought her back to earth by pinching her.

Charles turned red. But Samuel had gotten the contagion from the hilarity of the girl's reaction and could barely control his own laughter. He liked the idea that Mr. Song was making fun of the presumptuous Charles Perkins.

"You tell Mr. Song that we represent the United States government, and if he refuses to honor our subpoena, I can have him thrown in jail!" Charles threatened.

This frightened the girl, who translated what Charles said, gesturing hysterically, but Mr. Song answered, unmoved, his arms folded across his chest with his hands inside his sleeves.

"He says the same thing. 'No ticky, no laundry'. He doesn't care if you represent the president of the United States."

Samuel tugged at Charles's sleeve and whispered to him. "Don't antagonize him. Don't you see this is some kind of private depository? Look at all those double padlocks on the jars and boxes. He is just protecting his clients. We can get the medical examiner to come up here with the other half of the claim check. That way the word won't get out that he caved in."

"At least tell me this, Mr. Song," Charles demanded, showing him the two keys they had gotten from Engel's. "Does one of these keys here open something that belongs to

Mr. Rockwood?"

Mr. Song picked up half of the claim check and shook it in Charles's face.

"All right, Mister. We'll go and get the other half. Just make sure you don't do anything with whatever belongs to Mr. Rockwood. We'll be back tomorrow," said Charles, fuming.

Charles stuffed the subpoena back in his briefcase and dragged Samuel toward the exit. Just as they were walking out, the girl called out to Samuel. She was smiling. "My honorable uncle, Mr. Song, says that you have a bad cigarette cough. If you will take this Chinese medicine three times a week for a month, you'll get better. But, he says if you don't stop smoking you'll die young." She handed him a half-pint bottle with Chinese writing on it. Samuel nodded in appreciation and took out his wallet in an attempt to pay, but the albino waved him off.

"Ask Mr. Song if he wants to buy an advertisement in my newspaper," said Samuel.

The girl translated. "No Chinese person reads your newspaper, and an ad wouldn't help his business. If his clients read such an advertisement in the press, they'd think that his business was bad, and they'd stop coming. That's not very convenient."

"That's too bad," sighed Samuel, putting the bottle of medicine in his jacket pocket.

Once outside, they stood talking on the sidewalk. Charles was clearly unhappy, but Samuel convinced him they were making progress.

"I'll subpoena that examiner bastard up here tomorrow morning, and he'll have to bring the claim check with him," said Charles. "Then we'll see if this asshole still thinks he can make fun of me." And he turned and walked off down Pacific toward Montgomery.

\* \* \*

# The Chinese Jars

When Samuel arrived at Mr. Song's herb shop the next day, he couldn't believe what he saw. There, on the sidewalk, was Charles, dressed in the same clothes he had had on the day before, unshaven, with two federal marshals next to him. An upset-looking medical examiner was pacing back and forth, trying to argue with him. A Chinese gentleman dressed in a Brooks Brothers three-piece suit leaned against the shop storefront with one leg bent and the heel of that foot resting against the low sill that held the plate-glass window with Mr. Song's sign on it. He seemed to be the only one who wasn't in a hurry.

"You didn't have to do it this way!" exclaimed the examiner, red in the face and breathing heavily.

"You wouldn't cooperate," said Charles. "That's why I had to stay up all night and prepare the lengthy affidavit I took to the magistrate. So now I have a search warrant."

"Did you have to serve me at six in the morning?" asked the examiner, glaring again at Charles.

"I need the claim check, I can't keep wasting time. If you'd given it to me when I asked for it, we'd both have been able to sleep in," said Charles.

"But you didn't need me!" exclaimed the examiner.

"I'm sure you remember the chain of evidence argument," Charles teased.

At ten o'clock sharp, Mr. Song's assistant unbolted at least five locks from the inside, and the small man stepped aside as Charles, the medical examiner, the two marshals, the elegant Chinese man, and Samuel entered the establishment. The bell on the door tingled wildly, welcoming the procession.

Once they were all inside, the assistant hobbled through the blue beaded curtain and, within a couple of minutes, Mr. Song appeared carrying a cup of steaming tea with a top on it; he opened the top from time to time to breath in the aroma and take a sip. His black suit with a Mandarin collar emphasized his whiteness. He had on his head what looked like a black Chinese skullcap. He bowed slightly and mumbled something in his language.

"He says good morning, and he hopes you have many male children and live long lives," said the Chinese man in the suit, who introduced himself as an official federal government interpreter.

"Tell him we are here to examine the contents of the jar. We have both halves of the claim check," said Charles.

"You must put them here so he can see them," said the interpreter.

Charles summoned the examiner to the counter, and they both put down their respective half's of the claim check. Mr. Song pulled a pair of wire-rimmed spectacles with thick lenses out of his sleeve and put them on over his pink eyes. This had the eerie effect of enlarging them, making him look like an ostrich. Mr. Song stared at the two pieces for a long time, while the others tried to control their impatience. "This is claim check number 85. Now you need the key," he said, through the interpreter.

"Shit!" exclaimed Charles.

"I think we have the key. It's one of those Mr. Engel copied for us," said Samuel, fishing around in the manila envelope from Charles's briefcase and pulling out two keys.

The assistant pulled the ladder over to the middle of the stack of clay jars on the eastern wall. Mr. Song pointed with a long bony finger to number 85.

"He says to climb up and see if one of the keys opens the top. It's the second from the last one up there, a little to the left."

They looked at each other and, since no one volunteered, Samuel scurried up the wooden ladder that creaked with each step. He started inserting keys into the band that held the top fast on the jar, not an easy task because the ladder moved and his hands shook. He also didn't like heights. At first none worked, but as he calmed down and was more careful, he found one that did. He then started inserting keys into the band that held the container against the wall. A scream from Mr. Song stopped him. The albino was gesturing like a madman with both his arms in front of his face as he talked to the interpreter.

"No, no," said the interpreter, "Mr. Song says he will take care of the rest."

"Why didn't you bring it down in the first place?' asked Charles.

"If you didn't have the key to open the jar, no need to bring it down because it wouldn't have belonged to you," said Mr. Song through the interpreter.

Samuel came down quickly, while the assistant brought a huge key ring from behind the beaded curtain. Mr. Song sorted through the keys and chose one, which he gave to the assistant. With startling agility, given his age, he went up the creaking ladder, unfastened the band that held the jar to the wall, brought it down, and placed it on the counter. Mr. Song checked to make sure it was the right number and then stepped back.

"He says you are welcome to examine it, the contents belong to you," said the interpreter.

"No, no," said Charles, "we want him to open it. It might be booby trapped or something."

This interchange produced a hilarious moment between the interpreter and the assistant. Mr. Song joined by smiling slightly, which consisted of his showing a row of pointed teeth for an instant. Finally, the small man removed the top, tipped it over until it was lying lengthwise on the counter, and started removing the contents. The first to come out was a vegetable material. There was a lot of it, and it had a strange musty odor.

"What's this?" asked Charles warily. "Is it a narcotic?" He

picked up a small amount and smelled it, suspiciously.

"Mr. Song says it is a Chinese herb called Chai Hu used to treat liver problems," said the interpreter. "In English it is called Bupleurum."

The assistant then took out several packages. One was wrapped in white tissue paper and held fast with string. There were also five small bundles of hundred dollar bills, each held by rubber bands, some so old they were on the verge of disintegrating.

Samuel watched intently to see if any plane tickets were hidden in the jar, but there were none.

The examiner, who had been sulking in the corner, with his turtle's head slumped between his shoulders, perked up when he heard about the herb that was a treatment for hepatic problems. Rockwood's pathology slides showed that his liver was in its last stages. The herbs reinforced his opinion as to the cause of death. But from the looks of the situation, it was more complicated than one supposed, which meant that he'd have to hold on to the cadaver.

"I'll examine the material, if you like," he said.

"Be my guest," said Charles. He went on to the package wrapped in white tissue paper. He carefully unwrapped it and found a velvet box. It had three gleaming green stones in it, one the size of a bean and two smaller ones.

Charles whistled, "Emeralds! And they look to be of good quality. They must be worth thousands of dollars. How did they come to be in the hands of a janitor, I ask? How much cash is there?"

The examiner counted out the hundred dollar bills in each packet. "Ten thousand."

"And a like amount in these stones," added Charles. "How much is the medicine worth?"

"Mr. Song says it's worth about thirty dollars," said the interpreter.

# The Chinese Jars

"Thirty dollars for some grass. What times we live in!" exclaimed Charles.

"Just a minute," said Samuel. "You see that piece of paper holding one of the packets of bills? It has some printing on it. It looks like part of an address. It has the number 838 and nothing else." He took his notepad out and wrote down the number.

"It doesn't mean much," said the examiner. "It was just used to hold the bills together."

"You never know," said Samuel.

Charles puffed up as much as his tired frame allowed. "We're going to take possession of this evidence in the name of the people of the United States of America. This document allows us to do that."

He showed the search warrant to the interpreter, who in turn showed it to Mr. Song.

"You are welcome to the entire contents of the jar," said Mr. Song, through the interpreter, "because you presented the claim check. But the jar belongs to the shop, so you can't take it."

"I'm sorry, Mr. Song, we must take it," said Charles. "We'll hold the evidence in it until we decide if a federal crime has been committed. If there is no reason to hold onto it, we'll return it to you."

"The material in the jar is not mine, it is yours," responded Mr. Song through the interpreter. "But the jar belongs to Mr. Song's Many Chinese Herbs, and it will not leave here."

"We can pay you for it," suggested Samuel.

"It's not for sale," replied Mr. Song, who by now had lost the proverbial patience of his race and was furrowing his brow.

"I'll give you a receipt for the jar from the United States government," said Charles. He took a sheet of Justice Department stationary from his briefcase and wrote a detailed list of all the items he was taking from the shop. The interpreter read them off to Mr. Song.

"Is this white man deaf or demented?" Mr. Song asked.

But the interpreter thought better than to translate it. Instead he explained, "Mr. Song is desolate because if the people on the street see you leave with his jar they will spread the word, and he will lose his good reputation. How could the people confide in him if he allowed just any white man to leave his establishment with one of his jars underneath his arm?"

"Listen, Mr. Song," interrupted Charles. "Here's the receipt for everything. You keep it until the case is over. Then, everything of yours will be returned to you," and he slammed the paper down on the countertop.

Exhausted, Charles motioned to the examiner, the two marshals, and the interpreter that they should follow him out of the shop while at the same time he was cursing the albino, his assistant, and the infernal bells above the door that wouldn't stop tingling.

"Call me tomorrow, Samuel. I can't think straight right now," he said.

# 7

## Rafael in a Muddle

SAMUEL WENT to Camelot at an ungodly hour of the morning because Melba had woken him up with the bad news that Rafael had been arrested. He found Blanche effortlessly carrying cases of beer from the storeroom to the bar dressed only in a top, short pants and work boots. He tried to help her but the boxes were too heavy for him. Then Melba came out of the office. Samuel heard her. She'd been on the phone talking to important clients of the bar, trying to find someone who could help Rafael.

"What happened?" asked Samuel.

"I told him a thousand times to take that goddamned net off his head!" exclaimed Melba.

"They arrested him because of that?"

"No, they caught him with a stolen machine. I don't know what kind, but it looks like it's valuable. They searched the bar and his house. His mother was beside herself," explained Blanche.

"What can we do?" asked Melba.

"He needs a lawyer. He has a right to a defense," said Blanche.

"Who'll pay for that?" asked Samuel.

"We'll see. This thing has to be cleared up fast," said Melba.

"On the assumption that he's innocent," pointed out Blanche.

"You don't think Rafael's a thief, child!" exclaimed Melba.

\* \* \*

Days later Samuel watched the criminal court judge sitting on the dais in his black robe pounding the gavel. "The clerk will call the roll. Please give time estimates. We have a full calendar this morning."

The sleepy female clerk looked through the sheets of paper in front of her. "The People of the State of California versus Rafael Garcia, docket number 54321702."

Rafael—in handcuffs, with his ankles shackled, and wearing a San Francisco County Jail jumpsuit—was let out of the holding cell at the side of the courtroom by the bailiff. In the meantime, the well-dressed attorney sitting next to Samuel, in his expensive double-breasted Walter Fong suit, looked at his watch and pulled his Day-Timer out of his jacket pocket. He was heavyset with curly hair, a bulbous nose, and capped white teeth that matched the porcelain of a bathtub. He smiled all the time to show them off, as they had no doubt been expensive. He sauntered up to the podium inside the railing and the swinging door that separated the observers from the participants at the daily cattle call.

"Hiram Goldberg of the Law Offices of Hiram Goldberg representing defendant Rafael Garcia." He was one of the best criminal lawyers in the city. He stood there waiting for the prisoner to make his way slowly to a place beside him, followed by the deputy closely guarding him.

When Rafael arrived, he looked at the attorney suspiciously. He'd never seen him before. Then he quickly glanced around the courtroom, saw Samuel in the rear, and waved with a slight smile of recognition. He guessed that the fancy attorney standing next to him was Samuel's doing, so he relaxed a little.

The municipal court judge, who had a florid face and the reputation of being irascible, looked over his reading glasses at the defendant with a total lack of sympathy. He didn't trust Mexicans or other immigrants of color; it was a matter of principal with him. "To the charge of violating section 496 of the California Penal Code, receiving stolen property, a felony, how do you plead?"

"The defendant pleads not guilty to the charge, Your Honor, waives time to a speedy trial and asks that bail be reduced from $5,000 to $1,500, which we're prepared to post this morning."

"He's charged with a felony, Mr. Goldberg. The words have to come out of his mouth, not yours," the judge chided. "Do you plead not guilty and waive time, Mr. Garcia?"

Rafael had a whispering session with his attorney and remained silent for almost a minute. Samuel guessed from a distance that they were having an argument. It was too bad that Hiram couldn't have talked to his client beforehand.

"Do you speak English, young man?" asked the judge, impatiently. "I have a full calendar this morning, and if you need an interpreter, we'll have to pass on this matter."

"I understand everything you said, Your Honor, except about the time thing. That's what I was asking about. You wouldn't want someone to agree to something he didn't understand, would you?" Rafael asked, sarcastically.

Hiram nudged Rafael to shut up, but he straightened his shoulders in defiance and gave a penetrating glance at the bench. He was scared because he'd never been in front of a judge before, and he knew he was in trouble. Nonetheless, he wanted the judge to know he was his own man.

"We'll pass this matter," said the judge. "You need to consult with your attorney."

As Hiram slammed his Day-Timer on his thigh, the ruby in his pinky ring gave off a glint from the fluorescent light above. This messed up his whole morning calendar. Now he'd have to wait until the end of the hearing. He whispered something in Rafael's ear and reminded the judge, "I'm scheduled to appear in departments 15, 16 and 17, Your Honor."

"That's okay. We'll see you back here at eleven. The defendant's not going anywhere."

Rafael was shuffled back to the holding cell in cuffs and shackles, and Hiram walked quickly through the swinging gate doors that separated the working part of the courtroom from the audience. He motioned to Samuel to follow him out into the hall.

"That guy's a smart-ass Mexican," he complained.

"He's a friend of mine," said Samuel, "and Melba wants him out of jail. That's why she sent me here and why she retained you."

"I'm only a lawyer, not a magician," Hiram said. His jowls hung over the high, stiffly starched collar of his white shirt. His gold cufflinks matched the tie tack. Samuel felt a wave of dislike for him.

"It's hard to deal with smart-ass Mexicans. They make my job a lot harder even when they can afford me. This is a kiss-ass business. Melba paid me a lot of money to get this prick off, but he wants to know every fucking detail about what goes on around him, and I don't have time for that shit. You go and talk to that greaser and tell him how things are in this town. Mexicans are in last place, along with the queers. It's the Jews, the Irish, and the Italians that run it, in case you hadn't noticed."

"Calm down," Samuel interrupted. "He's a good kid. You know I won't be able to talk to him until court is over. Just get his bail reduced so we can get him out."

"That's not going to be easy, not now. Don't you see, he's

questioning the judge's authority, and he's not one of the boys. He may have fucked himself," said Hiram.

"I'll straighten him out. You get him a bail hearing. We have good character witnesses. He's a hard-working citizen and not a flight risk," said Samuel.

"I gotta go. See ya at eleven," said Hiram, and he waddled down the hall.

Putting his hand on the swinging outer door, Samuel yelled at him, "How 'bout buying an ad in my paper? I'm busting my ass to sell slots. You look like a guy with a lot of dough!"

"Jesus Christ, man, you know lawyers can't advertise in this state," replied Hiram, over his shoulder, as he disappeared into another courtroom, the door flapping behind him.

When Hiram returned at eleven, Rafael's bail hearing was set by the court for the following Thursday at two-thirty.

\* \* \*

When court next convened in Rafael's case, Hiram Goldberg entered with a large entourage. There was Melba; her daughter, Blanche; Rafael's mother, brother, and his two sisters; Sofia; the parish priest; and Samuel. They were all prepared to testify what a good and reliable person he was, following Hiram's carefully scripted preparation of each of them.

The judge called the court to order, and the clerk called the case.

"Bail is presently set at five thousand dollars. Mr. Garcia is accused of having a stolen X-ray machine in his possession worth over ten thousand dollars. Why should the people reduce his bail?" asked the judge, squinting at the defendant.

"For several reasons," answered Hiram, rising heavily to his feet. "In the first place, the state has absolutely no proof he stole the machine. The most the D.A. can say is that he was in the vicinity of the machine when the police arrived."

"Your Honor," interrupted the assistant district attorney, who stood up from his place at the table next to the podium where Hiram was lecturing the court. He had the gaunt look of the zealot, with sunken cheeks and deep shadows surrounding his eye sockets. "Mr. Goldberg will have a hard time disputing Mr. Garcia's involvement in this crime, since the X-ray machine was in a truck he rented in his own name. The only thing we don't know, and he won't tell us, is where he got it and where he was taking it. But we do know where it came from, and it certainly didn't come into Mr. Garcia's possession in an arm's length transaction."

"Before I was interrupted, Your Honor," said Hiram, "I was about to explain to the court that it wasn't my intention to try the case at this time. My idea was merely to present the flimsiness of the evidence against my client. But even more importantly, the record needs to reflect that Mr. Garcia has absolutely no criminal record. In fact, quite the contrary, he's a pillar of his community and is no flight risk whatsoever. He has a long-standing job with Melba Sundling, a well-known and respected saloonkeeper of Your Honor's Irish persuasion, and she is here to confirm that. He's heavily involved in the activities of his local Catholic Church, as his parish priest will attest. In addition, he helps support his mother and three siblings, which, by the way, he can't do if he's in jail."

"Before we clutter the record with lengthy testimony," said the judge, looking at the plethora of witnesses filling his courtroom and calculating the hours of testimony that he would have to listen to, "I want to see the lawyers in chambers, and bring the probation officer with you."

They all crowded into the judge's chambers. "Counting the number of witnesses in the courtroom, Mr. Goldberg is prepared to load the boat, counsel," said the judge. "Why did you make the bail so high in the first place?"

"This is a serious crime," said the gaunt attorney, starting again to give his prepared speech about the well-known evils of stealing from others.

"Hold on! This isn't the trial," shouted Hiram. "We're here to talk about bail, just bail."

"Where there's smoke, there's fire, Judge," the attorney responded, his thin lips quivering with disdain for both Hiram and Rafael.

"Oh, bullshit. This is the crappiest case I've seen in years," Hiram cut in. "You just want to hold Mr. Garcia's feet to the fire in the hopes you'll get some hot evidence of a big theft ring. It's not there. This guy was just in the wrong place at the wrong time. You'll see."

"What does the probation department have to say?" asked the judge.

"He's definitely not a flight risk," answered the probation officer. "He's a pretty stable guy, and he seems really close to his family."

The prosecutor interrupted, "I didn't come here to hear this prisoner praised. He's a common thief who should have to stay behind bars. Remember, Judge, your job is to protect the citizens of this city, not to coddle the criminals."

"That's enough!" shot back the judge. "You gentlemen wait outside. I want to think about this one. Mr. Probation Officer, leave your report with me. I'll file it after I've read it."

The attorneys left the judge's office, and Hiram walked down the aisle toward the drinking fountain outside the flapping main doors. As he passed Samuel, he winked at him.

Alone in the quiet of his chambers, the judge quickly turned the pages of the document he had been handed. He didn't like greasers, the name he gave to Mexicans in private, but he decided to lower his bail to two thousand dollars. It remained to be seen if the prisoner could post it. In any event, he was sure Rafael would end up behind bars.

# 8

## Xsing Ching Surrenders

Xsing Ching pushed hard on the doorbell of Virginia Dimitri's Grant Avenue apartment. His palms were sweaty and his muscular shoulders hunched as he concentrated on the button. He couldn't remember a time in his life when his nerves were so shot. He struggled to control his emotions. The carved wooden door looked immense to him in the sunlight. On the other six or seven occasions he'd visited Virginia, as he remembered, it was night. His encounters had become more intimate and pleasurable, but still formal. This was the first time that he'd broken the strict protocol that Virginia had laid down for his visits. It was clear that he shouldn't get involved with her. His life was too complicated and the last thing he should allow himself was a passionate love affair, but he had a lot in common with her. Both were sensual, refined, and ambitious. Virginia had never asked anything of him. What did that beautiful woman want from him? On his third visit, he'd brought her a crocodile purse that cost him a small fortune. She thanked him formally and later, after they'd made love, she begged him never to repeat the gesture. "I like you a lot Xsing, and you make me happy. I don't need anything from you except your presence. I prefer that you don't give me presents because that changes the tone of our relationship. It makes me feel like you're trying to pay me."

At first he was insulted. But after he thought about it, he understood that she was right. From that moment on he viewed her differently.

On his third ring, the one-armed servant, Fu Fung Fat, opened the door a crack. "Is Miss Virginia in? I need to speak with her," said Xsing in Mandarin.

Fu Fung Fat listened to his Chinese compatriot with a cold eye. "The mistress does not accept visitors without an appointment. Those are her instructions."

"It's urgent. Tell her I'm here, and let her decide," Xsing responded with such authority that the other couldn't ignore his request.

While he was waiting, Xsing continued his pacing. Was Virginia with another man? He felt ridiculous. She was free to do what she wanted, just as he was. Just the same, the agonies of jealousy left a sour taste in his mouth. He took out a white handkerchief and wiped his clammy hands and dabbed at the beads of sweat on his forehead.

Several minutes passed before Fu Fung Fat returned. Again he only partially opened the door. "The mistress says to come back at three o'clock," and he closed the door before Xsing Ching could further plead his case.

Xsing Ching walked the streets in a daze until it was time; at exactly three, he reappeared at Virginia's door and heavily pushed the bell. He was more composed than he had been on his morning visit, but the undershirt he wore beneath his expensive suit was soaking wet from perspiration.

The manservant opened the front door, unlocked the chain, and ushered him inside with a smile. Now he was a welcome guest: he had an appointment. Walking down the hallway, Xsing reexamined the giant vases; he noticed details on them that had escaped him in the evening light. Sun from a skylight illuminated a collection of jade statues in niches of the wall. Even though he was an expert in antiques, he didn't bother to examine them. His mind was on something else.

The servant showed him a seat and went to call Virginia. Half a minute later she came out of the bedroom with the fresh air of an innocent girl. If she was with another lover during the time he was wandering the streets, there was no evidence of it. She was dressed in black toreador pants that came to her knees, a gray silk belt around her waist, ballet slippers on her feet, and a man's white shirt. She didn't have on any jewelry or noticeable makeup. Xsing Ching got up quickly to greet her. For an instant he thought of making her his mistress and taking her to New York and installing her in an apartment facing Central Park, like a queen, and loving her the way both deserved to be loved. But his immediate concern was the urgent matter that brought him there.

"I'm very sorry I couldn't see you this morning, Xsing. Why didn't you call me first?" asked Virginia.

He came to her and kissed her on the forehead. "Thank you for seeing me, Virginia."

"Fu Fung Fat told me it was something urgent," she said, taking him by the arm to the sofa, where they sat down together.

"Yes, I have to talk with you." He was so nervous his hands were shaking. "Thank you for seeing me, Virginia. My son is here in San Francisco. I brought him because he suffered another relapse of his leukemia, and the doctors in New York told me that California is the only place where they can do a bone marrow transplant. We didn't expect this because lately he seemed to be getting better and his condition was in remission. But now I'm afraid he is gravely ill."

"Oh, Xsing! How can I help you?" exclaimed Virginia. "Where is the boy? What's his name?"

## The Chinese Jars

"His name is Ren Shen Ching. He's in the Children's Hospital on California Street. I remember that you offered to put me in contact with some doctors from here...," and his voice broke.

Virginia caressed his neck. Xsing saw she was as moved as he was.

"I'll take care of this immediately," she said. "Just give me a few moments."

She retired to her bedroom and closed the door. The minutes she was gone seemed like an eternity for Xsing Ching. When she returned, she found him on the sofa with his legs apart, his elbows on his knees, and his head cradled in his hands—the image of total desperation. She kneeled at his side and embraced him.

"Xsing, I've just spoken to Dr. Stephen Roland. You are to meet him at Children's Hospital at four thirty. That's in about half an hour from now. He's one of the foremost authorities on leukemia. I explained the case to him, and he promised me that he would do everything in his power to help your son. He'll meet with his treating doctor to see if he is a good candidate for a transplant. He did tell me that this treatment is still in the experimental stage."

"I understand, Virginia, but we must try it. It's the last recourse."

As disconcerted as Xsing Ching was, he noticed that Virginia was crying. The tears rolled down her cheeks and fell onto her shirt. Could his misfortune have moved this apparently cold woman?

"What's the matter? Do you think Ren will die?"

"No, it's not that, Xsing. He'll be in the best hands, and I think they'll save him. There are cases of miraculous recovery with the transplant."

"Then why do you cry?"

"You see, I lost my only child some years ago from an

illness. This brings back many painful memories. I know exactly how you feel. That's why I'm so happy to help you."

"I don't know how to thank you, Virginia," and he hugged her tightly, as they cried together.

* * *

A few days later Mathew went to the apartment. When he saw Virginia, he grabbed her around the waist and picked her up and kissed her on the mouth. She pushed him away and smoothed her clothes. She didn't like displays of exuberance.

"We've got this guy in the palm of our hands," said Mathew, taking off his jacket and loosening his tie. "He's ready to do business on my terms. He's insinuated that he won't divide the shipment of art, he'll give me priority, and I'll be able to have all I want before he offers any to the rest of his clients. This is formidable! How did you do it? He seemed as cold as a crab and you made him lose his head. Is he in love with you?"

"I don't think it has anything to do with love."

"What then?"

"Gratitude."

"Gratitude for what?"

"I found a specialist for his son who's suffering from leukemia. They're doing tests on all the family to see who's a compatible donor for a bone marrow transplant."

"What do you know about that? How did you get him a doctor?" asked Mathew.

"Let's just say I have an old friend. It was just a matter of giving him a call to remind him of moments we shared in the past."

"Was he your lover? Did you blackmail him?"

"It's none of your business. I've given you what you needed. How I did it is my business."

Mathew shrugged his shoulders. Virginia's methods

were irrelevant to him as long as she got results, and that's what he paid her for. But he was curious and a little jealous. Virginia was attractive to him because she was a mystery. They had ceased to be lovers a long time ago and, since they were working together on many business deals, it was better not to mix in love or sex. Nevertheless, Virginia saw the slight bulge in her partner's tan gabardine slacks, and she smiled to herself, sure she still had power over this man. Sooner or later she would have the need to use it.

"Have you had any news from Xsing Ching?" asked Mathew.

"Yes. He called this morning to thank me for getting him help so fast. The doctor was encouraging and felt the boy would survive the crisis. He told me as soon as his son was better he would come and see me so we could celebrate."

"Good. We'll close the deal for the complete shipment and you charge your commission. Congratulations, you've shined as usual," said Mathew. He got up from the sofa, leaned over and kissed Virginia on the cheek, then began to walk toward the door. Fu Fung Fat accompanied him. Mathew had the impression that the strange servant always treated him with disdain, but he had nothing to complain about because he did his job and Virginia trusted him completely.

\* \* \*

After Mathew left, Virginia went quickly to her bedroom, opened her clothes closet, dug deeply into the rear and brought out a box with two black bands around it. She opened a jewelry box in the first drawer of her dresser and pulled out a claim check with the number 120 on it and a padlock key. She then called Fu Fung Fat to her bedroom. "You know what to do," she ordered.

Fu Fung Fat, nodded and put the key and the claim check

in his jacket pocket and put the box in a travel bag that he slung on over his shoulder, then he headed for the back stairs. He reached the narrow streets of Chinatown.

The tingle of the bell announced him. Mr. Song's assistant greeted him as if he were an old friend and called for his master. Fu Fung Fat showed him the claim check. Mr. Song found the relevant key on his huge key ring and instructed his assistant to access jar number 120. The man climbed the ladder, unlocked the outer band, and brought the jar down, then carried it to a small curtained area behind the blue beaded curtain. Fu Fung Fat went in, unlocked the jar, and opened the box he'd brought from the apartment. He stuffed its cash contents into the jar, closed and locked the band, and announced that he was finished. He picked up the empty box and took back the claim check from Mr. Song. He watched as Mr. Song's assistant climbed the ladder and locked the jar in place; he then put the key and claim check in his pocket, put the empty box in his travel bag, paid his respects, and walked out the noisy door.

# 9

## The Missing Page

On a Sunday afternoon in early January 1961, Samuel sat at the round table at Camelot talking with Melba. Excalibur, under the table, had not only stopped growling at him but now followed him around. Currently, he was gnawing on one of his shoelaces. Samuel pulled it away.

"I can't believe this fucking dog. First he wants to attack me, and now he wants to slobber all over me. Can't you keep him under control?"

"I assume that you didn't come here to discuss my dog's etiquette," said Melba.

There was an accordion file on the table next to Samuel. Its contents spilled out onto the oak tabletop, covering the stains of the liquor spills that had been absorbed over the decades.

Samuel had a one-page police report in his hand. "You see, Melba, this is perplexing."

"What do you mean by that?" she asked.

"I mean, it doesn't end, it just stops, almost like it was cut off."

"Maybe it was. Maybe someone deep-sixed the rest of it," she said.

"They couldn't do that. It's an official document."

Melba smirked. "You're a cherry, Samuel. There's all sorts of shit that goes on in this town. It just depends on what kind of influence people have. It's always been that way."

"You know as well as I do that Rockwood didn't have that kind of influence. I've shown you that he lived in a closet, for chrissake," said Samuel, as he finished pulling his shoestring out of Excalibur's reach. He took a cocktail napkin from the table and wiped the slobber off the slimy lace, then tied his shoe.

"I'm not talking about Rockwood. He's dead! Besides, he wouldn't be the one trying to cover it up, would he? It'd be the person who did him in. I bet if you do a bit more snooping, you'll find out there's more to this," she suggested.

"Listen to this description of the accident," said Samuel.

"What accident?" asked Melba.

"You remember, he was killed by a trolley bus. It hit him in the street out by General Hospital."

"I remember that. Go ahead, read it to me." She put her cigarette in the ashtray, which had several butts already in it, and blew the last puff of smoke out her nose. She then took a sip of beer from her glass.

"'The victim and two others appeared directly in front of me. It was dark, and they came out of nowhere. I applied my brakes but couldn't stop. I hit the victim. The other two got out of the way.' That's it," said Samuel.

"Who said that?" asked Melba.

"It must have been the bus driver, but it's not signed by anyone."

"Is his name on the report?" asked Melba.

"Yeah, it's right here at the top," said Samuel.

"Well, genius, take the report to him and go over it."

"I'd already thought of that, but I like to talk things over with you first, is all," said Samuel. He started stuffing the pile of papers back into the accordion folder and, in turn, put it into his bulging briefcase. He said his goodbyes to Melba and a few of the patrons while looking in vain toward the back of the bar, hoping to catch a glimpse of Blanche, whom he hadn't seen around there for several days. To him it seemed like decades.

He hopped on a cable car and rode it down to Market, set his watch by the clock in the Ferry Building, and jumped on a number 5 McAllister trolley bus, rode it past city hall and the plaza in front of it with its grove of bare trees, all the way up to the imposing Saint Ignatius Church on top of the hill. From there he walked down by the University of San Francisco Law School to Grove Street, where he found the address he was looking for on the south side of the street. It was a typical duplex of flats with bay windows on both the lower and upper floors. He rang the doorbell several times until an attractive Negro woman in her mid-thirties answered the door of the upper flat. She was holding a baby in her arms.

"I'm sorry to disturb you, ma'am," said Samuel. "I'm looking for Mr. Butler. Is he home?"

"Who are you?"

"Samuel Hamilton from the local newspaper."

She turned and yelled up the stairs, "Jim, there's a man down here lookin' to talk to you."

"Who wanna talk to me?" came a voice from deep inside the flat.

"A man from the newspaper," she said, and the baby started crying from all the commotion.

"What he want?" asked the voice, loudly.

"You gotta come deal with this, Jim. The baby's crying. Hurry up!" and she went back upstairs, leaving Samuel at the door.

"All right, all right." A huge Negro man, wearing a red Pendleton shirt and suspenders holding up his loose denim trousers, appeared at the top of the stairs. "What you want?' he said loudly from his perch, as he looked suspiciously down at Samuel framed in the doorway with his wrinkled khaki sports

Foley and find out what he knew about the missing page. Instead, he went to Chop Suey Louie's for dinner. Louie greeted him at the door with his usual smile, while Louie's mother stared at him with disgust.

"Hi Samuel, we have a great special tonight, Chinese fried rice with shrimp. Go and say hello to Goldie, she been asking for you. She wants to know why you don't pay attention to her, like before."

"That fish doesn't bring me good luck."

"In love or in work?"

"In either. Blanche doesn't even know I exist, and I haven't sold an ad in days. At his rate you'll have to vouch for me so I don't die of hunger. Plus, I've been working hard on an investigation, and I don't have much to show for it. The case is more complicated than an old hag's hair bun. No offense to your mother," he said, nodding toward the seat where the old woman sat watching him.

"If you want Goldie to bring you good luck, you have to spoil her a little, Samuel. I went to the pet shop and bought this food for her. Climb up on the step ladder next to the aquarium and give her some; not much mind you."

"Like this?" asked Samuel, pouring some of the food into his hand

"Less. Do you want Miss Goldie to get fat?"

"How do you know it's a she?"

"By the affectionate way she looks at you," and he started to laugh.

Samuel climbed up on the stepladder and put a pinch of food in the tank. "Okay, Goldie, make a little effort to change things. I'm fed up with this streak of bad luck, it's lasted too long."

* * *

The next morning, realizing he'd been neglecting his job, he went to the newspaper office. He put his briefcase on the chair and rifled through his latest messages and requests. He hadn't made a sale for a week. He was worried that at any minute his boss would call to fire him, but he had the crazy hope that when that moment came he'd be able to announce that he'd solved a big criminal case. His boss would then promote him to reporter, he would dedicate himself to the police beat, and nothing would escape his bloodhound instincts. He would become a celebrity. Even Blanche would come to him on her knees begging for his love. He slapped himself on the forehead and tried to concentrate on his work, but he was obsessed with the death of Reginald Rockwood III.

With one telephone call he found out that Officer Foley was on the swing shift, which gave him several hours to work before trying to see him. He made several phone calls, attempting to convince uninterested potential clients to sign up, but all he was able to sell was an insignificant mattress ad. At least this futile exercise in monotony assuaged his guilt and cleared his mind.

At four o'clock sharp he put on his sport coat and ran out. When he arrived at the new Hall of Justice on Bryant Street, he went directly to the police department and asked for Officer Foley, who turned out to be much younger than he thought. He looked like a pimply teenager. "I'm Samuel Hamilton. I saw your name on this police report," he announced, handing him the sheet of paper he carried. "Do you remember the incident?"

The officer read it over and saw his name at the bottom. "Yes, sir, this is my report. Where are the other pages? I remember there being three; two in writing and a diagram."

"That's all I have," answered Samuel. "Can you take a look in the file and see if the rest of it's in there?"

Foley left the room for several minutes and returned shaking his head. "Not there. You'd better check with my supervisor. I turn over all my reports to him, and he signs off on them at the end. That's why his name's not on this page."

"You do remember the incident?" asked Samuel.

"I remember it well. This was only my third accident. I knew it was above my head. I'm only a rookie and traffic was my first assignment. Let me think," he said, scratching the pimples on his chin. "There were three guys, two Chinese and the white guy dressed in the tuxedo who got killed. The question was whether the Chinese guys pushed him into the path of the bus. I also seem to remember that the bus driver said one of the Chinese guys had something wrong with his face. He must have been really ugly for the driver to notice his looks at a time like that. My supervisor's job was to review the facts and turn the matter over to the right department. You'll have to ask him what he found out and what he did with the information," said Foley.

"Who was your supervisor?" asked Samuel.

"Sergeant Maurice Sandovich," answered Foley.

"Where can I find him?" asked Samuel.

"He's back on the Vice Squad now. They switched him to days," answered Foley.

"What do you mean, he's back on the Vice Squad?"

"Not for me to say, you'll have to take that up with him. Sorry I can't do more for you," he said, and waved Samuel off.

\* \* \*

Samuel knew he wasn't going to get anything out of the police department by himself, so the next day he went to the U.S. attorney's office to ask for help.

Charles Perkins was feeling good about himself. He had gotten a spread in the newspaper that Samuel worked for as a result of being the lead attorney on the conviction of a group of drug smugglers from Central America. So when Samuel showed up at his office unannounced, Charles received him in good humor. His office was full of boxes concerning his recently completed case, and piles of stacked mail on his desk awaited his attention. He was seated in the swivel chair with his feet up on the desk.

"Hi, Charles. Busy as usual, I see," said Samuel. He was looking right at the hole in the right sole of Charles's weathered-looking Florsheim black wingtips. The worn look of the shoes matched the dullness of the tired blue suit he was wearing. Those details awoke a certain sympathy in Samuel for his arrogant friend.

"You again. I haven't heard from you in a while. I thought maybe your case just went away," he said with his usual air of superiority, balancing a cup of coffee in his right hand.

"Not quite," said Samuel. "It gets more complicated all the time. Remember the one-page police report?"

"Yeah, that was a no-brainer," said Charles. "It just told us what happened."

"That's what I thought at the beginning, but I learned there are pages missing," said Samuel.

"Is that right," said Charles, taking his feet off the desk and sitting upright in his chair. "How did you find that out?"

"I talked to the trolley bus driver and the police officer who made out the report."

"And?"

"The police officer was a rookie, and he turned his report over to his supervisor. But he remembered the accident, and when he went to look for the rest of the report, it wasn't in the file," said Samuel.

"Who was his supervisor?" asked Charles.

"Maurice Sandovich."

Charles jumped to his feet. Half of his coffee spilled on the papers on his desk. "You've got to be kidding!"

"I'm not kidding. Why would you say that?" asked Samuel.

"Maurice Sandovich is one of the crookedist cops I've investigated since I've been on this job. He's up to his neck in rackets connected with Chinatown. Tell me about the one-pager."

"The driver told the cop that two Chinese guys might have pushed Rockwood into the path of the trolley bus," Samuel explained.

"What did Sandovich have to do with all this?" asked Charles.

"He was supposed to approve the report and file it, but instead two-thirds disappeared."

"Where's Sandovich now?" asked Charles.

"He's back on the Vice Squad."

Charles cursed. "I can't believe they put that bastard back on Vice. I bet he weaseled his way onto the Chinatown beat again, and now he's back to work for the gangsters down there. Who would've approved that move?" Then he thought for a minute. Actually, that's beside the point. We still have to prove he was involved and that he did something wrong. But most of all, we have to figure out why," said Charles.

"For the last couple of days I was thinking about coming to see you," said Samuel, "and now I know why."

"Why is that?"

"Because you always ask the right questions," said Samuel.

"You came just at the right time. Before today I couldn't have done anything. Did you read the story about me in the paper this morning?" Charles crowed.

"Sure," Samuel lied, knowing Charles would recount whatever had happened in more detail than the paper had told it anyway. He was correct. He spent the next half hour rehashing all the excitement of his trial victory, while Samuel was stealing glances at the clock on the wall.

"What do we do now?" asked Samuel when Charles finally

stopped talking.

The lawyer came back down to earth and thought for a minute. "Believe it or not, we have to be careful not to step on local law enforcement's toes. You see, there's a delicate balance between the San Francisco P.D. and the federal government. We have to respect their territory. Otherwise, when we need something from them, it won't be available. I think the best thing to do is to go to the chief of police and explain to him what the problem is. Of course, if there's an innocent explanation for the disappearance, or if it turns out that the report was just misfiled, then Sandovich gets tipped off that we're watching him."

"From the sound of it, it doesn't matter," said Samuel.

"What d'ya mean?" asked Charles.

"If this guy's as bad as you say, then if he's not caught for this, it's bound to be for something else, so why not just take the shot. Besides, it's not your office that's investigating him. I stumbled on this by accident. If worse comes to worse, you can blame me."

Charles laughed, brushing the lock of blond hair back from his forehead. "I like that approach. There's no doubt this guy is bad. I bet he's way more involved than we actually figure right now. But we have to be careful not to make him suspicious, because he can attack like a scorpion"

\* \* \*

Charles made a few phone calls. A few days later, he and Samuel had a meeting with the assistant chief of police, Sandovich, and Officer Foley. Charles Perkins started the discussion. "Mr. Hamilton here has been looking into the death of Reginald Rockwood III. He was killed at the end of November when he was hit by a trolley bus, late at night, down by General Hospital. Officer Foley made a several-page report about the accident. His supervisor at that time was Sergeant Maurice Sandovich, the gentleman sitting over there. Foley turned his report in to the sergeant and that's the last he saw of it. When Mr. Hamilton interviewed Officer Foley, and Foley went to get the file, only the first page was there, which is the reason for this meeting."

"Sergeant Sandovich, will you explain the procedure for Mr. Perkins?" asked the assistant chief.

"Yes, sir," answered Sandovich. He was a big man. He had gray hair barbered in a crew cut. His puffy cheeks and blotchy complexion gave away his enjoyment of drink, but he had a steely look in his blue eyes that couldn't be ignored. He took in everything, forgot nothing, and was not happy being the object of the grilling that was taking place.

"Here's the way it works. The traffic officer, Mr. Foley, was under my supervision 'cause he was new to the beat. I don't particularly recall the accident, so I have to tell you what I generally did at that time. I would go over the report with the officer in charge of the scene and, if I found everything in order, I'd sign at the bottom of the second page or at the end of however many pages there were." His head turned slowly around the room so he made sure he had made eye contact with everyone there.

"Wait a minute," said Charles. "What if there was only one page?"

"That would only happen if someone called in and there was no officer at the scene. In that case, no supervisor would be involved," said Sandovich. "In a major accident, there would always be at least two pages. You see; there would always be a diagram. If this was a big accident, you can count on there being at least two pages. After my review, I would decide if it needed further investigation and, if it did, I would turn it over to the appropriate internal department or I would file it."

"It's not in the file, Sergeant," said the assistant chief.

# The Chinese Jars

"Maybe I turned it over to one of the departments," said Sandovich. "What was the nature of the injuries?"

Charles zeroed in. "The man died, and Foley says that the trolley bus driver, a Mr. Butler, told him that Rockwood was pushed in front of the bus by two Chinese guys, or at least held him there until the last second."

"I don't remember the incident or the report," said Sandovich. "But if it was a potential homicide, I probably turned the report over to them," he said coolly, shrugging his shoulders.

"Homicide has no file on this case, and there's no record of anyone ever contacting them," said the assistant chief, noticeably annoyed.

"I don't know what to tell you, Chief. I don't remember anything about this case; I was in charge of a lot of cases then," said Sandovich, and he tilted his seat back with the attitude that he was starting to get bored.

Samuel had been watching the interchange, and he noted the cool way Sandovich handled everyone, sure they couldn't touch him. He treated everyone with equal disdain. It was apparent that he knew more than he was letting on, but he acted as though he always covered his tracks perfectly, and it would be difficult to catch him. That much impunity to violate the law by someone whose job it was to uphold it really frosted him.

"All right, gentlemen," said the assistant chief. "Officer Foley, you take this one-page report over to Homicide and explain to them there is at least a page missing, and tell them what was on it as best you can remember.

"I assume you'll fill them in on whatever you know," he said, looking at Samuel.

"Always glad to help," said Samuel, controlling his anger. "Butler gave a sworn statement to the Municipal Railway investigators."

The chief asked Sandovich to stay with him. And when all the others had gone, Samuel lingered near the door on the pretext of lighting a cigarette and he heard part of the conversation.

"I don't like this shit, Maurice. I pulled you off Vice and the Chinatown beat 'cause you were acting slimy. You got a reprieve and got your job back, but this sounds like the same old crap. You better get this straightened out and you better not be double-dealing, I warn you."

"You got nothing to worry about, Chief, I'm clean," he answered, giving him an intense stare. He got up and hurried out of the office.

* * *

Samuel and Charles took a cab to Stockton Street in Chinatown. The street was full of Chinese shoppers, and the occasional white bargain hunter, or the groups of tourists with cameras around their necks. The vegetable stands were crammed with mountains of fruits, brightly colored vegetables—including leeks, chard, and mushrooms of all kinds, to name just a few. The fish stalls put tanks of water on the street where fish and shellfish waited their turn. At a sign from a shopper, the fish merchant stuck in a net and took out what was requested. Giant lobsters, their pincers tied, struggled as if they knew what was in store for them. In the window of the butcher shops and restaurants hung Peking ducks and other delicacies waiting to be purchased for the evening meal or devoured at lunch. The smells of ginger, cilantro, and roasted fowl lingered in the air.

Samuel had convinced Charles to try the culinary art of Chop Suey Louie's, which he thought was the best, mostly because he didn't have anything to compare it to. They pushed their way through the crowd and entered the place, which at that hour was packed and noisier than usual because of the yelling of the crowd listening to the horse races on the radio. It was part of the place's attraction because most of the clientele bet with Louie on the outcome.

The owner warmly welcomed them and squeezed them in between other customers at the counter. Samuel ordered for them, and they were quickly served a variety of plates that Charles couldn't identify.

"I see what you mean. Sandovich is a lying son of a bitch. What are we going to do about it?" asked Samuel with his mouth full.

"It's not so important, now that the truth's come out and the case is in the hands of Homicide. I just went there today to scare the shit out of Maurice so he'll make a mistake. I have a lot of accounts to settle with that bastard, and with a little luck I'll be able to trap him," said Charles.

"I thought he was pretty sure of himself. If we knew who he was protecting, we could solve this case," said Samuel.

"What interests me is if there's been a federal crime committed. Otherwise, I can't get involved."

"Two guys pushing a man in front of a trolley bus isn't a federal crime. Is that what you're saying?" asked Samuel.

Charles laughed. "It's been a busy day, ol' buddy. Now we just have to wait for Sandovich to stick his foot in it."

"If he's so shrewd, what makes you so sure he'll make a mistake?"

"Because I know that bastard. He can't keep his hands out of the cookie jar, and you can bet he got paid plenty for deep-sixing that report," said Charles. "Now whoever paid him will want their money back or at least more bang for their buck."

# 10

## The King of Wands

ROBERTO, Count Maestro de Guinesso Bacigalupi Slotnik de Transylvania, was sitting at the round table of Camelot talking with Melba when Samuel walked in on another Sunday afternoon a couple of weeks later.

"What a surprise to see you, Maestro Bob. Where the hell you been?" asked Samuel.

"That's a good question, young man. I could beat around the bush, but I'll be honest with you. I've been drying out," said Maestro, without his usual Slavic accent.

"Drying out? I had no idea you had that problem."

Samuel took a seat next to him. Maestro had on his old black pinstripe suit and heavily starched shirt with slightly tattered cuffs, which didn't look white anymore. He still had the beginnings of his handlebar mustache, but his hair had turned almost completely gray. Samuel thought he was mortally ill or had had a brutal trauma, one of those that turns one's head gray overnight. Noticing the difference, Samuel pointed to his hair, "You look different."

"I just let it grow out. I got tired of dyeing it. I learned a lot about myself up at Duffy's, the dry-out place," said Maestro, with a sigh.

Excalibur got up from under the table and put his head in between Samuel's legs. Samuel tried to push him away, but the dog started licking his hands affectionately.

"Get away from me, you goddamned mutt," said Samuel. But the dog stayed where he was, and started scratching his absent ear.

"How long were you there?" interrupted Melba.

"Eight weeks."

"Isn't that a long time?" asked Samuel.

"Not when the booze has taken control of your life," said Maestro. "I needed to get it out of my system and start over again on the right track."

"That must have cost a fortune," said Samuel.

"Luckily, a kind patron helped me pay the bill. You know I couldn't have afforded it all by myself," he said with teary eyes.

"Who was the good Samaritan?" asked Samuel.

"No one you know," said Melba, and Samuel saw her exchange glances with Maestro.

"I'm really surprised. I never thought of you as a drunk."

"Everyone has his moments of darkness, friend. I just couldn't make ends meet. My magic wasn't paying the bills and no one came to see me for notary work, so I started buying that cheap Gallo Tokay, and pretty soon I was drinking for a living."

"Besides your gray hair, you look great now," said Melba. "Are you cured?"

"Unfortunately, being cured is a life-long struggle. I just have to make sure I stay away from it today, then tomorrow, and then the day after," sighed the Maestro.

"Are you sure this is the right place to be, with that constant temptation?" asked Samuel, pointing to the liquor behind the bar.

"These surroundings are kind of my home. I don't have any other place to go. Here is where my friends are," said Maestro.

"So far, I'm okay."

"We're here to make sure that he only drinks soda water. No one is going to give Bob any booze," said Melba.

"What's in that little black bundle over there?" asked Samuel.

"Those are Tarot cards," said Maestro. "I learned how to use them when I was at the clinic. They're an ancient way of telling fortunes," said Maestro, unwrapping them from the black handkerchief.

"What do you mean, ancient? A hundred years?" asked Samuel, looking at the beautifully rendered cards. He pictured Gypsy women in an Old West setting with a sign outside a broken-down shack, agreeing to read one's fortune for a nickel or a dollar or whatever the freight would bear.

"Hundreds maybe thousands of years old," explained Maestro. "I figured, since my two businesses weren't doing so well, I'd spend my spare time learning the ropes so I could create another source of income."

"How long did you study?" asked Samuel, touching the cards, drawn in by curiosity.

"Almost the whole time I was there. There was a fortune-teller who was also drying out. She had a spare deck of cards, and I found three books on the origins and meaning of the Tarot in Duffy's library. The fortune-teller makes a living by charging for a reading. She said with my background as a magician, I was a natural. Figure it out. I can do a reading in half an hour. I can do sixteen a day, easy, and I can charge two dollars per session. I'll have it made.

"That is if you get sixteen takers," laughed Melba.

"Two bucks, huh?" said Samuel. "Will you do a reading for me at that price?"

"Certainly, young man. Let's go over here to get away from the crowd."

"Before you leave this afternoon, talk to me, Samuel. I've

some news for you," said Melba, as she got up and walked toward the bar.

Samuel and Maestro sat down at an out-of-the-way table in the rear of the bar, and Maestro shuffled the Tarot cards. They were bigger than playing cards, and each had a human figure or a combined human and animal figure on it.

"You'll understand more as I help you unravel the mysteries of your life," he said with such a serious look that Samuel felt it was inevitable he was going to be duped.

"Separate them into three piles and shuffle 'em, not the way you would playing cards, but gently so they have some of your energy on them," said Maestro, as he took off his suit coat.

"Now take ten cards out of the semicircle I've put them in," he added as he fanned the cards out. "Make sure you give them to me in the order that you picked them."

After Samuel chose his cards, he handed them to Maestro Bob, who then began to spread them out on the silk cloth.

"You see the first card goes directly on top of and across the second card.

"There's a process to interpreting Tarot cards, Samuel. Each reading is a voyage of discovery. Only you can know the true meaning of what we see before us. I am just a facilitator here to help you."

"Okay," said Samuel, feeling skeptical. "I'm listening."

"The first card is the King of Wands."

Samuel saw an impressive figure dressed in a red robe with a crown on his head. He was seated on a golden throne in a green pasture with a lit torch in his left hand.

"This usually signifies a tremendous surge of creative energy. It's kind of lurking beneath the surface of your consciousness, but it hasn't been formulated," said Maestro Bob. "Does that ring any kind of a bell with you?"

"Don't know yet, keep going," said Samuel, interested.

"The second card is the crossing card."

Maestro pointed to the Tower card. It showed a powerful crowned male figure erupting from the sea with a three-pronged spear in his hand. In front of him was a tower on a small island starting to crumble.

"This is the only card that has a building on it. It represents what's stopping you from getting to your really creative urges. It could be your present job. The idea is that your employment may be stable and constant, and you don't want to jeopardize losing it," said Maestro Bob.

Samuel whistled. The magician had hit a sensitive point. He'd never told him about wanting to become a reporter, but it seemed that the card was referring to that. Selling ads in the newspaper didn't pay much, but he'd held onto the job because it at least offered him a paycheck. "You've caught my interest, Maestro," he sighed.

"The third card is the Knight of Pentacles. It means you go about your business in a diligent and conscientious manner. I would imagine, although I don't know you well, that you are like a dog that gets hold of a bone and won't let go. The most important message this card gives is that there is someone watching over you who will help you achieve what you are after."

"What's next?"

"The fourth card represents the base of the matter," continued the Maestro. "This card is the King of Pentacles. It indicates you are on a mission, or that someone will come into your life to help you develop the special talent or pursuit of higher goals you possess but has been asleep within you. In fact, I wouldn't be surprised if the same person who is watching over you is also pushing you closer to the limelight."

That could only be Melba, concluded Samuel enthusiastically. Whenever he would be going around in circles, not seeing the light from any side, she would set him on the right path.

# The Chinese Jars

"The fifth card is the Three of Cups. This indicates past influences. This is a letting-go card. It means that whatever way you were heading in terms of career or in matters of the heart, you are letting go and are willing to start on a new path. Let's take a break here. Please order me a club soda."

Samuel lit a cigarette and sauntered up to the bar. "Scotch over the rocks and a club soda," he told Melba, as he caught his reflection in the mirror behind her. When she put the orders on the bar, he impulsively took her hands in his and kissed them.

"What the hell's wrong with you? Are you drunk?"

"You have no idea what the cards have just told me!" He returned quickly to the table. Maestro Bob was cleaning his fingernails with a small pocketknife. He noticed that Maestro no longer had polished fingernails. He thought the magician had really changed.

"Are you ready to begin again?" asked the Maestro, as he drank half the glass of soda in one gulp. "The sixth card is the Devil. We call it the card of forthcoming influences."

The card was menacing. It displayed a creature that was half-human and half-animal with horns and hoofs in a dark underground setting. The grotesque figure held humans on short strings and at the same time it was blowing into a conch.

"I don't like what I see," said Samuel.

"It has several meanings. It could mean coming in contact with shadowy and corrupt figures, literally from the underworld."

"Am I in physical danger?" asked Samuel.

"It could mean that, so watch out. It could also mean there are conflicting forces awakening within you, such as love and sex."

What did the magician know of his relationship with Blanche? A conflict between love and sex said the crappy card. He always thought that his attraction to Blanche was closer to love than lust, but he had to admit that it had a sexual component, especially at night when he had fantasies about her.

"What else do the Tarot cards say about this woman?" he asked anxiously.

"He who doesn't get his feet wet never crosses the river. It's a Slavic saying. In other words, you have to be more aggressive if you want to have her. Who is the woman?"

"No one for the moment. We're talking about the future in hypothetical terms, aren't we?"

"The seventh card is the Page of Cups. This is where you find yourself right now. Something new is happening in your life. It's just beginning."

Samuel agreed. For sure, it was time for a change. It was time to get out of the basement of the newspaper, he needed another date with Blanche, and he also needed a healthier life. He smoked and drank too much, and he should stop eating those rolls and Chinese soups. In short, he should stop living like an animal.

"Tell me, Maestro, do you say the same thing to everyone?" asked Samuel, nervously.

"I say nothing. You picked the cards and the cards talk. They have their own meaning. It's what they say," said the Maestro, "not me. This is the Four of Swords. It has to do with your hopes and fears. It shows you in a time of quiet reflection—a place where you're weighing things, deciding which way to go and in no hurry, either. It looks to me like you're building up strength."

"You're right about that. The last card says Judgment. What does Judgment mean?" asked Samuel, looking at the golden-haired, crowned woman sitting on a throne with a sword in one hand and the scales of justice in the other. "Am I going to be involved in a lawsuit?"

"No, no, it has to do with the final outcome. It's a good card for you. That doesn't mean it's always good; it depends. But you are about to come to terms with whatever has held you back in the past. It's like you're at the end of one chapter in life and ready to start a new one."

"What else?"

"That's it for now," said Maestro Bob.

"You've earned your two dollars, and one more as a tip, plus another soda water," said Samuel, putting the money on the table and ordering him another drink.

\* \* \*

Samuel wandered back to the round table where Melba sat looking out the plate-glass window at the view of the park and, beyond it, the bay, and nursing her usual glass of beer.

"You wanted to talk to me, Melba?" he asked, sitting down alongside her. Excalibur started to get up, but Melba intercepted him by grabbing his collar.

"I have some news for you," she said.

"Really?"

"The word on the street is that you caught Maurice Sandovich with his pants down."

"He's hiding something big in this case, Melba. He got rid of some pages of the Rockwood police report. Those pages showed Rockwood might have been murdered."

"Take it easy, Samuel," said Melba. "Don't get too excited about Maurice Sandovich. He's small potatoes. He's been involved in Chinatown graft for a long time. If he did something, he did it on orders from somebody who had him by the balls, or is also involved in one of the rackets he has his fingers in."

"What d'ya mean, one of the rackets?" he asked.

"Maurice protects a lot of interests in Chinatown. He's on the Vice Squad. It could be prostitution, drugs, but it's probably gambling. You have no idea the amount of gambling that goes on in that small area of the city. He makes a good living doing that. So he owes a lot of favors. But the ultimate person or persons you're looking for isn't Maurice," explained Melba. "On the other hand, looking in Chinatown isn't a bad idea."

They drank in silence, she, her beer, and he, the last of his Scotch. He'd promised himself he'd only drink two a day, and this was his second.

"Have you heard from Blanche?" asked Samuel in the most casual tone he could affect.

"Starting tomorrow she'll be here every day. She says that until Rafael's case is settled, she's willing to help me."

"To clean the bar?"

"No. Rafael is here now, but we don't know for how long. There are a lot of other things he does that I may not be able to count on from him. I need someone to back me up. This isn't a job for a single woman."

"You can count on me, if I can help in any way," Samuel offered.

"Yeah. I know I can count on you as soon as Blanche shows up," Melba laughed.

"Don't make fun of me, Melba. Your daughter treats me like a louse."

"You have to change the focus, Buster. I heard it didn't go so well when you went running in the park with her."

"Did she tell you that?"

"You need to find a common ground that's not athletics. Something that you both enjoy that doesn't make you look ridiculous."

"Does she like music?"

"Depends," said Melba.

"There's the symphony, but that's pretty highbrow," said Samuel.

"It would be for both of you. How 'bout the Blackhawk? Dave Brubeck's there a lot and that cat knows how to do it, and Blanche likes him" said Melba.

"I like 'm too."

"You'll have to start somewhere. There's also an art theatre near it on Larkin, where they show foreign films. Try that, too. I haven't raised my daughter in a total cultural wasteland, you know," said Melba.

Samuel walked to his den, thinking of the Tarot cards.

# 11

## Rafael's Luck Runs Out

HIRAM GOLDBERG made all the moves he had in his bag of tricks during the final argument of Rafael's criminal trial. He put on a dark suit and lavender-scented cologne, and he took off his gold chains and cufflinks in order to make the jurors feel sympathy for his client's social class. His enthusiasm made him almost levitate, and at one point he got so close to the jurors that the judge warned him he couldn't sit in their laps. He lamented, pleaded, and cajoled, trying to twist the evidence in his client's favor like a Jesuit would, going so far as to preach the melodrama of the crippled mother, the siblings without a father, and the pregnant wife. He even cried; yet when all was said and done, Rafael was convicted of receiving stolen property.

Rafael had no illusions; he knew where he came from and where his kind stood in the community. Besides, he wasn't a whiner. He was caught with the goods; that couldn't be changed. The probation officer tried in vain to get him to talk, but he wouldn't squeal so that bigger fish up the line could be snagged in exchange for a lighter sentence or dismissal of the charges. Everyone in his community knew that if he did that, the consequences could be fatal.

He stood at the bar with his lawyer, waiting for the judge to pronounce sentence. The courtroom was crowded with his family and friends. He noted that his brother Juan showed up without a pompadour or a chain hanging from his belt, and in a suit and tie. Surely that was on instructions from the lawyer. Sitting with his mother and sisters was his wife, Sofia, who was now big with child. Melba was there with her daughter, Blanche, and Samuel was next to her. Several of his companions from the neighborhood were there to lend him support. They were at once courageous and nervous at having to show their faces, since they were perpetually trying to escape from the police. To them, as to him, honor was more important than the consequences of a public appearance in front of the law, which was hostile to them.

"Hear ye, hear ye, the Superior Court of the State of California, in and for the City and County of San Francisco is now in session, the Honorable Guido Carduloni, presiding," announced the clerk.

A young man in a black robe came out of one of the two back doors and took his seat on the dais. He was of medium height, had short black hair, and was clean-shaven. He had a strong jaw line of a boxer, but his brown eyes were amiable. Carduloni had presided over Rafael's criminal trial; he knew all the details of the case and had painstakingly read the probation report, which he had in one hand. The court file with all his notes was in the other.

Hiram and Rafael were already at the counsel table, and the assistant district attorney was seated at the table next to the jury box.

"As you know, Mr. Garcia," announced the judge, "this is the day set aside for sentencing. I assume your attorney has explained the procedure to you and allowed you to read the probation report."

"Yes, Your Honor," answered Rafael, standing erect.

"Is there anything you want to say before sentence is pronounced?"

"No, Your Honor."

"Is there any reason why sentence should not be pronounced at this time, Counsel?"

"No, Your Honor, there is none," answered Hiram.

"Very well," said the judge. "Mr. Garcia, you shouldn't be here. But a jury of your peers has found that you violated the laws of this state.

"The district attorney offered to agree to a reduction in your sentence; and frankly, I was willing to go along with it, if you would provide information about the person or persons who actually stole the X-ray machine so they could be prosecuted. But you have refused to even discuss the matter. Therefore, the probation department and the district attorney both take the position that you should be given the maximum sentence. Are you aware of their recommendations?"

"Yes, sir," said Rafael.

"Do you wish now to make any statement concerning others' involvement or provide the district attorney with the requested information? If so, I'll continue this hearing."

"May I have a moment with my client, Your Honor?" asked Hiram Goldberg.

"Of course," said the judge. "We'll take a five-minute recess." He put his glasses on, got up from his cushioned seat, grabbed the two files, and left the courtroom.

Hiram leaned over and whispered in Rafael's ear. "Okay, Rafael, this is it. Last chance to give up whoever it was that got you here. The judge wants to help you, but the D.A. wants information. It's stupid to protect some gangsters. They wouldn't do it for you."

"No dice. My life wouldn't be worth shit if I opened my mouth," said Rafael. "These things happen. Let's get on with the show."

## The Chinese Jars

Hiram shrugged and motioned to the bailiff. In short order the judge was back on the bench.

"My client has nothing to add to what's already on the record."

The judge put his glasses to the side. "The probation department and the district attorney have asked that you be sentenced to four years in state prison. I feel that's steep, since you have no previous record and in all other respects seem to be a good citizen. I therefore sentence you to three years in state prison. Since you did not appeal the judgment against you, you will be taken into custody forthwith, and I instruct the bailiff to do that right now."

There were gasps from the part of the crowd that wanted a stiffer sentence and moans from his friends and family who hoped for a much lighter one.

"Your Honor," chimed in the assistant district attorney, "we feel that the sentence is too light. This man has been convicted, and he's shown absolutely no contrition."

"I know what your position is, Counsel. The sentence will stand. Bailiff, take this man into custody.

"Next case!"

Rafael was carted off. Hiram walked slowly out of the courtroom surrounded by Rafael's friends and relatives.

"That was a pretty stiff sentence," said Melba, as she tried to comfort Sofia, who had her head down and was sobbing.

"Not as tough as it might have been," said Hiram. "They had the goods on him, and he wouldn't give anybody up."

"Is there anything we can do?" asked Samuel, as he and Blanche stood together in the hallway looking downcast.

"Go and visit him once he gets to San Quentin and tell him to give information. That way the D.A. will agree to shorten his sentence," said Hiram.

Samuel was glad Rafael would at least be close so he could see him, but he knew better than to suppose his friend would ever disclose what the D.A. and the court wanted from him. He tried to comfort Rafael's mother, but there wasn't much he could say. The breadwinner for the entire family, the person who'd kept them out of poverty, had been taken out of the equation for three years. How were they going to survive during that period?

"Why would Rafael stand by his word of honor when he knows what his absence means to all these people?" asked Samuel.

"For these cholos, it's a question of honor," sighed Hiram, and he walked away.

\* \* \*

San Quentin was already falling apart in 1961. It was over a hundred years old and it looked it. It sat at the foot of the new Richmond San Rafael Bridge overlooking the San Francisco Bay, mostly to the south, where one could see the back side of the Tiburon Peninsula and Point Richmond looking east. On a clear day even Berkeley and Oakland were visible. What a view! The only problem was that it was from behind bars and barbed-wire fences.

Rafael sat with his hands and feet shackled in the San Francisco sheriff's bus as it wound its way on Highway 101 into Marin County, then turned east on Sir Francis Drake Boulevard. While the bus meandered along the narrow road after it left the highway, its motor chugging and the gears grinding, Rafael couldn't help contrasting the abundantly green hills bursting with multicolored wildflowers and orange California poppies with the drab yellow stucco of the prison he saw in the distance. The bus crept to a halt as it approached the main gate, and he saw two boys sitting on the rocks, holding bamboo-fishing poles. He watched the calm bay waters splashing gently against the rocks as the boys threw their lines out and hauled in big striped bass. He thought that one day he would go there with his son to fish like those kids were doing.

The driver, a big burley sheriff's deputy, commented as he saw the pile of fish next to the pair. "Like shooting ducks in a pond."

Rafael turned and looked at him through the ten-gage wire cage that separated them. All of a sudden, he felt a sob well up in his chest. He gritted his teeth.

The gate opened slowly. Rafael saw the guard in the watchtower above them pointing his weapon down and looking at them through binoculars. The bus stopped in front of the reception center. There were ten inmates shackled inside the vehicle plus three guards and the driver. On the outside were seven more guards, heavily armed, waiting patiently for the doors of the bus to open.

When they did, the prisoners waddled off as best they could with their legs bound together. Once on the ground, they were put in a single file and patted down then directed to file in the door of the reception center, one at a time.

Rafael was shuffled inside and found himself in a room with three oversized white guards. There were iron bars on all the windows and on the door that he had just walked through. His chains were removed, and he was strip-searched by two of his captors while the other kept a keen eye on the process and a finger on the trigger of his firearm. He was issued the blue denim garb of the San Quentin prisoner with his individual number stenciled on the back of the shirt. He was then photographed and fingerprinted.

"All right," said the big sergeant behind the steel cage from where the uniform had come. "I don't have to tell you where you are, you know that. We have rules here, and in order to get along, you'll have to follow them. You understand that?"

"Yes, sir."

"This here's a pair of earphones, and a sheet, towel, and blanket. The cellblock lights go out at ten o'clock, but not the lights in your cell. That way we keep an eye on you," he warned, as he pointed his finger at Rafael in an absentminded rote way he had done hundreds if not thousands of times before. "You can listen to the radio all night, if you're one of those guys with a guilty conscious who don't sleep. But tomorrow you'll be interviewed for job placement. And when you get a job, you're expected to show up on time every day and perform. So don't stay up all night listening to bullshit. We collect the sheet and towel every two weeks to be washed. If you don't turn 'em in, you're up shits creek. Understand so far?"

"Yes, sir."

"You're expected to behave. If you do, you'll get some privileges, like exercise in the yard. If you fuck up, not only will you lose your job, but we've got a special place for you, and it's not nice down there. Understand that?"

"Yes, sir."

"We're going to put you with another Mexican boy from Southern California. That way there's no excuse for the racial crap that you prisoners are always complaining about. So we don't want any of those problems with you. Get it, Greaser?" he said, as he squinted hard at the prisoner, frowning.

"Yes, sir," said Rafael, with a deadpan expression on his face, looking the big man right in the eye.

"I don't like that kind of defiance. You'd better be careful. This Sergeant here is gonna take you to your cell. You understand you'll be locked up when you're not working for the People of the State of California or you're not exercising the privileges you earned for being a good boy?"

"Yes, sir."

"Follow him!"

The first guard unlocked a door and started down a corridor. Rafael followed. His nostrils began to fill with the acrid smell of the musty building and of men living together in a limited space. Behind him was another guard. Neither was armed. They walked through several buildings until they came to a giant cell door guarded by two armed men on a catwalk above it, completely separated from the ground below. They paced back and forth in what looked like a self-contained environment; no one could get to them, even if they wanted to. An electronic buzzer opened a large barred gate, and Rafael saw the cellblock where he would be living.

The two guards walked down the aisle with Rafael sandwiched in between them until they reached cell number 677. One of the armed guards on the catwalk pressed a button and another buzzer sounded. The one in front of Rafael then lifted a bar from in front of the cell door and unlocked it with a key.

"Here's your home, Spic," said the second guard. "You take the top bunk. Your amigo already laid claim to the bottom one. He'll be back at four-thirty. He works in the laundry. You make sure you guys get along. Any questions, you save 'em up. But don't make the list too long. The warden don't have time for bullshit. Got it?"

"Yes, sir," said Rafael. Turning, he put his sheet and blanket on the bunk, hung his towel by the small sink with a piece of metal above it that took the place of a proper mirror, and plugged the earphones into the radio jack by one of the two small tables in the cell.

"Ya wanna shave every day?" asked the first guard.

"Yes, sir."

"You'll get a razor early each morning. Don't expect no hot water. This ain't no hotel, so you'll have to shave with cold. The razor will be collected just as soon as you're done, so don't get no ideas, you can't use the blade for anything 'cept shaving. Trying to fuck around with it will mean losing privileges, understand?" said the bigger of the two men, chewing a wad of tobacco. His pot hung over his belt and he had some trouble moving.

"Yes, sir," said Rafael.

\* \* \*

The cell door slammed. He saw the steel bar come down and heard it clang. Then they were gone. He grabbed hold of the bars and looked out until his knuckles were white, but he couldn't see much. He could hear the sound of other cell doors opening or shutting; he wasn't sure which, as his ear was not yet finely tuned. There were sounds of footsteps on the metal catwalk above, which could only be the guards, and he assumed he'd get used to hearing them night and day. He could also hear the muffled sounds of people talking, but he couldn't make out a word of what was said.

He went back to his bunk, made it, laid down, and watched the ceiling for a long time. He thought of Sofia and the baby. Tears of anger and despair flowed down the sides of his face into his sideburns, then down his earlobes onto his pillow. Fifteen minutes later, he got up, wiped his face, and blew his nose with a piece of toilet paper. The commode was in one corner, in full view of the front of the cell—a porcelain bowl, a chrome handle, and no seat. He flushed the tissue down the toilet and went back and laid down on his bunk again, staring at the ceiling. He swore that he would never shed another tear for the rest of his life.

At four thirty-five, footsteps approached the cell. The buzzer sounded; there was the sound of the bar opening and a key being inserted in the lock, and a short Mexican man with close-cropped black hair and the evasive eyes of a rabbit was ushered in by a guard. He was dark-skinned and wore a mustache. The sleeves of his prison-issue shirt were rolled up above his elbows and his forearms were covered with scars and tattoos.

# The Chinese Jars

"Órale pues, carnal, me llamo Pancho Alarcón. Soy de Canta Ranas. They tol me about you, the vato from San Francisco, right?"

"Yeah. My name is Rafael," he said, as he extended his hand. "Where's Canta Ranas?"

"You're kidding. You northern vatos don't know nothing. Canta Ranas is right next to Los Nietos, just outside of Los Angeles.

"They say you got nailed with an X-ray machine. Que cabrón. What the fuck were you doing driving around with a pinche máquina as big as an elephant in broad daylight?"

"Where did you get all this shit on me?" asked Rafael, noting a large blue dot tattooed on Pancho's cheekbone next to his right eye.

"Oh, alalva, carnal, there ain't no secrets in here, 'cept for the child molesters, and we fix them. Everybody knows you're a good vato. You took the rap for the other cabrones, and you never squealed. That gets you points, mano."

"It also keeps me alive," said Rafael, laughing.

He talked a long time to Pancho that afternoon and evening, and got the lowdown on how to survive in the hostile environment in which he found himself. He mused: it wasn't so different from the outside except, if he fucked up, they always knew where to find him. Pancho was an old hand and knew his way around. He was worth listening to.

The next day Rafael was sent to the prison employment committee. He was told he qualified for three different positions. The first was the machine shop, where the license plates for the state were made. The second was working for the prison library, but the third interested him the most: it involved working in the doctor's office.

He accepted the medical job. He liked the idea of dealing with the men who needed help with their physical ailments. He would, in effect, become the doctor's Man Friday. He was to be in charge of appointments and would administer rudimentary first aid. He also had access to the medical library. Even though the treatises were, for the most part, outdated, he could read them in his spare time. And, by the end of his sentence, he envisioned having enough of a background that he could apply to train for a degree as a registered nurse. But he shouldn't make long-range plans, he decided.

The doctor liked him immediately. Rafael made an excellent impression, and being Mexican was an advantage. He would get along well with the ever-increasing Hispanic population of the prison, many of whom didn't speak English. He would work alongside a Negro nurse who came from the outside and together they would ethnically represent a majority of their patients.

Rafael also met with the priest, who already knew of Rafael's good relationship with the church because he had received a letter of praise from his parish at Mission Dolores. Rafael volunteered to help the Father with Mass and teaching catechism, or in any other way he could be of assistance. Since the priest was not at San Quentin on a daily basis and he had confidence in Rafael, he trained him to handle the spiritual crises of the inmates in his absence.

\* \* \*

After several weeks, Rafael fell into the routine of working at the doctor's office and helping the priest tend to the flock. He made no real friends other than Pancho, preferring instead to study the old medical texts and read books borrowed from the library or a romance novel if he could get one.

His cellmate was not particularly smart, but Rafael liked him, since he thought him loyal and he'd given him invaluable information on how the institution worked. There was always another twist, something new to learn.

## The Chinese Jars

One evening after dinner, the two were in their cell talking when there was a clanging of the bars from next door and a voice yelled out.

"Hey, Pancho, Cerdo's calling you."

"Thanks, carnal," said Pancho. He got up from his bunk, walked over to the cell door and took a small mirror out of his pocket.

"What are you doing?" asked Rafael.

"Communicating with the brothers, carnal."

"With that mirror?"

"Yeah. Just watch."

Pancho stuck the mirror out of the cell door, into the aisle and put two fingers in front of it facing in a vertical position. Then he turned them sideways so they were parallel to the ground. He watched the mirror intently until he got the answer to his signal that he was looking for from a cell down the row. He then withdrew the mirror and put it back in his pocket.

"I thought mirrors were illegal," said Rafael.

"So, who gives a fuck, carnal. It's a free country, isn't it?"

"Yeah, I guess so."

"You want some yesca?"

"No. No thanks, don't use it," said Rafael.

"You don't mind if this vato has a few tokes, right, ese?"

"Be my guest, carnal, you live here, too."

Pancho took his shoe off and hit the wall behind the toilet three times with the heel. Then he lifted his mattress and grabbed a wire coat hanger, straightened it out and created a hook at the end of it.

Rafael started to say something, but Pancho interrupted, "Shh, it's about to happen." He rushed to the commode and stuck the hanger in as far as it would go, hook end first. He put his finger up to his lips asking for continued silence. They both heard a toilet flush above them, and within two seconds

Pancho's experienced hand was pulling a small waterproof pouch out of the toilet. It was attached to a long string. He squeezed as much water out of the string as he could, then wrapped it in his towel and wrung it out. Afterwards, he hung the string at the back of the bunk to dry, so it wasn't visible from outside the cell.

He opened the pouch and felt the marijuana with his fingers. He raised it to his nose and smelled it.

"This is some good shit, carnal. Sure you don't want to smoke some with your compadre?"

"No, thanks, mano, it's not my thing," said Rafael.

Pancho took a package of Zig Zags off his small table, rolled a joint and lit up. He reclined on his bunk enjoying every minute of it as the smoke wafted up toward Rafael's bed and the ceiling beyond it. "Life is good, carnal," he said, after three tokes.

# 12

## Something's Cooking

XSING CHING was lounging on Virginia Dimitri's comfortable couch long after they had made love. His shirt was unbuttoned at the top, exposing part of his hairless chest. He looked totally relaxed, unusual for such a guarded person. Virginia entered the room dressed in a pair of navy-blue bell-bottom slacks. She had on a soft white shirt, the tails tied in a knot in front, exposing just enough of her midsection to tease any onlooker.

"Can I freshen your drink, Xsing?" she asked

"No, thank you. I'm comfortable just the way I am."

"Mathew will be here any minute. He's always late." She sat down beside him and patted him on the knee.

"How's Ren?"

"The crisis passed, as you know. Doctor Rolland is ready to do the bone marrow transplant when necessary. I don't know how I'll ever be able to pay you for what you've done for my son, Virginia."

"Don't try, Xsing. Not everything has a price. Sometimes one just has to resign oneself to being in debt," she joked, kissing him on the neck.

She heard a key unlock the front door. Mathew walked

quickly down the hallway into the foyer of the apartment, while Fu Fung Fat stood silently by the kitchen door, watching him.

"I'll have a bourbon and soda," Mathew instructed him.

He kissed Virginia on the cheek and extended his hand to Xsing Ching. "Sorry I'm late; too many things going on in my world. But I'm sure you two haven't missed me. I understood from Virginia that you wanted to see me, Xsing?"

"Yes, Mr. O'Hara, we need to talk. You know we have to be discreet."

"Here we can talk freely. Virginia is my partner."

"Of course, I wasn't referring to Miss Dimitri. As you no doubt know, I have already been in contact with other clients and have some offers. It would be very discourteous on my part to ignore them."

"We can offer you a better deal," said Mathew.

"I think I've convinced Mr. Ching to deal only with us, Matt. The fewer people who know of the shipment the fewer risks there are," said Virginia.

"I agree with Virginia. This makes the most sense," said Mathew. "You and I are businessmen, Mr. Ching. There won't be any problems. We both have experience and know that discretion is indispensable in these cases. I assure you that no one will ever know where these items came from or how they got here."

"I don't usually sell a whole shipment to one person. I try to be more subtle about that much quality merchandise coming into the same part of the country at one time," explained Xsing.

"I understand your concerns, but I insist on obtaining the entire shipment. Virginia has explained my motives to you, and I understand that you agree," said Mathew.

The discussion went on for almost an hour. Mathew kept turning the conversation over to Virginia whose soft exchanges with Xsing seemed to hold the key. Finally he gave up. "Okay,

okay, I've decided to sell the whole shipment to you. I want to emphasize that I'm doing it because it is very important to Miss Dimitri. I'm indebted to her. Because of her intervention my son's life may be saved."

"Of course!"

"She knows better than anyone what this means to me, because she's also lost a child," said Ching, putting his hand on top of Virginia's.

"Virginia? A child?" Mathew seemed lost.

"Let's not talk about that. It's a loss that I haven't been able to overcome," interrupted Virginia, shooting a look of warning at Mathew.

"We must be careful," Ching said, nervously. "You know I had to pay a large sum to keep this quiet?"

"What do you mean?" asked Mathew.

"Blackmail."

"That's impossible!"

"My organization was approached by an anonymous source who knew there was going to be a large shipment delivered to the United States. We had to buy their silence. We worked behind the scenes to find out who was in charge of the blackmail. Fortunately, that person has been taken care of. But you must understand that we are nervous about going forward, for fear that other things may pop up."

"How do I know this person is out of the picture?" asked Mathew, very upset.

"Our source is reliable. If I tell you this has been resolved, you can believe me."

"I'm not happy to learn this, Mr. Ching. I like my business deals to be clean, without complications. I need to know there won't be any trouble with an interloper. Who was this person, anyway?"

"I never learned who the blackmailer was, but he will not bother us again. You have my word for it, Mr. O'Hara."

"How long has it been?" asked Mathew.

"Long enough so that we know there are no repercussions."

This twist represented new risks that Mathew needed to consider. Blackmail? How much did that person know? How had Ching eliminated him? The business deal wasn't so clean now, but it was still juicy. Now came the hard part; agreeing on the price. "Do I understand correctly that you will sell me the entire shipment for $300,000 dollars?"

"Oh, no, Mr. O'Hara, the price has always been $700,000!"

Mathew jumped up immediately. "That's more than twice what I understood it to be!" he exclaimed.

"You have been misinformed, Mr. O'Hara. It's $700,000. When you see the pieces you'll see they're worth much more," answered Ching, making an effort to control his anger.

"Go back to your people. Tell them I will go to $350,000, and not a penny more," offered Mathew. "Tell them they'll have a few days to think it over. We'll meet here again on Saturday evening."

"I'll take your message to them, but I assure you we cannot accept such a low price," said Xsing Ching. "Remember that we had to pay a high price to shut up the blackmailer."

"And you want me to pay for that?

"We have other buyers who are very interested," said Xsing Ching.

"Maybe you can get more by dividing up the merchandise, Mr. Ching, but it will also be riskier and more difficult for you. And remember, it will take much more time. A bird in the hand is worth two in the bush, as the saying goes. Besides, in me you will have a sure thing. We can make deals in the future, since I know these aren't the only objects you intend to sell in this country, right?"

"That I can't discuss with you. As you can imagine, it

doesn't depend on me alone."

"That's my offer. Take it or leave it," said Mathew

\* \* \*

After Xsing Ching left, Mathew showed his irritation. "What the hell was he talking about, Virginia?"

"I lied to him, of course. To soften him up, I told him that I'd lost a child," she replied.

"I'm not referring to that. What's this about blackmail?"

"I don't know. That was the first I'd heard of it. He did say it has been taken care of, didn't he?"

"Do you believe him? We can't be sure."

"He said we could take his word for it. He's running a bigger risk than we are, and he has more to lose. It doesn't surprise me that he took personal charge of the blackmailer."

"He said he didn't know who it was," said Mathew.

"What did you want? For him to give us a first and last name?"

"I don't know, Virginia. This smells bad to me. We can't go forward if there are spies out there threatening to expose us," said Mathew, drying his forehead with the back of his hand.

"Calm down and try to think clearly, Matt. The blackmail scheme gives you a certain advantage because Ching feels exposed. It makes more sense for him to get rid of the merchandise than look for new clients. Take advantage of what's happened to negotiate the price, but don't push it too far. We can't back out now, there's too much at stake," she said dryly.

\* \* \*

Mathew O'Hara didn't sleep for several days. He shut himself in his office and made hundreds of telephone calls, going through all his contacts to try and find out the person or persons who were trying to interfere with his business deal and how they had planned it so carefully. It took him three days to get results. From his network, established over many years of making illicit deals, he finally was able to find an informant who had connections with Chinatown. He made arrangements to meet him at Camelot at six o'clock on Friday evening.

Mathew was there early, fidgeting at the bar, nursing his drink. Six o'clock came and went and no one showed up. He finished one drink and ordered another, conversing briefly with Melba. Finally, at seven fifteen, a short Chinese man in a double-breasted dark gray Hong Kong–tailored suit with a hat almost covering his eyes came in. In spite of the dim light and his hat, he stood out, not only because he was the only Asian in the place but also because his face was severely scarred. It was a burn or a bad case of smallpox, concluded Mathew. Mathew watched him as he made his way toward him, but Excalibur reacted quickly by showing his teeth at the intruder. He was growling fiercely and about to take a chunk out of the strange man when Melba grabbed him by the collar and pulled him off his feet.

The man, furious, let out a chain of expletives in Chinese and retreated toward the door. He was bowlegged and pigeon-toed. Mathew stopped him at the door and identified himself. The man straightened his suit coat, picked up his hat, which he'd lost in his flight, and, still festering with anger, followed Mathew to Melba's office.

"Didn't I tell you Excalibur was a great watchdog?" Melba said to anyone who was listening, without releasing the dog, who continued to kick as he hung by his collar.

Once in the office, Mathew shut the door and turned on the lights. The man peered carefully into every corner of the small enclosure and, only when he was satisfied there was no one inside and there were no visible microphones, he locked the door and sat where Mathew indicated.

"What do you know?" asked Mathew, without introduction.

"Where money?" the man asked.

"There's plenty of time for that. First, let's find out what you know."

"No money, no 'fomation," the man said.

"How do I know you have information that will help me?" asked Mathew.

The response was a disdainful shrug. They were sizing each other up. The Chinese man stuck a finger in his ear and manipulated it meticulously then examined the waxy material on his fingernail that he extracted. He didn't seem to be in a hurry. Mathew noticed his huge hands that were out of proportion to the rest of his body and concluded that this man was a gangster. He figured he was one of those tough guys who are hired cheaply in Chinatown for all sorts of dirty work. He looked dumb, and was probably too unsophisticated to be a con man. Mathew pulled an envelope out of his inside pocket and extended it. The man took it, flung it open, and started counting the hundred-dollar bills. He counted them twice and put them in his suit pocket then pushed his hat back and smiled. He had very bad teeth. That scarred face and those awful teeth would scare the bravest of men. Mathew trembled. He wasn't used to dealing with people like this.

"There was man who cause a lot of trouble for Chinese merchant. Tall white man who dress in tuxedo. Paid a lot of money for be quiet," he said, with a laugh that sounded like a dog's bark.

"What's a lot of money?" demanded Mathew.

"Fifty-thousand dollar!"

Mathew's head and chest jerked back and his eyes opened wide in surprise. That was a lot of money. If Xsing Ching was willing to pay that sum, the situation was more serious than he thought. That meant that the blackmailer could prove that he knew all the details about the contraband.

"Man got too greedy. He no problem now," said the Chinese man, passing a finger in front of his own neck.

"What does that mean?" asked Mathew. "That you killed him?"

"Meeting over, goo' night, Mister." He opened the office door and walked briskly toward the front of the bar, leaving Mathew flatfooted. Regaining his composure, Mathew rushed after the bowlegged man and caught up with him just outside the front entrance to the bar.

"Just a minute, buddy. I need to get a couple more answers."

"You want more, you pay more."

"Did this man act alone or with others?" asked Mathew.

"One hundred dollars," said the Chinese man, holding out his hand.

"That wasn't part of the deal. I paid for information about who the blackmailer was."

"You got 'fomation. Man in tuxedo. You want more, you pay more!"

Furious, Mathew realized that if the man disappeared, he would never see him again. "All right," he said, as he peeled another five twenty's off the wad he was carrying.

The man quickly counted it and stuffed it in the same pocket. Mathew turned his head just in case the man decided to show his teeth again. "Man act alone. Never with anyone, never contact anyone. Me follow many times."

By then Mathew had connected the information with the death of Reginald Rockwood. He'd heard about his death, but he asked all the same.

"What happened to the guy in the tuxedo?"

"Taken care of. Out of picture. Our business finish. Goo' night," he said, and disappeared into the darkness of the spring evening.

## The Chinese Jars

That bastard Reginald, Mathew thought. How did he know Xsing Ching even existed? I have to find out how he got that information. What an asshole!

\* \* \*

For once, Mathew arrived at his Grant Avenue penthouse early. He had bags under his eyes. He made his way to the living room and yelled for Virginia. "Did you know that Reginald blackmailed Xsing and got $50,000 dollars?"

Virginia arched her left eyebrow. "I wasn't aware they even knew each other."

"According to my sources, it looks like Xsing took care of him."

"Does that mean they killed him?" asked Virginia with a jolt.

"Let's just say he's no longer a problem. I'd rather not know more."

"What does this discovery mean about closing the deal?" she asked.

"It depends on what kind of guarantee Ching can give me that there was no one else involved," said Mathew.

At that moment the doorbell rang; seconds later, Xsing entered. He was sporting a dark gray suit with a matching yellow tie and handkerchief. "Good evening to you both," he said, and took a seat in an armchair directly across from the sofa where the other two were sitting. If he was taken aback by Mathew's disheveled appearance, he made no comment.

"This blackmail incident has complicated our arrangement," said Mathew, trying to control his bad mood and his nerves.

"No need for complications, Mr. O'Hara. Everything is in order, I assure you."

"I've done my own checking on this, and I suspect that there was someone else involved. I learned that you paid a fortune. The money was never recovered, was it?"

"An unfortunate detail. My sources looked everywhere. Considering the total value of the transaction, let's just say that was the sales commission," said Ching sarcastically. "I understand the federal government recovered a part of it, but no one knows where the rest is. Why should this concern you?"

"How do you know what the feds recovered?"

"As I've told you, my sources are well placed."

"Let's change the subject," said Mathew. "Did you communicate my offer to your people?"

"Yes. They say they will be pleased to sell you the merchandise for $600,000. You can't complain, Mr. O'Hara. That's quite a reduction."

"That's not what I offered," said Mathew, "and now that there's a dead man in the middle of all this, I'm not sure I even want to go through with this deal."

Virginia listened intently to the men talking, taking mental notes. Mathew was about to lose his head. She called Fu Fung Fat and asked him to bring drinks for everybody. The pause and the alcohol calmed down the atmosphere, and the negotiations started again in a calmer tone.

"Here's what I'm willing to do, Xsing. I'm willing to come up to $450,000."

"That's not enough, I'm afraid," answered Xsing.

"It doesn't do me any good for you to tell me that. How much do they really want?" asked Mathew, again at the point of being impatient.

"I will have to make a call," said Xsing Ching. "May I use your phone?"

"Yes, of course. You can use the one in the bedroom back there, where you'll have some privacy," said Virginia.

Xsing left the room.

"I don't recognize you, Mathew. You're not usually so impulsive."

"I don't have all the strings in my hand. I don't know

what's going on behind my back. These guys are playing hard to get. What's their bottom line?"

"It looks as though for once you've found players who are just as good as you. Relax, you just have to bluff like in poker, and you're a master at that, Mathew. Use Rockwell to your advantage."

"How?"

"It's obvious that they killed him. Just as I've told you, Xsing Ching will do everything possible to finish this deal and get out of here. You, on the other hand, can take your time. Make him nervous," she said.

After a short while, Xsing Ching came back from the bedroom. His blank expression didn't give away anything, but Virginia learned to guess his state of mind. She took his hand and led him to the dining room table. "Let's have something to eat," she said, ringing the jade bell.

"I'd rather finish with this first," said Xsing Ching.

"Oh, no. There's time to enjoy dinner," said Mathew, smiling, taking off his tie, and throwing it on the back of one of the chairs.

Virginia invited them to sit down, and in a few minutes Fu Fung Fat brought the first course to the table: halibut cooked in dill and white wine and wrapped in banana leaves. He served very well with only with one arm but had to make several trips to the kitchen to serve the dishes one by one. Then he served the wine. He already knew that Xsing Ching drank only Chablis. Virginia prolonged the dinner an extra forty-five minutes by talking banalities, while Xsing Ching became more and more tense, just as she had calculated. He refused desert but had to sit patiently while the other two slowly savored their ice cream.

"We'll drink coffee in the living room," she decided.

Xsing Ching was ready to have a nervous breakdown. She made a discreet signal to Mathew and he returned to the job at hand.

"What do your people say about my offer?"

"That it's not enough."

"How much will they accept?" he asked coolly. He felt in charge again.

"They said $550,000. As I explained to you, we lost $50,000 on the blackmail, which could have been prevented if people hadn't talked so much about the deal."

"What are you insinuating? Is that an accusation?"

"Simply stating the facts, Mr. O'Hara. It doesn't help you either if this matter is talked about outside these walls. The final price is $550,000."

"That's too much," said Mathew.

"Mathew is willing to make the purchase, Xsing, but he has his limits," interceded Virginia. "With what's happened, I mean with Rockwood, Matt will have expenses that he wouldn't have otherwise had. He'll have to quiet rumors and impede any potential investigation. Fortunately, in San Francisco it's always possible to arrange these things. You understand, don't you?"

"That's right," added Mathew. "We'll have to cover this up and grease many palms, and that will cost us a lot."

By the end of the evening, they agreed on a price, $500,000. Mathew calculated that his impatience and discomfort had cost him several thousand dollars, not to mention the money he'd had to pay the scarred thug. Fortunately, Virginia had played it like a true gambler. His partner was worth her weight in gold. He was satisfied. He already had buyers lined up for the merchandise at almost double what he would pay for it.

\* \* \*

The meeting was set for the following Wednesday at nine p.m. at Pier 12 in the industrial district, south of Market. Xsing Ching agreed to have the merchandise there in crates, separated according to Mathew's specifications, making it easy to transship wherever and to whomever he wished. Xsing advised he could not be present because of other commitments, but he gave the account number of the Hong Kong bank where he wanted the money deposited via Western Union, once Mathew verified the authenticity of the pieces. After the transfer was made, the vases would belong to him, and he could make separate arrangements to pick them up.

Mathew was nervous all day. In the evening he went to Camelot for a couple of stiff drinks to calm his nerves before heading for Pier 12. Although unusual for him, he took a seat at the round table at the front of the bar and shortly Melba joined him. They sat there talking and watching the fog slowly invade the bay. Mathew guessed the temperature would drop, and he had on only a linen suit jacket. The fog was already blocking out the view of the bridge, and little by little the city lights were becoming blurred.

"This must be the only city in the world where one shivers from the cold all year," said Mathew, as he cracked his knuckles.

"Don't you like the fog? It looks like cotton," said Melba.

"I prefer the sun."

"You should live in the Mission," she said. "Why are you so nervous? I've been watching you the past several days and you've been acting weird."

"A lot of stuff going on, Melba. It'll be over soon, and I'll take the family to Hawaii for a vacation."

"I saw you talking to a tough-looking Chinese guy the other night. I hope he wasn't part of whatever you're up to."

"No, quite the contrary. I was just buying information. I got what I wanted."

"You had me worried. He wasn't your typical upstanding citizen. Did you see his face? Those looked like acid burns."

"We can't always choose who we do business with,

Melba."

"Would you like another drink? It's on the house."

Mathew hesitated, calculating how much another drink would affect his judgment. "What the hell, I've got time to kill," he decided, relaxing back into the chair.

"You've made a real success out of this place, Melba. I should reduce my take," he added.

"No need for that. It's a fair deal. I've enough to live on, and business's a hell of a lot better than it was in the Mission."

She waved two fingers in the air. The bartender caught her drift and soon brought bourbon on the rocks and a beer to the table.

"Where's the Mexican guy who used to stock the bar? What's his name? I haven't seen him around lately," said Mathew.

"You mean Rafael. Poor bastard, he's in San Quentin."

"No kidding? What for?"

"It's a long story. Mostly because he wouldn't squeal on his buddies," she explained.

"It's not for anything violent, is it?"

"Rafael? No way. He's the gentlest guy in the world."

"When's he get out?" asked Mathew.

"Not for a while. He actually just went there."

Mathew was not really paying attention anymore. He looked at his watch and realized it was eight thirty, time to go. He stood up, finished his drink in two gulps, and turned up the collar of his suit jacket, preparing to encounter the chilly evening.

"See ya tomorrow, Melba."

"Okay, Mathew, drive carefully in the fog," she said.

\* \* \*

Pier 12 was on the San Francisco waterfront south of the Bay Bridge At the time it was a dilapidated warehouse quay, used for unloading and depositing several inbound ships' cargos. Although still used for storage, its days of hustle and bustle were gone. Most of the unloading had shifted to Oakland.

It was a dark night, and there was heavy fog and limited visibility. Mathew's Packard approached the entrance and the headlights illuminated a chain-link fence and gate with three padlocks on it. Through the links, Mathew could make out the outline of a building with a single light on the top of its north corner that shone down through the mist to the dock level below.

There was a guard shack a few feet from the gate on the driver's side. An Italian man, square like an armoire, with several days' stubble, came out of the door with a flashlight in his hand. He had on a wool cap that covered his ears and a pea coat. As he approached the car, Mathew's chauffer, who'd loyally served him for fifteen years, rolled down the window. "We're here to meet some people and take a look at some merchandise," explained the driver.

"Yeah. Who sent you?" asked the guard.

The driver turned to Mathew, since he didn't have an answer.

"Xsing Ching," barked Mathew impatiently from the back seat.

"Don't get mad at me, Mister. I'm jus' doin' ma job. You gots to watch it in this neighborhood." He unlocked the three padlocks and swung the gate inward, hooking both sides so the car could pass. "Dey said dey'd meet you down by door number 3. Yous'll have to drive down dare a ways. Be careful. Dare ain't no lights out dare. Dat one up dare's da only one. Not many peoples come down dis way at night."

"Okay, man. Thanks for your help," said Mathew, reaching over the left shoulder of the driver and handing the guard a tip. "This is for your troubles."

"T'anks, Mister. Every little bit helps. When yous wants

to come out, drive up to the gate and honk. I gots to keep it locked. Boss's orders!"

Once the car was through the gates, the guard closed and locked them. The driver put on his brights but only caught the fog, so he lowered the beams and used the light on the corner of the building as his guide after he put on the windshield wipers.

The car crept along the pier. Mathew sat hunched forward on the back seat with his hands clenched on the seat in front of him. He squinted to see the outline of the warehouse doors as the car inched along. He could hear several foghorns moaning their litany from various parts of the bay.

"Nasty night to be down here," he commented.

"Yes, sir," replied the driver.

"Here it is. Stop."

The driver stopped in front of door number 3, which was partly open. Mathew stepped carefully out of the car onto the uneven and worn wooden planks of the old dock. He peered inside the door and could see what looked like a flashlight moving around the other side of the warehouse some three hundred feet away. "Hello! Anybody home?" he yelled.

"Over here," a voice responded, and the only light in the building shone in his direction.

"Is it safe to walk from here to there?" asked Mathew.

"Hold on, I'll come and get you," the voice answered and began to get louder as it approached the place where Mathew was standing. He watched the flashlight reflecting off the cobwebs in the rafters as it bobbed up and down with the person's movement.

When the voice arrived, Mathew saw a man in a raincoat and hat that looked Chinese. All around him, it was completely dark. There was an eerie silence, except for the occasional foghorn sounding in the distance.

The man introduced himself in perfect English. "How do

you do. I am Wing Su, Mr. Ching's representative. It's nice to finally meet you. All our conversations have been on the phone. Hard to see in here, so you'd better follow me. I have been removing some of the packing so you can examine the merchandise. You will be pleased."

Mathew strained to get a look at the man's face but there just wasn't enough light.

With the man leading and holding the flashlight, they slowly walked through rows of cargo stacked randomly in the huge space, none more than three or four feet high. When they arrived at the other side, where Mathew had first seen the light, there were three workmen dressed in overalls, two with crowbars and another with a claw hammer, removing pieces of wood from the twenty or so crates spread over a thirty-square-foot area. The man in the raincoat was told to direct his flashlight at one of the partially open crates by one of the workmen. Under the light Mathew saw a delicately carved vase.

"It's more than a thousand years old," said Wing Su. He picked it up and put it on top of a nearby crate while another man shined his light on it. Even in that poor light Mathew could appreciate its translucence and richness of color and it exquisite form. The figures depicted on its side almost jumped out at him as they performed the perfunctory chores of daily life in ancient China with such perfection that they seemed ready to move.

"Have you ever seen anything so beautiful?" he asked Wing Su.

Wing Su then pulled out another vase, even older than the first, and had them shine a light on it. Mathew wasn't an expert or a collector, but the beauty of those objects produced such emotion in him that he could hardly talk.

"Mr. Ching wants you to get your money's worth. Here's a list of the inventory," said Wing Su, handing him a folder. "He asks that you make sure all the pieces are here and in good shape. Of course, you understand that before they can be delivered, you will have to transfer the money."

"Yes, I understand," said Mathew, still fumbling for words.

"You will be depositing the $500,000 this week, will you not?" asked Wing Su.

"I'm not at liberty to discuss the details with you," answered Mathew. "Let's just say I'll live up to my end of the bargain."

"That's all we can ask for, Mr. O'Hara, and all we need to hear at this point. My next job is to inform you that you are under arrest for trafficking in illegal art from Communist China."

"How's that? What the shit do you mean?" exclaimed Mathew.

"I repeat. You're under arrest. Put your hands behind your back. I have to handcuff you."

"This is unheard of."

"Do what you're told. We don't want to get rough with you."

Mathew shook off the paralysis that had initially weakened his legs, turned quickly, and pushed the man in the raincoat, knocking him backwards onto one of the boxes. With four quick strides he was lost in the darkness. Three federal U.S. Customs agents came out of the shadows with flashlights and went after him. As they approached him, he started running. He reached the entry door and flew past the Packard, which only had its parking lights on, and started running down the vacant dock with the feds in hot pursuit. He was gaining strength that he didn't even know he had until they finally tackled him. It took all three to pin him up against the wall of the vacant warehouse, where he continued to struggle and scream obscenities at them.

"You fuckers don't know who you're messing with," he yelled, as he continued to battle. "I want to talk to the mayor, right now. This is a violation of my constitutional rights..." Suddenly he seemed to calm down. He tried to explain that there must have been some mistake. He was an honorable man, well known in the city. He recited a list of important people—senators, bankers, the governor—all would vouch for him. This could all be fixed among friends; there was no need for the scandal. He had resources and could be generous.

"I have my rights," he said. "I demand to talk to my lawyer!"

Then another figure came out of the shadows into the small circle of light created by the flashlights of the agents. It was Charles Perkins.

"Good evening, Mr. O'Hara. I'd like to introduce you to Agent Tong," pointing to the man in the raincoat. "Good job, Mr. Tong. You were very convincing in your role as Mr. Wing Su. And what's more important is that you fixed it so that Mr. Ching never suspected that you infiltrated his organization."

"Yes, but we didn't catch him. We should have had him here tonight, but he got away."

"It doesn't matter. When he tries to do another deal in the U.S., and surely he will, we'll get him. But it'll take time because his organization is shattered, and it will cost him a lot to put it back on its feet. We have the works of art and Mr. O'Hara here. I'm sure that this will guarantee you a promotion, Agent Tong."

"Thank you Mr. Perkins. Now it's your turn to prosecute Mr. O'Hara. He has a lot of influence and money. I hope he doesn't slip through your fingers."

Mathew took advantage of the brief moment of distraction, broke free, and again started running blindly down the pier, now stumbling, now falling, now getting up, with three U.S. Customs agents in hot pursuit.

"Don't shoot him," yelled Charles Perkins in an authoritarian voice from the shadows.

There were flashlights bobbing up and down and the sound of feet pounding on the timbers as they chased Mathew down the dark planks. Suddenly there was a splash and everyone knew that he had jumped or fallen into the water.

Charles yelled, "Get the fire department down here with blankets. And one of you agents jump in after him. He won't last long in that cold water. We have to pull him out."

Mathew was, in fact, struggling. It was freezing cold. He started to swim under the pilings, but his clothes became saturated with water, and his legs felt like lead pillars. He started to go under and he thought it was all over, so he yelled, "Over here! I give up! I'm drowning!"

As soon as they knew where he was, one of the agents jumped in. When he reached Mathew's side, he said, "Stop fighting or we'll both go under." The two other agents shone their flashlights on the two men in the water, and Charles Perkins, with his authoritarian voice, came out onto the pier with his flashlight and caught them in its light. "Bring him to shore."

"I can't do it by myself, Chief," said the Customs agent in the water.

Before Charles could take the initative to send another man into the water, the chauffer from the Packard went running past the others and jumped into the bay to rescue his boss. By then Mathew had lost all his strength. Between his loyal chauffer and the Customs agent, they were able to get him to a place where he could be pulled ashore. Soon after that they heard the sirens from the fire department near the entrance gate. Together they dragged him to shore and began slapping him on the back just as a fire engine showed up at the gate.

Charles yelled at the gatekeeper, "Open the goddamned gate. This is police business."

He complied, and a minute later the fire truck shed plenty of light on the scene. Three firemen jumped down with blankets. One immediately started to revive Mathew, who'd sucked in a lot of water, and the others made sure the two wet rescuers were made warm so they wouldn't suffer from hypothermia. The ambulance took about fifteen minutes to arrive and by then Mathew had made a pretty good recovery. He was handcuffed, wrapped in blankets, and still shivering.

* * *

While Mathew O'Hara spent that first night handcuffed in the jail section of the hospital, Xsing Ching was flying toward the Far East on a Pan Am Boeing 707, sitting in the first-class section of the new jet plane with his wife and children. He thought he had just completed the most lucrative deal of his life and the money would be waiting for him when he arrived in Hong Kong. Perhaps the only thing that was lacking to make him completely happy was Virginia Dimitri, but he knew he couldn't have everything.

He rang the call button. "Will you please bring a bottle of your best champagne? We want to celebrate something very special," he said to the stewardess.

# 13

## Chinatown Mourns

SAMUEL LEARNED of Mathew O'Hara's arrest in the newspaper and saw that Charles Perkins was involved. He called him from the phone booth at the rear of Camelot.

"Hello, Charles, this is Samuel."

"I know that. Don't you think they tell me who's calling?" he answered haughtily.

"That was quite a coup!"

"Yeah, I thought so, too. It took some time, but it wasn't until the last minute that I got the tip that broke the case."

"What kind of a tip?" asked Samuel, fumbling for his package of cigarettes.

"I can't discuss details of an ongoing case with you, Samuel, sorry."

"Just a second," said Samuel, coughing while he lit a cigarette. "Do you think O'Hara had anything to do with Reginald's death?"

"Why do you think that?"

"They knew each other. Reginald came to O'Hara's bar almost every night. I saw them talking on more than one occasion," explained Samuel, blowing the smoke out of the open folding door.

"That's interesting," said Charles, "but I don't see any connection yet. We searched all of O'Hara's apartments and found nothing that would even point in that direction."

"Oh, really? Which apartments?"

"One on Grant, and the other south of Market, one of those lofts in the old industrial part of town. Why did he have so many apartments? That's the question."

"So, no connection with Rockwood?"

"Not so far, but keep snooping. You never know where the trail will lead," replied Charles, and he hung up.

Samuel stayed in the booth mulling over what they'd talked about and decided it didn't amount to much. He supposed that Charles would be obsessed with getting a conviction against O'Hara. It was a juicy scandal and would be a big advancement to his career if he got one. He also knew that Charles would keep most of the leads to himself. If anything, it would have to be him providing the insights to Charles.

He went back to the round table through the empty bar, ordered a cup of coffee, and picked up a discarded newspaper on one of the empty tables. He sat down and started a crossword puzzle he found on the back page. Halfway through the puzzle, Melba arrived. She was perky, alert, and dressed in an awful blue nylon pantsuit whose only virtue was that it matched the color of her eyes. Excalibur followed her closely.

"Have a cup of coffee with me, Melba."

She went behind the bar, opened a beer, and went back to sit next to him.

"Blanche didn't come today?' he asked, trying to be casual.

"She had to go and pick up an order of liquor that wasn't delivered. Have you made any progress with her?"

"I don't know if you can call it progress, Melba, but at least she agreed to go out with me tomorrow," he answered, blushing, in spite of himself.

"Good luck. You're going to need it, sweetie."

"This thing with O'Hara hit me like a rock, Melba," said Samuel, in order to change the subject. "I suppose that creates problems for you. Isn't he your partner in the bar?"

"It doesn't affect me. Everything is the same."

"Why would a guy with that much money get involved in something like that?"

"Sometimes people get too big for their britches."

"Was he involved in shady deals before?"

"Well, that's evident. I suspected something. A couple of weeks ago, he met here with a Chinese thug. When I saw him, I knew he was trouble," said Melba.

"Why?"

"I have an eye for that kind of person. He looked like he killed people for a living. His face was severely marked. Like from a case of smallpox, or a burn, but a real bad case, for sure."

"Really?" asked Samuel, thinking of the description of one of the men that pushed Reginald. "When was that?"

"A couple of weeks ago. When he came in here, Excalibur almost ate him. It surprised me because he's never attacked anyone here at Camelot."

"Except me," Samuel reminded her.

"Don't be silly. He only growled at you, he never tried to bite."

Samuel stood straight up. If Melba said anything else, he didn't hear it. He rushed back to the phone booth and got through to Charles. "I think I have a lead on the guy who pushed Reginald into the path of the trolley bus," and he proceeded to explain what he had just learned.

"That's good information. But it won't do much good to ask O'Hara about it right now. He has that smart-ass attorney, Hiram Goldberg, and so far he's taking the Fifth on everything," Charles replied.

"Isn't there anything we can do?"

# The Chinese Jars

"I have an idea," added Charles. "I'm going to talk to Homicide. Remember our old friend Sandovich? They can pull him in for questioning and people from my office will be there, too. I have to hand it to you, Samuel. You're a persistent son of a bitch."

"I think you're wasting your time. Melba told me he's a small fry; he doesn't swim with the big fish," answered Samuel.

"That may be, but we've got to start somewhere. You know the old saying: if you don't shake the tree, you have to wait for the fruit to fall. Let's shake that fucker."

"Okay with me," said Samuel. "Keep me informed," and he hung up.

\* \* \*

After being very persistent with his entreaties, Samuel was able to observe the interrogation of Sandovich through a two-way mirror. The room where it took place was small and without ventilation. There were several people present: a detective from Homicide, Charles Perkins, a U.S. Customs agent representing the federal government, and Sandovich. On the table was a tape recorder and several ashtrays with smoldering cigarette butts in them, which made the air sticky, and almost brown. The space behind the mirror where Samuel was observing was even smaller and more stifling. It had two old chairs, a side table, an ashtray, and a pitcher of water with a dirty glass. The walls were covered with soundproofing so noise couldn't get out; and thanks to a speaker above the opaque mirror, a person sitting in the room could not only observe the goings-on but could hear them as well. Samuel struggled against the urge to smoke, because in that enclosure he wouldn't be able to control his cough, which in the last few weeks had gone from bad to worse.

"Maurice, my name is Charles Perkins, from the U.S. attorney's office. We've met before."

Sandovich nodded. He was dressed in his blue uniform with his prominent sergeant stripes displayed on both sleeves. He put his military-style hat on the table. Samuel noted that there were beads of perspiration on his brow.

"This gentleman on my right is from U.S. Customs. We have some questions to ask you."

Sandovich looked around suspiciously, especially at the mirror, and wiped his forehead with a handkerchief.

"It has to do with the death of Reginald Rockwood. You remember our last visit, don't you?"

"Yes, sir. I don't know how much help I can be, other than what I already told you," he said in a defiant tone. He lit a cigarette and smoothed his butch haircut with his sweaty left hand.

"We have new information, Maurice, and we want to go over it with you," said Charles.

"Yeah, sure. I got nothing better to do," said Sandovich, with a dry laugh.

Samuel noticed the friendly tone Charles was using, and he chuckled to himself. He knew the old trick. If you can't frighten 'em, seduce 'em.

"You see this, Maurice?" showing him a mug shot of a Chinese man with a severely pox-marked face. "Mr. Butler, the Muni driver, thinks he looks like the man who pushed Mr. Rockwood in front of the trolley bus. I grant you, he's not a hundred percent sure."

"You're asking the wrong guy, Counselor. I wasn't there. My job was to approve the report and pass it on, and I did that," he said. But he started to relax, as he saw that Charles's suspicions weren't directed at him.

"You know who this guy is, don't you, Maurice?"

"Never seen him before in my life," said Sandovich, "Can

you get me a cup of coffee? It looks like we're going to be here a while."

Charles ignored the request and sat down on the edge of the table next to Sandovich. One of his legs dangled over the other; his pant leg bunched up, exposing one of his socks with no elastic on top. "Let me tell you something about him," Charles began. "He's a notorious gunman for hire. He does all kinds of dirty work for the criminal elements in Chinatown. His name is Dong Wong. Have you ever heard that name before?"

"Not in public. Most people in Chinatown would never give the name of a person who did 'em harm. They'd be too afraid of reprisals. I've heard rumors that he was involved in this or that strong-arm kind of stuff, but never officially through the Vice Squad where I work. I understand other departments have been trying to get him for a few things, but they've never been able to pin anything on him."

"Do you know Mathew O'Hara?" asked Charles.

"Only from what I read in the newspaper. I don't deal with many white guys on my beat."

"So, Maurice, you've never met the gentleman? Is that correct?"

"That's correct, Counselor. I wouldn't know 'im from the next rich guy if I was sitting next to 'im on a cable car if I hadn't seen his picture in the paper," he said. A thin smile appeared on his blotchy face.

"How about Xsing Ching?" asked Charles, showing him another photograph.

Sandovich looked casually at the photograph. "Likewise, never laid eyes on him. I only know what I read in the paper."

"Ever hear his name mentioned around your beat?"

"Look, guys like O'Hara and Xsing Ching are out of the league of the ordinary stuff that goes on down there. If they were dealing, it was never in person and certainly neither of their names ever came up through any of my contacts," said Sandovich.

"Let's talk about your contacts. Will you let us interview them?" asked Charles.

Sandovich laughed. "You're kidding, aren't you? That'd be like giving 'em a death sentence. They'd be finished; they'd have to leave the country. I'm afraid not, Counselor."

"Okay, I have one more person I'd like to ask you about, Maurice." He pulled out another photograph, this one of a woman. "Do you recognize her?"

Sandovich looked at the photo for a minute or so. "Good looking broad. Who's she?"

"Virginia Dimitri," answered Charles.

"Never seen her or even heard her name. What you got on her?" he inquired.

"Nothing, frankly," said Charles. "But she's a girlfriend of O'Hara's, so we thought we'd ask."

"Is that all the questions you got? I've a busy afternoon," said Sandovich. He got up from his chair and put on his police hat.

"Yeah, that's all for now, Maurice. But you'll keep your eyes and ears open for us, won't you?" said Charles.

"Sure thing, Counselor." He shook hands with the Customs agent and Charles and left the room.

Samuel, feeling cheated, watched the small group of men on the other side of the mirror.

"We didn't get shit from that lying asshole," said the Customs agent.

"You're wrong. I wasn't looking for answers," said Charles, "If my instincts are correct, he'll spread the word about what he heard today. We'll have to wait and see how long it takes for it to filter into the neighborhood, and who responds."

Samuel let out a laugh. He'd underestimated Charles.

\* \* \*

# The Chinese Jars

When Mathew didn't return to the apartment the night he was arrested, Virginia didn't waste any time. She went to the bedroom, climbed a stepladder, removed a panel from the ceiling and took out two boxes of money that Mathew had left her. Then she replaced the panel. It was impossible to see where the crack was in the ceiling because it blended in with the wallpaper. She counted the stacks of hundred-dollar bills to assure herself there was half a million dollars. She never imagined she'd have to handle that much money. It was a cash transaction and her partner had to trust that she would make the deposit when it was time. She took a roll of butcher paper and twine from the utility closet and began to put the money in packages, wrapping each with the resilient string and tying it with a perfect square knot so it wouldn't come unraveled. When she finished, she put the packages into two canvas bags and tied the tops with quarter-inch rope and another knot.

Early the next morning, she sent Fu Fung Fat to Mr. Song's with instructions to deposit in her receptacle the packages she had prepared as soon as he opened. She told him to contract for an additional jar in her name, since it wouldn't all fit in the one she had.

The one-armed man had to make two trips. He loaded the first sack on his back, gained his balance, and staggered to his destination; he then came back for the other. After he finished, he gave Virginia the two claim checks and two keys. She hid them behind the same panel in the ceiling, sticking them to the beam with adhesive tape. She then calmly waited for events to unfold as she anticipated they would.

It didn't take long for the authorities to show up at the Grant Avenue apartment. She received the agents without fuss when she was taken into custody and acted like the ride in the police car was a social event. She underwent hours of interrogation by Charles Perkins and the U.S. Customs agents. They already knew Xsing Ching had spent time with her, including how many times and on what dates, but she could tell they didn't know much else, and certainly nothing of her involvement. She easily deducted that they'd had him under surveillance. She admitted that she had been Mathew O'Hara's lover, but for some time now she only worked for him. Her interrogators thought she had all the attributes to please such a rich and refined man as O'Hara, and they felt a certain sense of envy. She wore a green silk blouse with the top button undone, and Charles and the Customs agent were having trouble concentrating on the questions.

"What discussions did you have with Mr. Xsing in connection with the delivery of the merchandise?" asked Charles.

She straightened up slightly and smiled seductively, looking Charles straight in the eye. Her nipples pressed up against the silk. "Perhaps I didn't make myself clear. I wasn't aware of the delivery of any merchandise, or whatever you want to call it. I only had dinner with Mr. Xsing and Mr. O'Hara. It was a social thing. It was my job to wine and dine the people from Hong Kong or anybody else who had business with Mr. O'Hara. It was public relations, nothing else. He was always there, and I never talked business with any of them. In fact, I had no idea what they were discussing. Mr. O'Hara never confided any of that to me."

"Were there others, besides Xsing Ching, at these meeting?" asked Charles.

"No, just him."

"What about the times when Mr. Ching came to your apartment when Mr. O'Hara wasn't there."

"He had a sick child and I was trying to get him medical help here in San Francisco. Check with Dr. Rolland from the University Medical Center if you don't believe me."

They had absolutely no luck in interrogating Fu Fung Fat

or the cook. They both claimed they spoke very little English. Both denied knowing anything other than that Mathew came to visit Virginia, and they only admitted that because it was common knowledge he owned the apartment. They both remembered that Xsing Ching had been there to dinner but couldn't remember any of the details. Their mistress and Mr. O'Hara received many guests, they added.

When the authorities searched the apartment, they looked in all the usual places: under the beds, in the back of the closets, behind the headboards. They rolled up the Persian carpets to see if there were any hidden trap doors, and removed all the pictures from the walls looking for secret vaults. They even tipped over the ancient Chinese vases, but they found nothing.

\* \* \*

"Would you like to go to a movie at the Larkin theatre tonight? I saw in the paper they were showing Rififi, a French movie," said Samuel to Blanche.

He had on his going-out suit, the most decent one he owned, and had just gotten a haircut. They agreed to meet at Camelot. Blanche also made an effort. Instead of pants and the usual tennis shoes, she had on a spring dress and a white blouse. To Samuel she looked more attractive than ever, although this new, more feminine and flirtatious Blanche intimidated him.

"I like the sound of it, but we're not going to understand a word," she said.

"It has subtitles, for sure. Afterwards, we can drop by the Blackhawk. Dave Brubeck's in town."

"How did you know I'm a big fan of his?" asked Blanche, surprised. "I have all his records."

During the movie, things didn't go quite as Samuel expected. After half an hour, he figured that he could put his arm on the back of her seat, and ten minutes later he let it fall casually to her shoulders. She looked at him out of the corner of her eye, but she didn't move. It would have been better if he could have held her hand but she was busy munching on popcorn like it was a lifesaver. There weren't many options left to Samuel, and he bravely tried to snuggle head-to-head with her. Blanche, sitting stiffly in her seat, didn't make things easy. Samuel stretched his neck as far as he could, but she was taller than he was, and he couldn't reach her unless he raised himself in the seat. He couldn't hold that position for too long, so he delicately pushed her head toward him, but with such bad luck that his glasses got caught in her hair. He tried to pull away, but Blanche couldn't stop laughing, and her volume kept rising as he struggled to free his glasses while he cursed in panic. People started to complain, and soon a voice told them to shut up. In the process, she started laughing louder and he got more confused. At that very moment the sound in the movie stopped. Two, three, five minutes, and nothing but silence with more shushes for Blanche to shut up. With a sigh of relief Samuel recouped his glasses and soon Blanche calmed down. Ten minutes passed and the movie was not only silent but was getting darker.

"You'd better talk to the management, there's something wrong with the sound," Blanche suggested.

Samuel left his seat and was gone for a couple of moments, and came back to tell her that Rififi had twenty minutes of silence.

"Oh, I suppose it's a French thing. Be patient," she said, trying not to make noise with her popcorn bag because the audience seemed absorbed.

By the time the movie was over, Samuel was worried, first that he hadn't understood it, then that Blanche hadn't liked it, and finally that he'd made a total fool of himself. He walked out behind her, dragging his feet.

# The Chinese Jars

"Would you still like to go to the Blackhawk?" he asked, apprehensively.

"Yes, of course," said Blanche. But her tone was less enthusiastic than before.

They walked the block and a half to the Blackhawk. He paid the cover charge, and they sat down at a table toward the rear of the nightclub. He ordered a Scotch on the rocks, and Blanche ordered a glass of orange juice.

As they listened to Dave Brubeck playing the piano and his musical companions backing him up, Samuel observed her out of the corner of his eye, happy that they didn't have to talk because he couldn't think of anything to say. He motioned for the cocktail waitress. "I'll have another Scotch on the rocks," he said, nervously. He swallowed the drink in two gulps. In a little while, he ordered another.

"Don't you think you've had enough," Blanche noted.

"Yeah, I guess you're right," he slurred. "Let's get out of here."

He hailed a cab right outside the club, and asked the cabbie to take them to her home in the Upper Castro. During the ride, she was stone-faced and silent, hugging the door as far away from him as possible.

"Are you going to say anything, Blanche?"

"What do you want me to say? You've had too much to drink. Frankly, I'm disappointed, because until we got to the club, I was having a wonderful time."

"You liked the movie?" he asked, surprised.

"Of course, I did."

By then they had reached her house. Samuel spent his last dollar on the cab fare. "I'm sorry, Blanche," he said, embarrassed.

"I'm sorry, too, Samuel. Go home and sleep it off, and don't drink so much when you're around me. Good night," she said, as she turned and bounded up the stairs, never looking back.

Samuel's hands were deep in his pockets and his shoulders were hunched over. Humiliated, he started walking the twenty blocks to his flat near Chinatown. He thought that he was not only broke—he didn't even have enough money to buy a pack of cigarettes—but he felt he'd blown his chance to make an impression on Blanche. He concluded that his courtship skills needed polishing, as Melba had often suggested, and that he also needed a better-paying job.

*  *  *

After a few days, Samuel became anxious to talk with Charles. He wanted to get as much information as he could about any leads Charles had that connected Mathew O'Hara with Reginald Rockwood's death. He borrowed money from Melba with the promise that he would pay her the following week, and he invited Charles to Chop Suey Louie's for lunch. It was the only restaurant he could afford.

They arrived at noon, and the place was almost empty, but they sat at the counter, Samuel's favorite spot.

"Where's your mother? This is one of the few times I haven't seen her in her corner," said Samuel.

"She went to the astrologer. She doesn't like my brother's fiancée."

"What can the astrologer do?"

"Maybe she can prove that they're not compatible. That would make my mother very happy," said Louie.

"You remember my friend Charles Perkins. He's an attorney with the federal government."

"Nice to see you again, Mr. Perkins. And you, Samuel? I see you're hanging around with big shots now. I hope you won't forget your old friends, and you'll continue betting with me," he said, laughing.

"Maybe that's not a good idea," replied Samuel, "I haven't

won a bet with you for the last three years."

Charles was seated on the end seat in front of the cash register where Louie usually held court, and Samuel was to his left. They were both drawn to the tropical fish swimming around in the giant aquarium directly in front of them. The big ones chased the small ones into the treasure boxes and holes in the lava rocks where they could hide. Goldie was immobile in one corner on top of some sand. Samuel thought she looked depressed, just like he was.

"Do you want today's special?"

"Sure," said Samuel, knowing it would be cheap, since he was paying.

"That's fine with me," said Charles.

Louie yelled something back to the kitchen in Cantonese.

"Has anything leaked onto the street that you could attribute to the interrogation of Sandovich?" asked Samuel, turning to Charles.

"Not a word," said Charles, "and that's surprising. I thought for sure by now it would have gotten out there and produced some results."

"I told you that before you brought him in. Melba said he was small potatoes," said Samuel.

"And who's that?"

"Just a friend. But she knows everything that goes on in this city. I'd really like to catch whoever killed Rockwood. He was my friend."

"Only that? Don't you want to get a promotion in the newspaper and become a reporter?" asked Charles.

"Some of that, too," admitted Samuel, blushing.

"I've already told you it puts me in a bind if I give you confidential information. But you've helped me on other occasions, and I want to give you a leg up, so I have kind of a half-assed solution. I'll provide you information off the record. If anyone tries to get your source, you play dumb. In other words, you didn't get it from me. Can we agree on that?" proposed Charles.

"That's great. You'll tell me everything then, and I won't say a word."

"No, not everything, but enough so you'll have the scoop on the whole story. That is, if we can ever figure out what it is."

At that very moment, Samuel glanced up at the aquarium and saw the reflection of two Chinese standing at the entrance. There was something about their attitude and something shiny in one of their hands. His mind delayed the connection of what his eyes had seen for a fraction of a second. It was a Tommy gun, and it was pointed directly at him. He reacted by instinct; "Down!" he yelled and pushed Charles off the seat to the floor, falling on top of him, just as the bullets came flying, shattering the counter where they'd been sitting, as well as the aquarium and the cash register where Louie was standing. They ended up blocking the small passageway leading to the kitchen.

Louie didn't know what hit him. He took six slugs in the chest and head and was dead before he hit the floor behind the counter.

There was pandemonium in the small restaurant. The few patrons there ducked under the tables or remained paralyzed and screaming with fear. And the water from the aquarium, mixed with Louie's blood and tropical fish, spread all over the floor. The assailants backed up as they fired, then got lost in Chinatown. The shooting only lasted a few seconds, but it seemed like forever.

Afterwards, Samuel remembered it like a photographic sequence, each one in its place for eternity. Several minutes passed before the people understood that the incident was over and they could react. Samuel shook Charles who was still under him, "Are you all right?" he asked, once he could speak.

"Yeah, I'm okay," said Charles, trembling. His mind still hadn't figured it all out.

"Louie!" yelled someone at that moment, and several people ran to the spot where he'd been.

Samuel, the closest to him, pounced on his dead body lying behind the counter, a mass of bloody carnage.

Miraculously, no one in the kitchen was hit, but the bullets had made a mess of it. The two people who were still there were hysterical, and the rest had run out the back door screaming. Someone called the police, and soon they heard the sirens of the patrol cars.

Charles pulled himself together and managed to get to a phone. He called the FBI.

"Get an ambulance! Get an ambulance!" yelled Samuel, as he tired desperately to revive his dead friend.

"Forget it, Samuel, he's gone," said Charles, reaching down and gently prying the crying man away from the body.

In the next few minutes a crowd gathered at the door, all trying to squeeze in to see what had happened. The police, the FBI, and an ambulance all arrived at the same time. The patrolmen pulled the curious away from the restaurant and started to block the street, while a young officer with a pad and pencil in hand tried to talk to potential witnesses. Two ambulance attendants tried to put Samuel in one of their vehicles. It was difficult to convince them that the blood was Louie's, not his. Charles showed them his identification and took Samuel by the arm and dragged him to the exit. As they passed a patrol car, parked with its lights flashing, Charles told a policeman to call the Medical Examiner because there was a dead man inside.

"Is he wounded?" asked the cop, referring to Samuel.

"No. But he needs to go home," he said, again identifying himself.

The policeman directed them to another patrol car, and Charles told the driver where to go. The car, its siren wailing, slowly took off, nudging its way through the gathering crowd.

"Who in the fuck did this?" asked Samuel, still in shock, looking at his clothes and hands, still full of blood.

"Don't you see, those bastards were after us!" exclaimed Charles.

"Was that the message you expected when you interrogated Sandovich?"

"Are you fuckin' crazy? If I could have anticipated this, I sure the shit wouldn't have gone to Chinatown," snapped Charles, still shaken.

"They killed Louie! He had nothing to do with any of this," murmured Samuel, with his head in his hands.

\* \* \*

Chop Suey Louie's death cast a pall over Chinatown; he was a popular and vibrant member of the community. Samuel couldn't forgive himself for what had happened. He felt responsible. He thought if he hadn't had the bad idea of going to the restaurant that day for lunch, his friend would still be alive.

He tried to get in touch with Louie's mother to give her his condolences, but she wouldn't see him. The person who opened the door let him know that the old lady blamed him for the assassination of her son. She'd always thought that Samuel's red hair was a sign of the devil, and events had confirmed it. He found out that the rest of his family lived in Waverly Place, but he couldn't muster up the courage to find them in the labyrinth of streets.

The next Sunday was set aside to mourn Louie's passing. Samuel couldn't face it alone so he invited Melba and Blanche to meet him at the Green Street Mortuary in North Beach, the Italian section. Both women were dressed in black and wore small hats of the same color, while Samuel had on his only suit, which for a change was neatly pressed. He wore it with a clean white shirt and a red striped tie. His red eyes were visible from quite a distance.

"Well, well, child, you look handsome," joked Melba, straightening his tie.

"I'm very sorry about your friend," said Blanche, moved by Samuel's obvious grief.

"Why is this happening at an Italian mortuary?" asked Melba.

"Most of their business is Chinese. The owner of the funeral home surely doesn't care which race his clients belong to," said Samuel.

"Is that a band outside the funeral home?" asked Blanche.

"That used to be the Chinese Marching Band. Now it's called the Green Street Mortuary Band. They play at most Chinese funerals," said Samuel.

"But there's no Chinese in that band," Blanche observed.

"That's because the Chinese didn't want to join Local 6 of the Musicians Union, so the white guys took over. It didn't matter to Louie. He loved their music. Every time a funeral passed his restaurant, he took me out onto the street and showed it to me with pride. He told me you could only get this kind of a reception in San Francisco's Chinatown, nowhere else in the country," explained Samuel, with tears in his eyes.

The mortuary hall still had its Italian decorations—copies of Renaissance paintings of saints on the walls and statues on pedestals in enclaves on either side of the seating area—a Catholic Church ambiance for Chinese clients. Up in front was Louie's closed coffin on a stand with several wreaths of different flowers placed on tripods, each with a red ribbon with Chinese writing placed diagonally across it. The hall was full of dignitaries and ordinary people. The mayor and the chief of police were sitting next to Louie's widow and their three children. The dead man's mother, seated in the front row, continued unmoved, mute and without shedding a tear. After a long sermon in Chinese, and a shorter one in English, the mourners filed out the front door, each person taking a piece of candy to help remove the taste of death, as Samuel explained it. The crowd went to one side of the stairs leading to the street while the band positioned itself on the other.

When the casket arrived at the top of the stairs, a drum roll started. The pallbearers took the coffin down the steps and put him into the hearse. They were followed by a group of ten women, all dressed in black with veils over their faces, sobbing uncontrollably.

"Poor man, he leaves behind a large family." Melba commented, moved.

"That's not his family. Those are wailers, hired by the family to cry for them. Chinese people don't like to openly express grief, so they pay people to do it for them," said Samuel.

After the wailers came the family, and further back, the rest of the crowd. Some were carrying paper houses, cars, and even a paper bridge down the steps of the mortuary.

"What's all that for?" asked Melba.

"These are things he'll need on the other side. They'll burn them at the gravesite. It's a way of releasing them so he can take them with him," Samuel explained.

"I thought he was a Taoist" said Blanche, when the band started playing a Christian hymn.

"He was, but Chinese people in San Francisco like the band to play Christian hymns and to make as much noise as possible," said Samuel. "It drives away the bad spirits."

In front of the hearse, but behind the band, was a red Cadillac convertible with its white top down and a huge photograph of a smiling Chop Suey Louie in the back seat.

## The Chinese Jars

After the hearse, limousines carrying the family moved into place, and then the autos of the rest of the attendees, including Melba's beaten-up two-door Ford coupe. The procession went down Green Street to Columbus, where it took a right on Stockton. When it crossed into Chinatown, a flurry of paper money was thrown at the funeral caravan.

"Look at that!" exclaimed Melba.

"It's fake. It's called spirit money. It has a slit in the middle so the pesky ghosts and spirits pass through it and get distracted. That way they can't prevent him from getting where he's going. You'll also notice that it didn't appear until we reached Chinatown. That's because it's against the law to litter in San Francisco, but it's allowed for Chinese funerals as long as it's done in Chinatown," Samuel informed her.

The crowds didn't stop their shopping as the funeral procession moved down Stockton and turned onto Clay and then again onto Grant Avenue, the main street of old Chinatown, with its exaggerated fake pagodas and bright red or green doors. It continued until it came to Waverly Place, where it finally stopped. There was a huge crowd on both sides of the street. The band didn't miss a note. The beat of the bass drum seemed to intensify, and the clash of the cymbals got louder. A burst of spirit money rained down everywhere, like confetti falling on a parade.

The band made one last stop in front of Chop Suey Louie's house to give him a chance to adjust to not being alive any longer. Naturally the spirit would be confused for a few days after death, so this one last trip to its former home gave it time to adjust to its new state. Then it could be on its way, explained Samuel to Blanche and Melba.

"Is that why they opened the door to the hearse?" asked Blanche.

"Exactly, and that's why they throw the spirit money, to distract the spirits again."

Samuel scanned the crowd and noticed policemen everywhere, some with cameras taking photographs of the bystanders. He recognized Mr. Song, and his loyal assistant, as well as his young niece, all with their heads bowed, paying their respects. He also saw a man with one arm standing on an orange crate taking in every detail of what was going on, more interested in observing the crowd than in following the funeral procession.

The music was so loud it made the street vibrate.

"This sounds like a hoedown more than a funeral procession," Melba commented.

"It is in a way," said Samuel. "It's a celebration of life, but it's supposed to help Louie get to the other side."

"If you gotta go, this way's as good as any," said Melba. "Good luck, Louie, and God speed!"

* * *

Charles Perkins was in a somber mood. He was sitting at a side table in his cluttered office, his shiny blue suit-jacket draped over the chair and the sleeves of his wrinkled white shirt rolled up to his elbows. His blond hair was greasier than usual. An armed marshal ushered Samuel in. Charles had moved the piles of papers with coffee cup stains on them to one side, making a clearing on the green leather table top for a game of dominoes. He was watching them collapse onto one another until finally all the pieces were down.

"Happy to get them all?" asked Samuel, trying to find a place to sit in all the chaos.

"Yeah. Wishful thinking," said Charles, noticing his guest for the first time. "I've been with the U.S. attorney's office for years. I've prosecuted lots of criminals, some of them really bad guys. But no one, Samuel, I mean, no one, has tried to kill me, not 'til now. It's unnerving," he added, with a look of anguish on his face.

"I know what you mean," said Samuel. "I haven't been sleeping so well myself." He took out his ruffled pack of Philip Morris's and put it up to his mouth, pulling a mangled cigarette out with his lips. "I've been racking my brain, trying to figure out if some piece of information you gave Sandovich could have caused those bastards to come after us." He coughed several times, putting his hand over his mouth.

"We went back and grilled him for six hours, but he wouldn't crack," said Charles.

"You're the boss, Charles," said Samuel, lighting the cigarette, "but I think you're barking up the wrong tree. Sandovich wouldn't risk getting involved in something like this and losing what he's got going."

"I know, Samuel, but the point of our spending time with the esteemed sergeant was not to accuse him but to get the names of all the people he talked to after our meeting a couple of weeks ago. He claimed he didn't talk to anyone, and that the only person who even knew he was there, outside of those present, was his watch commander. The captain who runs Chinatown Vice has an impeccable reputation. But just in case, we'll keep an eye on him," said Charles. "We've started to tap Sandovich's phone. Let's see what that produces."

"How about taking a longer view of this," suggested Samuel. "Melba reminded me of our discovery of Reginald's stash at Mr. Song's. What d'ya say we see if we can find out who knew about that? Although right now I can't, for the life of me, figure out who we might have exposed. Do you think that's who wanted to get us out of the way?"

"I'll leave that to you. Right now I've got my hands full with Mathew O'Hara. His lawyer says he wants to make a deal," replied Charles.

"What kind of a deal?"

"He's willing to plead guilty to a lesser offense,"

explained Charles.

"Does that mean he won't go to jail?" asked Samuel.

"No, that dude's gonna do time. He'll learn how the other half lives," said Charles, gesturing at Samuel with his index finger. "How much, depends on what he gives us."

# 14

## Mathew Tries to Deal

HIRAM GOLDBERG was his usual upbeat self as he flapped his Day-Timer against the pant leg of his double-breasted pinstripe charcoal brown suit. The smell of his sticky after-shaving lotion followed him around. The guard at the reception desk of the San Francisco County Jail, a beefy Irishman with his sergeant stripes tacked onto both sleeves of his faded blue uniform, smiled at his impatience.

"Here to see Mr. O'Hara again, Counselor? There must be things in the works," he said, showing the substantial gap between his two front teeth.

"Just another dreary day," replied Hiram, handing him a carton of Lucky Strikes. "Is my client well taken care of?"

"Of course, Counselor. Not just well taken care of, but well-protected by the band of brothers."

"It is true, you Irish stick together," said Hiram.

"It's more than that, Counselor. When one of us makes it big, like Mr. O'Hara, our pride gets involved, and we want him to come out okay," explained the man, made more loquacious by the cigarettes.

"Where am I on the visitor's list?"

"You're number three. There're only two attorney rooms. My guess is it'll be a half hour. If you have other things to do, I'll save a slot for ya."

"Thanks. I do have to check in down at Department 16. I'll be right back."

The guard stood up. His shirt barely contained his girth. He had the look of a bear but the hand he gave Hiram was limp.

"See ya later," said Hiram with a firm shake.

An hour later, Hiram was seated across a small table from Mathew O'Hara. The door had a small window, which allowed a sliver of sunlight from the hallway into the room. There were only two folding chairs and a table the same color as the gray concrete walls.

Mathew was grim-faced and had bags under his hazel eyes. His brown hair was still closely cropped, and he was clean-shaven. The drabness of his jailhouse garb did not diminish the authority that he always projected.

"Not getting enough sleep?" asked Hiram

"Who can sleep in this fuckin' place!" replied Mathew. "Besides, my wife says she's going to divorce me. That's all I need right now."

"You've got the best divorce lawyers in the city. That should make you feel better."

"Yeah," sneered Mathew. "I hired the five best, so she couldn't get her hands on any of them. You know about conflict of interest, don't you? But, so what? That doesn't help me out of this mess. Anyway, you're not here to talk to me about that crap. Why am I in this shit hole? Isn't this a federal rap?"

"The feds have a deal with San Francisco. The locals warehouse their prisoners for the short haul while their cases are pending."

"When do I leave here?" asked Mathew.

"When we make a deal or you beat the rap," said Hiram.

Mathew laughed cynically. "That's bullshit. You know as

well as I do, I can't beat this rap. They have me nailed to the wall. What's the best I can expect?" he asked.

"Probably six years plus a $40,000 fine and five years probation. That is if you cop a plea and give them something they can use."

"I am not sure I have anything they can use," said Mathew. "They already know about Xsing Ching. That's how they got me. I can confirm that's who I did business with."

"They want something more. For instance, some information about who in Chinatown tried to kill the U.S. attorney handling your case."

"What?" exclaimed Mathew.

Hiram saw the look of surprise come over Mathew's face and wondered if it was for real.

"And they think I had something to do with it?" Mathew asked. "I'm not a murderer!"

"I know that, man. Calm down. They're investigating to find out if the death of Reginald what-his-name was somehow tied into the deal you were in. They want everything you've got that could possibly connect the two."

"You mean Rockwood?" interrupted Mathew.

"That's the one, the guy who used to walk around in the tuxedos. Is it true that he lived in a janitor's closet?" asked Hiram.

"This is attorney-client stuff, right?"

"You've got it. Nothing goes outside this room, unless you want it to," replied Hiram.

"Frankly, I don't know much about the guy. I did hear that he lived in a closet at his workplace. I would see him at Camelot frequently, and I used to buy him a drink once in a while. I paid an informant to learn about the blackmailer, and that's how I heard that it was Rockwood."

"What kind of information did you get?" asked Hiram.

"Someone knew that illegal Chinese art was for sale; and

since I was the one who was buying it, I wouldn't go through with the deal unless there was no chance of discovery. A lot of good it did me," he said with a shrug. "My informant was Chinese. I can give you a description. Melba was in the bar the night he came in, and I am sure she can verify what he looked like. She wouldn't forget a guy who looked like him! But I think you should talk to Samuel Hamilton. I understand he sells ads in a newspaper. He was buddy-buddy with Rockwood. And if anybody knows what's happening in connection with his death, it's gotta be him."

"If you give 'em all you know about Rockwood's death, and your deal with Xsing Ching, and you agree to cooperate, they'll go for the six years," said Hiram. "You could be out in three, with credit for the time served and good behavior. But if they think you had anything to do with killing him, you're fucked. We have to be careful how we present this information."

"And if I give 'em nothin'?" asked Mathew.

"Assuming it's just the art and you go to the jury, if you're convicted you could get ten years and a $75,000 fine."

Mathew didn't have to think for long. He was now seated with his arms folded in front of him. "I risked a fortune on this fuckin' deal. To pay for that fine I'd have to sell stock that I want to keep. See if you can make a deal, just don't get me in more trouble than I'm already in."

* * *

After several unfruitful attempts to talk with Charles Perkins by phone, Hiram Goldberg made an appointment to see him in person at his office. He finally gained access after being searched by one of the three armed marshals protecting Charles, who had become paranoid since the shooting at Chop Suey Louie's.

When he walked in, Charles had his feet on his desk and

was leaning back in his chair, reading the newspaper. Hiram couldn't see his face. He only saw the many piles of papers on his desk with a space carved out for Charles to put his feet. To the side was a table with a green leather inset where dominoes lay scattered among the several groups of documents strewn about its top. In one corner of his office were boxes of files labeled with case names. He recognized several of them.

"Hiram Goldberg here, Mr. Perkins. I've come to discuss the O'Hara case with you. I'm his lawyer."

"I know who you are," said Charles, dropping the newspaper and removing his feet from the desk. He folded the paper and placed it in an already crowded drawer. "Sorry, I was just catching up on the news. You've been trying to reach me for several days, haven't you? What's on your mind?"

"Trying to see if we have any common ground on Mr. O'Hara's case."

"Depends on what he brings to the table," said Charles.

Hiram put his black leather briefcase with his initials stamped in gold on the floor and pulled at his overly tight shirt collar with a finger so he could catch his breath. Charles noticed the droplets of oil on his curly hair and the overwhelming fragrance of his cologne.

"Mr. O'Hara doesn't know much about the extraneous case you're inquiring about. I mean the one about the Rockwood fellow," replied Hiram. "The most he can do is give you a description of the man who said the tuxedo guy had been taken care of. But that was only a week or so before he was arrested."

"What was he doing with this man?"

"He was trying to get information. Apparently, this Rockwood guy was blackmailing Xsing Ching."

"How did Rockwood learn about the art deal?"

"That's exactly what my client would like to know."

"Did O'Hara pay Xsing Ching?"

"No way, the deal didn't go through. Guys like him always cover their backs. You must know that by now. My client wouldn't let go of the dough until the art was safely in his possession."

"We know he took half a million out of the bank," said Charles. "Where is it?"

"Why do you suppose that's related to the case?"

"Don't take me for a fool, Mr. Goldberg."

"I don't think he has to disclose to you what he does with his money as long as it's not illegal. I can guarantee Xsing Ching didn't get it. Look, even if he were convicted on all counts, what would the fine be?"

"We'll see about that," said Charles. "Tell me about the girl."

"Who?"

"You know who I mean, the Dimitri woman. How does she fit into all this?"

"The press said that she was O'Hara's lover, but he has assured me that they had only a business relationship. She entertained his clients," said Hiram.

"And you believe that fairy tale?"

"Why not? O'Hara isn't the kind of man that lets a sexual infatuation interfere with business. Anyhow, when his wife read about it in the papers, she filed for divorce. That's all you'll ever get against Dimitri: she's a home wrecker," replied Hiram with a sarcastic laugh.

"I need to look into this some more. If what you say bears out, I'll take the case up with the U.S. attorney."

"My client needs to know what he's looking at."

"What we talked about before. A $40,000 fine and six years in the poky," said Charles. "That is, if everything checks out."

"You'll let me know when?" asked Hiram.

"Within the week."

# 15

## Everybody's Two Cents

SAMUEL WALKED into Mr. Song's Many Chinese Herbs shop. The bell above his head announced his arrival at the threshold and kept tingling as he approached the black lacquer counter. The herbalist's assistant came out from behind the dangling rows of beads and craned his neck upward, straining to identify the visitor.

"I'd like to talk to Mr. Song," said Samuel.

The man disappeared behind the beaded curtain and shortly Mr. Song appeared. Samuel was again startled by the strange appearance of the Chinese albino dressed in a gray jacket with intricate embroidered designs woven into the fabric all the way up to the Mandarin collar. He had on black pants and a black gauze cap. He approached the counter and nodded his head slightly in an abbreviated bow. He'd recognized the visitor.

"I've come for some help with my smoking," said Samuel.

Mr. Song beckoned to his assistant to approach him and whispered something in his ear. The man quickly left the premises, and Mr. Song offered Samuel a seat on one of the two chairs he made available. Samuel sat while Mr. Song examined him with his red eyes, scrutinizing him with such precision that it was all he could do to keep from leaving.

He had no doubt that the albino would quickly see through his request for treatment to stop smoking as an excuse to see if he could get information. Most probably he was wasting his time. It was no small feat to get any facts from this secretive man who couldn't speak a word of English, although Samuel suspected he understood more than he let on.

Shortly, the employee returned with Mr. Song's niece. Samuel hardly recognized the girl with buckteeth. She wasn't wearing the Baptist church uniform and her black hair was cropped in a shorter cut with bangs. She saluted her uncle and turned to Samuel.

"My honorable uncle is at your disposal. What can he do for you?" she asked.

"I've come to ask for help to stop smoking," he said with a straight face, but in a hesitant tone.

She explained the purpose of the visit to Mr. Song. He nodded, knowingly, and replied in Cantonese, "He has come to the right place. Tell him to follow me."

The herbalist then went through the bead curtain and held it open with one arm so Samuel and the girl could follow. He ushered them into the back of the shop and pointed to an armchair in front of a Chinese screen painted with a picturesque mountain scene. Samuel was invited to sit down under a spotlight.

Buckteeth explained, "He will hypnotize you in order to help you stop smoking. Then he will give you Chinese herbs to reinforce the treatment."

"How much will all this cost me?"

Mr. Song put up two fingers.

"Two dollars a visit," she said, "and you will have to come every day for a week."

"Even on Saturday and Sunday?"

"Of course. This is a serious treatment," she explained.

# The Chinese Jars

Samuel saw Mr. Song's pink eyes looking at him intently over the rims of his glasses as he wound a delicate chain with a gold medallion on the end of it around his long pale fingers.

"Mr. Song says you have become well known in Chinatown," the girl translated.

"What does he mean by that?" asked Samuel defensively.

"He says people say you were a good friend of Louie's."

"I saw you and Mr. Song on the street, paying your respects the day of Louie's funeral. Tell him it was me and the lawyer from the U.S. attorney's office that they were really trying to kill."

"He already knows that," said the girl.

"And does he know why they tried to kill us?"

"He said maybe you were snooping where you shouldn't."

Samuel sat straight up. He could hardly believe that Mr. Song was coming out from behind his inscrutable façade and was willing to offer information.

"Does he mean getting too close to Xsing Ching's business with the Chinese art?"

The herbalist coughed slightly and lit his clay pipe. The irony was not lost on Samuel since he was there to try and stop smoking.

"He says not Xsing Ching, he is just a businessman, but to something much more ..." She abruptly stopped and had a lengthy discussion with Mr. Song in Cantonese. Samuel kept hearing them toss the same word back and forth with emphasis. Finally she said to Samuel, "You know the word sinister?"

"I do indeed. Why?"

They had another brief conversation in which the same Chinese word was used several times.

"My honorable uncle has nothing more to say on this subject. He wants to know if you are ready to begin your treatment?" she asked formally.

"Sure," said Samuel, mulling over the word sinister in his mind, as he watched the gold medallion hanging from the gold chain swing back and forth in Mr. Song's hand, until he lost all notion of time.

\* \* \*

Samuel had no faith in the bizarre treatment he subjected himself to for the entire week at the shop, but he didn't miss a session. He tried to engage the herbalist several times during their time together, but Song had retreated behind his shield of silence. Since the girl was not present to translate, their business was conducted in sign language, with Mr. Song pointing his finger to indicate that Samuel should consume the piles of herbs prescribed for him. To his amazement, by day six he not only felt slightly nauseated at the idea of smoking a cigarette but just the smell of tobacco bothered him. He decided it was now safe for him to show up at Camelot.

Excalibur began shaking his fanny with a happy rhythm from the moment he sensed Samuel's arrival. Samuel felt welcome, happy to once again be with his family. Melba smiled broadly from her perch at the bar and motioned for him to sit beside her, as she crushed her cigarette in the ashtray already full of butts with traces of her lipstick. She blew the smoke in Samuel's direction, and he, suddenly sick to his stomach, had to wait for it to clear before he sat down. She put a Scotch on the rocks on the counter, but he declined, asking instead for a club soda.

"Where the hell you been?" asked Melba. "And what happened to your fingers?"

"You won't believe it, Melba, I stopped smoking," he replied, looking at the ends of his fingers wrapped in adhesive tape.

"The hell, you say. Why would you do a thing like that?"

Samuel gave a nervous laugh and smoothed the sleeves of his new khaki jacket with no burn holes in it. He'd bought it secondhand, but it looked almost new. "The tape keeps me from biting my fingernails. My fingertips look like they've been in a meat grinder."

"So now you don't smoke but you bite your fingernails."

"But now I only try when I really want a cigarette. It's been a week. Mr. Song is responsible for this miracle. You should try it."

"Looks like the cure is worse than the disease." She reached for her pack of cigarettes and thought better of it, putting it back on the counter and tapping it with her index and middle fingers. "Did you ask Mr. Song if he could cure the biting, too?"

"Yeah, but he said it would cost more than stopping smoking, and it would probably just go away by itself, anyway," and he shrugged.

Melba laughed. "What a relief. For chrissake, there are so many complications that it isn't even worth trying."

"I need to talk to you," said Samuel, glancing in every corner of the bar. "But first, is Blanche in town?"

"Sure is. She'll be here anytime now. I hear you acted like a real jerk at the Blackhawk."

"She told you that? It's true. I drank too much. I was a little nervous. She must be furious with me."

"She doesn't hold grudges. She'll give you another chance."

"Great," said Samuel, biting his lower lip. "Stopping smoking was kind of a beneficial side effect. I really went to Mr. Song's to see if I could get information."

"Information about what?"

"About Reginald and Louie's death. Mr. Song started to talk but he quickly shut up, as if he'd said too much. The rest of the week was all hypnotism and no conversation. The first day his niece was there translating, and I asked him point blank if the people who tried to kill us were connected to Xsing Ching and the Chinese art. Song started to answer, but then he and his niece got hung up on a word and they went back and forth. It was like they were having a tug of war, the way they were talking to each other."

"What word?"

"Sinister."

"Did he use the word sinister?"

"Yes, he used it, in Chinese, of course. He said there was something much more sinister than the illegal Chinese art. That's why they tried to kill me and Perkins."

"Well, we all know that in this city even the police are involved in all kinds of crime and corruption. Imagine the things that go on in Chinatown," said Melba, grabbing another cigarette with one hand and scratching her blue-white coif with the other. She put the cigarette in her mouth but didn't light it.

"After that, Song wouldn't broach the subject. I saw him every day for a week, and I couldn't get another word out of him. He acted as if he had said too much in the first place."

"You told me that his shop is like a bank. That means that Song knows everything that goes on in Chinatown, but he won't tell you, of course. The security of his business and his clientele depend on his discretion," said Melba.

"I've racked my brain and I don't have a clue. That's why I came to you."

"The shooting in Louie's restaurant and the death of Reginald have to be connected," she stated at last. "The word sinister indicates that these are part of a more complicated plot than you ever imagined."

"Listen, Melba, we're not at the movies."

"Don't be naïve, Samuel. We're talking about crimes. If you want to solve them you have to think the worst and contemplate all the possibilities. You have to broaden your scope, see the bigger picture. You know what I mean?" she asked.

He was quiet for a moment, sucking on the ice in his glass,

and struggling with the desire to gnaw at his fingernails. At that moment Blanche came through the front door dressed in white running pants and a top and carrying a case of beer, which she dropped behind the counter. She had beads of sweat on her brow and as usual her hair was pulled back in a ponytail, secured with a rubber band. She tapped Samuel affectionately on his thinning head of red hair and disturbed a few flakes of dandruff, which floated gently to the shoulders of his new jacket.

"Hi, handsome. Hi, mom," she said cheerfully. "I ran all the way up Nob Hill."

"Why? Was someone chasing you?" asked Samuel, trying to ingratiate himself.

"I'm going to hire someone to replace Rafael," said Melba, pointing at the case.

"Come and see me when you're through here, Samuel," said Blanche, with a smile that left Samuel enchanted.

She sauntered off toward the office, greeting the patrons as she went and waiving at Maestro Bob, who was engrossed in a book on spiritualism. Samuel's eyes followed her with a desperate expression on his face.

"Go. Get your ass back there and breathe some life back into it," she ordered.

Excalibur sensed his new friend was about to leave, and he tried to follow him, but Melba held him down. "Stay, stupid dog. He's in love with somebody else."

\* \* \*

Samuel entered the small, cramped office, where the bar's pretensions of elegance ended. The outside door was made of polished mahogany, the same as the phone booth opposite it, but the inside was plywood and had a two-by-four nailed diagonally across its entire length. A steel spring snapped it closed. The back wall had studs and no covering other than tarpaper. Blanche sat in a swivel secretarial chair in front of a desk with her back to Samuel. She was hunched over piles of bills and receipts, lit by a small bedroom lamp with three circles of pink lace evenly spaced around the shade. An old kitchen chair next to the desk and a four-drawer filing cabinet completed the furnishing of the room.

He sat timidly in the vacant seat. The soft light from the lamp fell only on the desk, so both their faces were in the shadows. A whiff of her sweet smell, of perspiration and soap, a scent that had been mostly blocked by his smoking habit, hit his nostrils with the power of so much sexual suggestion that it took his breath away.

"Did you hurt yourself, Samuel?" she asked, pointing at his fingers.

"Nah. I stopped smoking," he replied, in a shaky voice.

"Oh, goody," she replied. "Nasty habit, that smoking. Why the tape?"

Samuel squirmed in his seat. "To stop me from biting my nails. It's only temporary."

"Maybe you'll be an inspiration to my mom's stopping. She admires you, you know."

"I didn't know that," said Samuel, very surprised.

"Yes. She's convinced you're going to be a famous reporter. She thinks you're brave to pursue the cause of Reginald's death after you were nearly killed."

"Well, I have more bad news," he blurted out. "Mr. Song, you know the albino herbalist I've told you about, says that the attempt to kill me and the U.S. attorney is only the tip of the iceberg. It's part of a much more sinister plot."

"Don't tell me!"

"They got Mathew O'Hara for smuggling. But the U.S. attorney, that Perkins guy, found out that they killed Reginald because he was blackmailing Xsing Ching, the man who took the art out of China."

"Mathew's not an assassin!" she said.

"I didn't say he was. He gave the attorney a description of the thug from Chinatown. He came to Camelot to talk to him and your mother saw him. From the description, it sounds pretty much like the guy who pushed Reginald in front of the trolley bus. He said he had taken care of Reginald."

"Wow. Reginald got that Xsing Ching guy to give him money?" she asked.

"It looks like he got several thousand."

"And where's all that money?" asked Blanche, taking a sip from her water glass. "Want some?" she asked absentmindedly, pushing the glass toward Samuel.

"Thanks," He carefully placed his lips where hers had been. "They found Reginald's stash at Mr. Song's, but it wasn't clear that it was from the blackmail."

Blanche was silent for a moment and then she smiled.

"Remember the movie you took me to? The one where I thought there was something wrong with the sound?"

"How could I forget? That was our first date," said Samuel, thankful she couldn't see him blushing again. He hoped she wouldn't remember all the disasters that befell him that night. "The twenty minutes of silence was a first in moviemaking, a throwback to the old days of the silents."

"That wasn't my point," said Blanche. "My point was, the robbers wanted to steal money, so they went to the place where it was kept, in a safe. You have sort of the same problem; it's like a riddle. You have to find out where the blackmailer put the money. Where's his safe?"

"Yeah," said Samuel, putting his right hand's taped fingers to the side of his face and feeling his stubble. "Maybe it's not even in his safe, maybe it's in someone else's."

"What do you mean?" asked Blanche.

"They found some of it at Mr. Song's but not all of it."

"Look for it then," she suggested.

Samuel hadn't come back to the office to talk about that, and he now realized it was better to be direct. "I'd like to take you to dinner next week," he managed to say as he stood up. He stayed in the shadows. Blanche swirled around in her chair and stood up. They were almost touching.

"I'd like that," she replied.

Samuel imagined putting his arms around her, standing on his tiptoes, and kissing her passionately on the lips. Instead he backed up as much as he could in the confined space. "You can pick the restaurant. I'd even take you to a vegetarian joint, where they serve carrots," he joked.

She half turned around and grabbed his jacket, pulled him toward her, and hugged him. Samuel went weak in the knees.

"I've missed you, Samuel," she said, letting go of him just as quickly as she'd grabbed him, and he almost fell.

"I've missed you, too," he stammered.

"If we go to dinner, it'll have to be before Wednesday, because I leave for Tahoe for a few days," said Blanche.

"I hope it won't be for long," he said hoarsely, shocked at his own audacity. "How about six on Tuesday? Where do I pick you up, here or at home?"

"Here, I have to help mom. Without Rafael, she's lost."

They squeezed hands and one of his tapes stuck to Blanche. Samuel was levitating as he pushed open the plywood door and left.

\* \* \*

Maestro Bob called out to Samuel and invited him to have a seat with him. His enormous handlebar mustache with the upturned ends, now without black die, made him look old. He put his book on spiritualism down next to a wrinkled brown paper bag and lifted his empty glass.

## The Chinese Jars

"You haven't consulted me for a long time, son."

"I'm sorry, Maestro, I've been tied up with some serious business."

"That doesn't surprise me. Remember, I've read your Tarot cards."

"The usual?" asked Samuel.

"Soda water, unfortunately," sighed the high priest of the occult.

Samuel went to get the drink and then installed himself at the table. He was still in the clouds. "What have you got in the bag? A snack?"

"No way. I'm now the proud owner of an object of rare value: a crystal ball. A person who seriously dedicates himself to the occult should have many resources."

"Everything helps. What can you do with a crystal ball?" asked Samuel, amused.

"I'm going to ask Melba to let us use her office for a while. The ball works better in private. That is, if you're interested in knowing your destiny."

"How much is it going to cost me?"

"The same as my other services. But if you don't have it, I'll give you credit."

"That won't be necessary. I placed a couple of ads, and I was even able to repay some of what I owe Melba."

"We'll do better in the office. The darkness attracts the spirits."

"Melba, can we use your office for a bit?" yelled Samuel in the direction of the bar.

"Sure," she answered. "But don't break anything."

Maestro left his book on the table with its spine open at the page he was reading. He grabbed the paper bag and his glass of club soda and followed his friend to the cluttered office. Samuel reached over the desk and clicked on the lamp with the pink ribbons on the shade, still thinking of his sweet encounter with Blanche.

"Perfect setup," said Maestro. He stuck his hands into the bag and pulled out a white-colored ball lodged in a wooden circular stand.

Samuel started laughing. "All that's missing is the house and the pine tree. It's one of those Christmas balls that you shake and it starts snowing."

"Not everything is as it seems, young man."

"How long will this take us?"

"A frequently asked question. These things can't be timed. It will depend on whether the spirits are free and then if they want to talk to us.  If we don't connect, I won't charge you," answered Maestro very seriously. He put the crystal ball on a piece of black silk under the lit lamp.

"Where do you want to start?"

"I'm stuck," said Samuel, and he explained the events of the previous few weeks. "I want to know where to look for some new leads."

Maestro started murmuring words in an ancient dead language as he caressed the white ball with his long fingers.

"The spirits are being resistant today," he said, after several attempts.

"What do you mean, resistant?"

"They won't give us much."

"Do they ever give anything at all?" asked Samuel, angrily.

"Of course. Now they only give me the name of Mathew O'Hara.

"Mathew O'Hara?" repeated Samuel.

"Just the name, nothing more. Oh, they also say that your love life is improving," said Maestro.

"Is that right? Or was it that you just saw me leave here with Blanche?"

Samuel fished through his baggy khaki's and handed

Maestro two crumpled bills. The magician put one in his pocket and returned the other.

"I wasn't able to help you much," he said, by way of explanation.

"You can answer this question for me without consulting your crystal ball because you spend a lot of time in this bar and you're pretty observant. Tell me how well O'Hara and Reginald knew each other."

"Just acquaintances. Sometimes they would have a drink together, as Mathew did with most of the locals."

"Do you think that Mathew could have ordered Rockwell's murder?"

"No," said Maestro emphatically.

*  *  *

To kill time, Samuel started taking the bandages off his fingers little by little even though he was far from controlling his urge to bite his fingernails. He was waiting at the East Gate of San Quentin prison. It was a Sunday, and he was being processed so he could visit his friend Rafael Garcia. He was at the small building by the iron gate for almost an hour and a half, standing in line with the other people who were there to visit other prisoners. He showed his driver's license, filled out the two-sided form, was searched and finally sent on the walk to the red brick building some two hundred yards away, which was at least as old as the prison itself.

Once inside, he was relegated to a cubicle with a large pane of thick glass that separated the visitors from the inmates. It was so scratched that in some places one couldn't see through to the other side. He sat on a metal seat next to a telephone for talking to someone on the other side of the glass. The pungent smell of pine-scented disinfectant and stale cigarette smoke lingered in the air, creating an invisible fog that made Samuel slightly nauseated, a direct result of Song's treatment. When Rafael arrived, Samuel almost didn't recognize him. His dark hair was cut and he wore a mustache. He also remembered him as wiry. Now he had rippling muscles.

"Have you been lifting weights?" Samuel asked through the phone.

"Yeah, just something to pass the time. There's not much to do in here, so I try and keep busy."

"We heard you had two jobs and never stop."

"That's me," said Rafael. "But remember I'm here twenty-four hours a day. No wife, no kids, just a bunch of punks to hang around with."

"I brought you some Mexican pastries, and enchiladas," said Samuel. "But they don't allow visitors to bring any of that stuff in, so I'll have a feast tonight. They did accept the romance novels that Melba sent you. The guard will give them to you later."

Rafael turned as red as a cooked lobster.

"Don't worry," said Samuel, "I took the covers off. No one will know."

"Thank you for coming, Samuel."

"Do you get visitors?"

"Yeah, Sofia and my mother come often."

"Melba told me to tell you she really misses you and is waiting for you to come back. You have a job as soon as you get out," said Samuel.

"Tell Melba I really appreciate the financial help she's giving my family and Sofia. They're all grateful for her weekly visits. Tell her I'm studying to be a nurse, so when I get out of here, I'll have a good job and I can pay her back."

"I doubt if she expects that, Rafael," Samuel responded.

"Well, that's the way I operate, Samuel."

"How can you study in here?" asked Samuel.

"The doctor lets me sit in on all his consultations, and I do a lot of reading about how to recognize and treat this or that. You'd be surprised how much I've learned. But that's enough talk about me. What've you been up to, Samuel?"

"I've been trying to find out who killed Reginald Rockwood. You remember him?"

"You mean the guy who used to come into the bar dressed in a tuxedo? The one who got hit by the trolley bus?"

"That's the one. Some Chinese thugs pushed him, but we can't find them. Maestro Bob looked in his crystal ball the other day and told me to check out Mathew O'Hara."

"A crystal ball?" laughed Rafael.

"Do you know O'Hara well?" asked Samuel, not wanting to get into Maestro Bob's methods.

"Not well. I only saw him at the bar, but he's coming here next week to spend part of the summer."

"To San Quentin? How did you know that?"

"Here, you know everything that goes on."

"Seriously? I knew he got six years, but I didn't think they'd send him to a state prison for a federal rap."

"Oh, no, he ain't staying. The rumor is he'll be moving on to Arizona next month. Maestro might be right," said Rafael.

"Right about what?"

"They knew each other, the guy in the tux and O'Hara."

"Sure, Reginald hung out at the bar and O'Hara would come in there all the time," said Samuel.

"No, I mean they were better friends than that, even. One time last year Melba had me deliver some cases of booze to O'Hara's penthouse on Grant Avenue for a fancy party he was throwing. I went there late, like the party had already started, and the guy in the tux was there, chumming it up with O'Hara and some really classy dame."

"Really? That could be important. Do you remember the address?"

"838 Grant Avenue, fifth floor. I'm sure. I have a good

memory for things like that."

"How many times did you see him there?" he asked.

"Just that one time.

"Why did you think they were close friends?" Samuel wanted to know.

"They acted like they'd known each other for a long time, real comfortable together."

"That number you mentioned sounds familiar to me," said Samuel, trying to remember where he had seen or heard 838 before.

The whistle sounded, indicating the visit was over. Samuel said goodbye to Rafael, with the promise that he would return.

\* \* \*

During the bus ride back to San Francisco, Samuel didn't stop thinking of the address on Grant Avenue that Rafael had given him. It triggered something in his memory, but he couldn't locate it. As soon as he got home, he started scouring his notes until he found it. O'Hara's address was the number on the scrap of paper that was wrapped around some of the money in Rockwood's jar at Mr. Song's. The next day he tried to reach Charles by telephone but had no luck, so he went to see him. He told the secretary that it was urgent, and she let him in. Charles had two bodyguards at the door, and it was obvious that he was still frightened. Samuel recounted the visit and what he'd learned from Rafael.

"Are you sure the numbers coincide?" asked Charles.

"I've checked my notes. Since Rafael said he saw Reginald at O'Hara's, maybe we should check Engel's invitations to see if anything shows up," Samuel suggested.

"That's not a bad idea. The problem is, I'm in trial. I've been going for the last two weeks, and I don't have a minute to spare." Charles held his brow with his middle finger and thumb and squeezed it in an attempt to stop the pounding of his headache.

"This is important, man. Did you know that O'Hara was headed to San Quentin?"

"He won't be there long."

"If we get new information about their connection, we can question him before he leaves for another state. Once he goes into the federal system, as you know he won't be available without a big hassle," said Samuel.

Charles took off his glasses, closed his eyes, and rubbed the bridge of his nose. He was very tired. "Here's the plan: you go down the hall and check the Engel's stuff to see if there's anything of interest that we missed. If you find a connection with O'Hara, we can go over and question him before he leaves."

"When can I look at it?" asked Samuel.

"I'll arrange for it right now," said Charles, picking up the phone.

Soon a marshal appeared at the door. The attorney ordered him to take Samuel to the evidence room, where he could look at some files without taking anything.

"Just make a note of what you find and report back to me," he said to Samuel, dismissing him.

The marshal took Samuel to the caged evidence locker, a large room with metal shelves from floor to ceiling labeled with numbers and names in conspicuous places so files could be easily found. The marshal went to a card file and looked up Rockwood, then went to the corresponding shelf, took three boxes out, and placed them on the metal table in the middle of the room.

Samuel rummaged through the evidence in the folder marked Mr. Song's Many Chinese Herbs until he found the scrap of paper that had been wrapped around Reginald's money. There he saw the number 838. He compared it to the printing on the other invitations in the shoebox from Engel's. He verified what he'd anticipated; the number 838 was engraved in exactly the same size and style as the hundreds of invitations he had seen several months before.

He continued through the box methodically, but saw no invitation with Mathew O'Hara's name or address on it, and that puzzled him. He decided that the number 838 in the same style meant that one probably existed somewhere, but where?

There wasn't anything else to accomplish there. He thanked the marshal and made his way to Camelot.

\* \* \*

The following day he was at Engel's before it opened and had to wait a quarter of an hour. The tidy Mr. Engel was the one who arrived to open the front door. Samuel approached him.

"Do you remember me, sir? I'm Samuel Hamilton."

The man squinted into the sun and cupped his right hand over his eyes, trying to identify him. "Name doesn't come to mind. How can I help you?"

"I was here a few months ago investigating your employee, Reginald Rockwood. Can I ask you a few questions?"

They were now in the reception area.

"Have you gentlemen figured out what actually happened to that unfortunate young man?"

"We're in the process, sir," said Samuel.

"I'm not sure I can be of any further help to you. The marshals took everything relating to Mr. Rockwood."

"I know that, but there's a piece of the puzzle missing, and that's why I'm here."

"Well, make it snappy," said Mr. Engel. "I've got a busy

day ahead."

"I'm looking for an invitation to a party at Mathew O'Hara's penthouse at 838 Grant Avenue. Can you look in your archives and see if there is one?"

"Ordinarily, I wouldn't give out that kind of information, but I know who you are and what you're trying to do, so come with me."

They left the Piranesi's behind and went down a long hallway to a light oak door with an etched glass panel in the upper half. Engel opened it and allowed Samuel to enter first. One wall of the room was filled with wood filing cabinets the same color as the door. On the other side of the room, there was a table and three chairs.

Mr. Engel went to a filing cabinet and fingered through the documents. "Here it is." He pulled one out that was encased in a plastic sleeve and put it on the table for Samuel to examine. It read:

838 Grant Avenue, 5th Floor, San Francisco

Mathew O'Hara cordially invites
You and a guest to a private cocktail party,
honoring Xsing Ching, world-renowned
Oriental Art Expert, who is visiting
the United States on a lecture tour.

Thursday June 10, 1960, 6:00–9:00 p.m.

R.S.V.P. SU-4-1878

"I'll be dammed," said Samuel. "So they knew each other even before this started."

"I beg your pardon?" said Mr. Engel.

"Can I take this with me?" asked Samuel.

"I'm afraid not. That's the only record I have of the transaction," said Mr. Engel firmly.

"Okay, but don't let anything happen to it," said Samuel.

"Here in my establishment, nothing will happen to it."

"I'd feel better if you took it out of the filing cabinet and locked it up," said Samuel. "It may be important."

"Very well," said Mr. Engel. Is there anything else I can do for you?" he asked with an impatient but polite smile.

"No, you've given me more than I expected," said Samuel.

# 16

## Rafael and Mathew

MATHEW O'HARA was used to the luxuries of life, to being surrounded by a coterie of "yes" men and getting what he wanted—not exactly the amenities San Quentin offered. Now he was just prison blues and a number, in a cell by himself. It was on the same floor and cellblock as Rafael, but he was cut off from the others and semi-isolated. The guard on the catwalk above pressed the buzzer, and the one accompanying Mathew lifted the bar and opened the enclosure.

"You have a private room, like in a hotel," the guard joked.

"Why?"

"'Cause you're important merchandise. If some of these guys found out who you were, we couldn't guarantee your safety. This here way we have some control over who can get to you," said the muscular guard.

Mathew flinched. "Do you think there are people here who want to hurt me?"

"Wouldn't be surprised. Different world than the one you're used to."

"But you don't know of any specific threat, do you?" Mathew insisted.

"Can't say I do." He went through the do's and don'ts list, then slammed the cell door, clanged down the iron bar, and Mathew was left alone with his thoughts.

The smell of food wafted through the block, making Mathew's nostrils quiver and his stomach growl. He realized he was hungry and wondered when it would be time to eat and what they would serve. He had a delicate stomach and watched his weight. He could hear the sounds of prisoners talking, singing, and yelling, mixed with the clang of cell doors, all made louder by the cavernous size of the building.

What a fucking mess, he thought. They told him he would only be at San Quentin for a week or so, but he hadn't realized what a shit hole it was until he got there. He never imagined that he would be thrust into such a cramped space with only a fold-down bunk, a metal table and chair, a toilet with no seat, and a piece of steel for a mirror.

Twenty-three hours a day in that dump "for his own safety." He knew he'd get to go outside each afternoon at five o'clock for an hour, but he didn't have any way to tell what time it was. He unhooked the chains that held the bunk to the wall, pulled it down, and sat on the bare mattress staring at the sheet and the single gray blanket that lay on the table. He noticed the irony of the stripes on the bedding running perpendicular to the bars on his cell. He tried to gauge the time from the position of the shadows on the floor, but couldn't figure it out.

\* \* \*

Time passed slowly for Mathew O'Hara until he finally heard the bar lifting. The door opened and two guards showed up at his cell. "Come with us, it's time for exercise," one of them ordered.

Handcuffed and with one on either side of him, Mathew

# The Chinese Jars

was escorted along eternal corridors, through several barred and locked doors, and then shoved into a courtyard of about two hundred square feet. On two sides, the one facing the bay to the south, and the one facing the Richmond Bridge to the east, there were chain-link fences with curls of barbed wire along the top. To the west was a gray cinderblock wall about ten feet high. From where he stood, Mathew couldn't see on the other side, but he figured it had to be the exercise yard for the rest of the prisoners of the cellblock. He could hear a chorus of voices coming from there. A guard tower loomed to the south on the other side of the chain-link fence. Two men holding rifles were inside its small glass enclosure. His handcuffs were taken off.

Mathew counted five other men in the yard with him, and he assumed they were separated for maximum-security reasons. They walked in circles or exercised without talking, under the guards' gaze. No one acknowledged his presence. He breathed deeply. He had not been out in the fresh air for over two months, and he missed it. It felt good. He thought about his boat, his lazy morning sails in the bay, and his beach house at Stinson. The afternoon was breezy, and he could see whitecaps on the bay through the fence and barbed wire. He watched freighters move northward under the bridge on their way to ports as far away as Stockton and Sacramento, and small fishing boats coming south, on their way back from the Delta, loaded with sturgeon and bass for San Francisco's fish markets.

The sun was still a reasonable distance from the top of Mount Tamalpais, and the air was crisp and invigorating. He walked slowly around the perimeter of the small yard, clockwise, first by the chain-link fences so he could enjoy the sun and the breeze. The part next to the ten-foot wall was in the shade, so when he traversed it, he moved more rapidly. He repeated the circle four times, accelerating his pace. Finally he could stretch his legs. He started jogging, lifting his knees, and filling his lungs.  He didn't know if talking was allowed, so when he passed the other prisoners he didn't look at them.

On the fifth turn, just as he was approaching the wall, there was a sudden loud explosion that shook the ground under his feet. Mathew didn't have time to think about what happened; the force of the blast lifted him and knocked him back several feet away. He flew along with the chunks of the wall, which seemed to disintegrate as if in slow motion. He landed, and the rubble fell all around, burying him. A cloud of dust covered the yard. He didn't hear screams, he didn't feel any pain, and he didn't try to move. There wasn't enough air for him to breathe. He closed his eyes and plunged into darkness.

When the dust started clearing, he was engulfed in an eerie silence like at the bottom of the sea. He lay there semiconscious and numb. I must be dead, he thought, with a sort of fascination. But he realized that he could open his eyes and felt his mouth full of grit, the pulverized cinderblock.

He didn't hear the sirens, the shots, or the screams because the explosion had left him numb and temporarily deaf. He opened his mouth and tried to call out but it seemed that no sound came from his lips. I'm dead, he repeated, but then a shooting pain on the left side of his body brought back some lucidity.  He remembered it like in a dream: the prison, the yard, the gray wall. With a gigantic effort, he managed to move his head and lift his shoulders out of the rubble but couldn't move the rest of the body. At that point he saw his lower left leg. It was twisted in an impossible angle, with two bones protruding and blood gushing from the gaping wound. I am going to bleed to death, he thought with indifference. He fainted again.

\* \* \*

## The Chinese Jars

Hell had broken loose in the prison. Later, they would find out that a missile of some kind had been fired from somewhere on the West Tower, but during those first moments no one knew what had happened, or what to do. Several guards ran around in total confusion, screaming orders that no one followed, while those in the tower south of the chain-link fence, who were not involved in the explosion, came out on their platform and started shooting in the air, thinking that would somehow restore order; it only contributed to the chaos. They looked toward the tower to the west, supposing that whatever hit the wall had come from there, but that was the extent of their reaction. If a guard from another tower had fired something, they thought, there had to be a good reason for it.

Rafael, who had been getting his daily exercise on the other side of the wall, was one of the first to react. He bolted over the pile of cinderblocks and entered the other yard. He saw five prisoners and a couple of guards who were just beginning to get back on their feet after being knocked down by the explosion, and he realized that they weren't injured. Then he noticed the man crushed under the rubble and the pool of blood gushing from him. Frantic, he started throwing material to one side to disengage him.

When Rafael was able to free the wounded man, he recognized, to his amazement, his former boss, Mathew O'Hara. One look was enough for him to realize that the man needed immediate first aid. He saw that the blood was spurting from his leg in rhythm with what he estimated was the man's heartbeat. The artery looked like it had been severed. He tried to stop the bleeding with his fingers but it was immediately obvious that a tourniquet was needed. Without hesitation he tore his own shirt and shredded a sleeve while he tried to reduce the bleeding by pressing the wound with his foot. He wrapped the fabric around Mathew's thigh and twisted it. The flow of blood diminished but didn't stop. Over his shoulder he saw his cellmate who, like himself, had come from the other yard.

"Pancho, ayúdame! This cat's on the way out."

"What do you want me to do, carnal?"

"Get a piece of wood! I have to tighten the tourniquet! Hurry up, vato!"

Pancho whistled and two other Mexicans showed up at the rubble.

"Corten un pedazo de leña, about six inches long!" Pancho ordered, measuring with his hands.

One of the men looked around, saw he was protected from the tower's view, and pulled a shiv out of his pants pocket. They got to one of the picnic tables. While the other one covered him from the view he sliced off a baton-sized piece of wood from the table and hid the knife back in his pants. He threw the wood to Pancho, who caught it in mid-flight and ran with it to Rafael. He then helped Rafael, who inserted it in the strip of shirt and twisted it until the bleeding stopped. Rafael realized that Mathew was in shock and started to shake and slap him.

"Wake up, Mr. O'Hara! Make an effort! Come on! Pancho, get some help!" he yelled, and Pancho ran off.

Finally the wounded man opened his lids. His eyes looked vacant and glazed in his dust-covered face. He yelled in pain.

"Help is coming," said Rafael, but even if Mathew could hear he wouldn't have understood the words. He was too dazed.

Only a few minutes had gone by but already there were armed guards in both yards shouting order at the inmates to stand back. One approached Rafael and pointed his gun at his head.

"Didn't you hear me, fucker? Hands up!"

"I can't let go of the tourniquet, sir. This man needs immediate help," he tried to explain.

# The Chinese Jars

"Goddammit, did you hear me?" the guard yelled, kicking him in the back and forcing him on top of Mathew.

"Leave him be," a voice came over a loudspeaker from the south tower. "He's the only help we got right now for the prisoner that's down."

The guard backed off, still pointing his gun. Rafael, now back on his knees, saw a blank and frightened look in the man's eyes that he recognized from his experience in the streets of his rough neighborhood. It meant that anything could tip the delicate balance in which they found themselves and make him start shooting. The other prisoners from Rafael's side of the yard recognized it, too, and they started moving in mass toward the cellblock gate to get back inside before any of the guards lost control.

At that moment, out of the crowd, came a shiv, thrown by an expert hand that no one saw, flying toward Mathew and Rafael. Maybe Rafael saw the metal shining in mid-air or maybe he acted by pure instinct. Without thinking, in a fraction of a second, he moved forward and the knife hit him in the neck. He fell back on top of Mathew.

The action was so swift, clean and silent, that several seconds went by before somebody in the yard reacted. The guard next to Rafael saw him fall, but he hesitated, confused. Then he bent over him and saw the knife in his neck. He poked Rafael with his knee and only then realized that he was dead. He cursed and automatically pressed the trigger of his gun. The bullets penetrated the ground, lifting shards of asphalt and cinderblock.

Panic broke out in the prison yard. The inmates ran to get into the building: pushing, falling, crawling. The guards kicked them and hit them with the butts of their guns, while the loudspeakers blasted away telling them to freeze and raise their hands. Nobody was about to wait around for that. All the alarms went off and a line of men in combat gear poured out of the building and occupied the yard, hitting left and right with their batons. Several of them rushed to Rafael and Mathew.

"What happened?" asked a sergeant.

"No fuckin' idea," replied the pale guard at the scene.

Soon the medical team arrived. By then Mathew O'Hara was unconscious. He had no idea that his Mexican janitor had saved his life twice in a span of fifteen minutes.

\* \* \*

Mathew was in the hospital for several weeks before he regained any semblance of mental coherence, numbed as he was by drugs, and hovering between life and death. Then, there was still the question of whether he would lose his leg. Grime from the pulverized cinderblocks contaminated his wounds, and there was severe vascular damage due to the comminuted fractures. But the medical staff at San Francisco General Hospital prison ward, where he was taken, included a woman doctor of Japanese descent who considered his case a personal challenge. She wanted to prove to her colleagues that she was as good as the best of them. During the war she had spent four of her teenage years in an internment camp for Japanese-American citizens. When everything else failed, she came up with the idea of using maggots to combat the gangrene that had set in, and then leaches to get rid of the stagnant blood.

They had fixed the fractures internally with steel plates and screws, but they couldn't close the wound because there was no live tissue surrounding it. While the other doctors were talking amputation she insisted on a graft technique to avoid osteomyelitis.

After three weeks, the orthopedist in charge was able to perform a cross-leg flap operation by taking Mathew's good leg, opening it up with a scalpel at the calf, and attaching it surgically to the injured area of his broken one. He hoped that after six weeks or so, the tissue of the legs would grow together. Then he would again operate to separate them, cutting off the part of the calf that had grown onto the injured site, literally transplanting it. Then only skin grafts would be required.

At that point in the treatment, Charles Perkins and Samuel Hamilton came to see Mathew. An armed U.S. marshal escorted them into his room that had bars on the windows on the sixth floor. Mathew had both his legs elevated by a pulley system, the right one crossed on top of the left shin where the legs were sutured together, all covered by bandages. When the visitors entered, a nurse was massaging both of his legs and feet, in an attempt to stimulate circulation.

"Gentlemen," saluted Mathew.

"Mr. O'Hara," responded Samuel and Charles at the same time.

"I bet you thought you'd never see me alive, eh?" said Mathew with visible effort.

Samuel knew him only slightly from the bar, but he noticed that the man had lost a lot of weight; his cheeks were sunken, his skin sallow, and his hair was growing out of the jailhouse buzz cut, like an unmowed lawn. Very little was left of the handsome and confident man that he'd been.

"I'm Samuel Hamilton, a patron of your bar, although now I drink mostly soda," was how he introduced himself.

"Melba talked to me about you."

The nurse adjusted the pillows to prop him up, then left the room.

"Mr. Hamilton is with me. He's helping me coordinate the investigation. He gives it an outsider's view," explained Charles.

"I see."

"You can speak openly in front of him with our usual understanding that everything you say is off the record," added Charles.

"Very well. But first you should tell me why I was almost killed at San Quentin."

"We have information that it was a Chinese operative, but we're not sure yet about the circumstances," admitted Charles. "As you probably know already, the explosion was caused by a man who shot a bazooka from one of the towers. He didn't act on his own; he was part of a well thought-out plan. But you know how difficult it is to get prisoners to talk. The man who we think threw the knife was found strangled the next day in one of the bathrooms."

"What knife? What are you talking about?"

"You don't know that Rafael Garcia, your former janitor, was killed by a knife that someone threw from the crowd of prisoners while he was protecting you?" asked Samuel.

"That's not what they told me! I thought there was a fight between the inmates. You say that he saved my life?"

"First he pulled you out of the rubble and stopped the bleeding in your leg. Then he stood between you and the knife."

"Oh, my God. He did that for me?" murmured Mathew, deeply moved.

Charles, anxious to get information, continued. "Someone, we don't know who yet, bribed a prison guard to allow an inmate access to the West Tower. From there he fired the weapon at the wall when you were behind it. We know this because the foolish guard put the money in his own bank account. Unfortunately, that by itself doesn't mean much because it was all cash. We're checking for serial numbers, and maybe fingerprints. The only thing the guard has been able to tell us is that a Chinese man with a badly scarred face, whom we think is Dong Wong, gave him the money and the instructions. He identified him from mug shots but couldn't tell us where to find him."

"That guard is fucked, he's an accomplice to murder,"

Samuel added.

"He's already told us everything he knows. These criminals had pretty good information of how the prison is run, and who the guards were and when they came on. They knew whom to bribe," said Charles.

"I know of the Chinese man with the scarred face. He's the one who told me they had eliminated Reginald for blackmailing Xsing Ching," said Mathew.

"I'm glad you brought that up," said Samuel. "I visited Rafael just a couple of weeks before he died, and he told me that he delivered some liquor to your apartment on Grant Avenue last year and saw Reginald there at a party for this person Xsing Ching. It looked to him like you and Reginald were old buddies."

"It's true that Reginald was at that party, now that I think about it," admitted Mathew. "But I'm not sure how he got there, unless I mentioned it to him one night at the bar. You know he spent a lot of time at Camelot, and I would buy him a drink occasionally," said Mathew.

"Rafael also said he was chummy with a good-looking woman at the party," Samuel insisted.

"You mean Virginia. She worked for me."

"The real question is what was the relationship between you, Reginald, and the Virginia woman."

"I told you, Virginia worked for me," repeated a weary Mathew. "And as far as I know, there was no relationship between Reginald and her. I don't remember them even talking at that party or at any other time."

"There's something we didn't understand before. Your connection with Xsing Ching went back quite a ways, didn't it?" asked Charles. "You two knew each other for a long time."

"Long enough," replied Mathew. "I worked on him for a while to get that artwork. Look, I'm pretty tired. Can we continue this tomorrow?"

Charles couldn't tell if Mathew was hiding something or if he was so drugged up that he was losing it. It didn't seem to make much sense to hammer at him, so he decided to call it quits for the time being.

"Okay," said Charles, "just a couple more questions. Don't you think Xsing Ching is pissed at you because he lost all that art to the federal government?"

"I'm sure he is," said Mathew.

"Pissed enough to try and kill you for revenge?"

"In light of what I've learned about what was done to Reginald and all that has happened since, that's a good probability. Honest, I can't go on," he added, slumping his head and shoulders back on the three pillows.

"We'll see you in a few days. Get some rest," said Charles, leading Samuel to the door.

# 17

## Samuel Takes Charge

SAMUEL LAMENTED Rafael's death as much as he had Reginald's or Louie's. He visited with Rafael's family several times—his widowed wife and baby, his inconsolable mother, and his siblings—and realized how important Rafael had been in all their lives. The grieving of those people produced a sad feeling of impotence in him; he didn't know how to help them. In addition, he felt guilty because he suspected that his intervention had provoked Rafael's death. His curiosity had started a chain reaction. He connected the two Chinese thugs who tried to kill him and Charles with the Chinese prisoner who threw the knife at Rafael. It seemed obvious to him that they all belonged to the same organization.

That evening, very downcast, he went to Camelot to tell his doubts to Melba. "I'm surrounded by dead people, Melba."

"I suppose this brings back bad memories. I'm referring to your parents. Maybe you never got over their tragic death."

"That could be."

"You've had a tough time of it, son."

"I learned something from Rafael about you, Melba, when I went to see him at San Quentin. He said you were helping his family."

"That's between you and me, buster, not for public consumption!" she ordered with her rough whisky voice.

"I only wanted to tell you that I'd like to help, too, but I'm always broke."

"That family needs more than just money. Your friendship will help them a lot," she said hoarsely.

"I just wanted you to know that I'm here to help, too," he said.

She got up and went quickly toward the bathroom. Samuel thought he saw tears running down her cheeks, but he dismissed the idea as preposterous. The only thing that could make Melba cry was an onion.

He stared blankly out the window toward the bay while Excalibur edged over to his side. Samuel absentmindedly started scratching the dog's head. When Melba returned several minutes later she realized where the dog was and called the mutt in her gravelly voice.

"Leave 'im be," said Samuel. "I'm getting used to his fleas."

"Time heals all wounds, son. Rafael was a great guy and we'll miss him. Now's the time to help his family."

"This has gone too far. Reginald was just the beginning. Then it was two innocents, Louie and Rafael, who had nothing to do with this mess. And it could have been Mathew O'Hara like it could have been Charles and I."

"That's quite a lineup," admitted Melba. "It's clear you haven't found the central piece of the puzzle yet."

"I've a hunch where to look for what's missing. I've had some time to think about it. Truth is, I got fired. I was a lousy ad salesman."

"I'm sorry, man."

"I always hated that damn job. Not working doesn't help my depression; but, honestly, all I think about is this case."

"What're you gonna do?"

"I'm gonna keep my eye on Mr. Song's, that's what I'm gonna do. I think that's where we'll find the clue that we're looking for. Sooner or later, someone of interest is bound to show up there."

Melba watched Samuel still petting the dog, who couldn't have been happier. He was wagging his tailless bottom and blinking his eyes in ecstasy.

"Don't worry about food. You can always eat here at cocktail time.

"Thanks a lot. I'll try not to take advantage. Fortunately, my landlord is also a good guy. He'll give me some leeway on the rent. I'll be able to survive for a short while."

"You can come and clean up in the evenings like Rafael used to do. It would mean some extra cash. And you'll see more of Blanche," Melba offered.

\* \* \*

Losing his job was a relief, but he couldn't help feeling that he was a loser. There wasn't any reason why Blanche would ever care for him. Why had she embraced him that time in Melba's office? The date at the vegetarian restaurant had been very nice, but it didn't help advance his plan to win her over. He didn't have a single drink, and Blanche noticed it but didn't say anything.

He might not have been making much progress with Blanche, but his relationship with Excalibur was marvelous. The dog followed him around when he worked at the bar, and he learned to depend on that constant presence, like a shadow, behind him. The physical work of stocking liquor and the companionship of the mutt did wonders for his depression. He couldn't believe it when he found himself explaining to the dog his existential worries and his ideas about the case. He could no longer call it "The Reginald Rockwood Case" because it now involved three dead people. It was sinister, as the Chinese albino herbalist had defined it.

He looked back at his life and realized that he had always been a loner, since his early days in Nebraska, all the way through his two years at Stanford and his boring, desperate job selling ads at the newspaper. He gradually realized that he didn't like his isolation. That became evident to him as he spent time with Rafael's family.

He started showing up at the bar, even when he wasn't working, to pick up the dog and take him for walks in Chinatown. One day in a market, he discovered that the sight of live fish fascinated Excalibur, so he bought him a striped tropical fish in a bowl. The animal spent so many intense hours with his nose pressed up against the glass, watching the fish swim in circles, that the fish died of fright. After replacing it three times, Samuel decided Excalibur would have to stare at a carrot in the bowl or get some other avocation. The flea-bitten mutt, who resembled an Airedale, and the disheveled, failed newspaper ad salesman with the thinning red hair made quite a picturesque couple.

\* \* \*

Samuel wasn't just taking walks in Chinatown to satisfy Excalibur's obsession with fish. He sized up the street where Mr. Song had his shop. He'd walked though the neighborhood using dark glasses as a disguise and Excalibur as a companion. He found several places where he could station himself to watch, among them a laundromat where he washed his sheets so many times while he was spying that they ended up threadbare. He also ate at a shabby Chinese restaurant called the Won Ton Café kitty-corner from Mr. Song's.

The name of the establishment was painted on the inside of the flyspecked plate-glass window in red letters a foot high framed by a yellow border. Inside, above the name, were four faded pink Chinese lanterns made from cheap paper with lights burning in only two of them. Before entering, he looked through the window and saw three tables, any one of which gave him the view he wanted. He figured if he wasn't too conspicuous and if he came in at different times of the day while Mr. Song's was open, he could accomplish his objective of keeping an eye on those who came and went. Since the menu posted on the door was cheap, he could also afford the prices for the greasy fare. The first time he entered, he tripped on the door jam and the owner thought he was blind.

"You no can see?" he asked, fooled by the dog and the dark glasses.

It took Samuel a second to figure out that there was a certain advantage to this confusion.

"That's it, I see very little, almost nothing, really. This is a seeing-eye dog," he said, smiling sheepishly behind his dark glasses.

"Okay. Sit there," and he directed Samuel by his elbow to a dark corner of the café.

"No, no, dog needs light," said Samuel, pointing to one of the tables in front of the plate-glass window.

He thought he'd blown his cover because the man looked skeptical, but he led Samuel and the dog toward the window. He handed him a menu written in Chinese and gave a brief explanation of each dish in broken English. Samuel pretended he couldn't see.

"We have Won Ton special," the owner offered.

"Yeah, I'll have the special and some green tea."

In the days that followed, the Won Ton Café turned out to be perfect for what Samuel had in mind. Hidden behind his dark glasses, he ate lunch there every day, making the plate he ordered last as long as possible. The fat in the food congealed in a thick layer that was almost impossible to swallow. Fortunately, he didn't have to wait long. One afternoon around two o'clock, when he calculated he couldn't extend the lunch any longer and was about to pay the bill, a

Chinese man with one arm appeared as if out of nowhere in the middle of the Won Ton Café. Samuel was sure he hadn't seen him come in. He supposed there was a back door with access to the kitchen. He noticed him immediately because he was sure he'd seen him before. At first he couldn't place him, but then he remembered where: at Louie's funeral. He'd seen him standing there on an orange crate and later when he mentioned it to Charles, he'd been told that the description fit Fu Fung Fat, Virgina Demitri's servant, someone whom Charles had questioned after Mathew's arrest. The one-armed man made a gesture of hello to the owner, but he didn't sit down to eat; he left immediately, crossed the street, and entered Mr. Song's Many Chinese Herbs shop.

Samuel was in the perfect place to accomplish what he wanted. He could see the man talking to Mr. Song, who was standing behind the black lacquer counter. The sun shed enough light on the interior of the shop to give him an idea of what was going on. He knew the routine. The servant handed Mr. Song something, no doubt a claim check. The albino looked on his huge key ring, and the assistant climbed up the ladder and returned with an earthen jar. The one-armed man took it behind the beaded curtain and came back with it in a few minutes. He talked briefly to Mr. Song, who placed the jar underneath the counter. Samuel assumed it was empty because on other occasions the patron waited until the jar was returned to its place in the wall and locked in by the assistant before leaving.

Fu Fung Fat left the shop, crossed the street with a bulging package that he could barely carry and, to Samuel's surprise, came back into the Won Ton Café. But instead of sitting at a table, he went behind the blue oilcloth curtain in the back. Samuel assumed he had gone to the restroom, but when the man hadn't returned after a half an hour, he realized the man wasn't coming back. He called the owner.

# The Chinese Jars

"Want to pay?" the owner asked.

"Yes, but I need to use your bathroom first," said Samuel, getting up with exaggerated clumsiness.

"Back there," but he immediately remembered that his guest was almost blind so he took him by the arm and led him through the oilcloth curtain. Excalibur had learned to walk in front of the supposed blind man.

They found themselves in a long, poorly lit hallway with several closed doors, all painted a sickening parrot-green color. There was an accumulation of dirt around the knobs. The smell of grease and untidy restrooms was nauseating. Samuel swore that a couple of cockroaches ran in front of him but he couldn't be sure. The man stopped in front of a door with a decal of a Chinese warrior on it. On the door next to it was one of a damsel from the imperial court, which was really out of place in that disgusting passageway.

"This is it," he said, as he nudged Samuel toward the door.

Samuel pulled Excalibur into the small room and had to hold his nose because the smell almost knocked him over. Fortunately, he was alone. Excalibur showed no signs of being uncomfortable because of the stench. On the contrary, he sniffed in the corners with pleasure. After a short while, Samuel decided not to waste any more time. He walked out of the bathroom, pulling Excalibur by the leash, walked down the dark hallway, opened the oilcloth curtain, and summoned the owner with his dark glasses in hand.

The owner looked at him with more anger than surprise because he'd never totally believed the story of his being blind.

"You see?" he spit out.

"Yes, I can see," said Samuel, "and I have a problem. A man with one arm went through that curtain and has disappeared. I need to know where he went."

"I see no one," said the owner.

"This is very important. If you won't show me where he

went, I'll have to bring the police here. Do you understand?"

"Police no bother me. They my friend."

Samuel's face turned red with anger, "I don't mean the local police. I mean the federal police. Get it?"

The owner's casual sneer changed immediately into a worried expression.

"I know very well that you pay protection money to Maurice Sandovich, but he won't be able to help you if I call the federal cops," threatened Samuel.

The owner squinted and wiped his palms on his white apron. "What you want?'

"I want to know where the man went," said Samuel. "I promise you, if you cooperate you won't have problems with the authorities."

"How I know you keep you word?"

"You just have to trust me. You don't have a choice. If the federal police come, you're through. We can fix this between the two of us without any problems. So what's it going to be?" He put his hands on his hips and started tapping his foot, as he looked the owner in the eyes.

"Okay," said the owner, frightened.

"It's a deal," replied Samuel.

The owner guided him down the hallway to the last door and knocked several times. The door opened a crack and when someone saw it was the owner of the Won Ton Café, the door opened. They entered a room whose size couldn't be determined because there was so much cigarette smoke. Coughing, Samuel saw, through watery eyes and the smoky atmosphere, several round tables with felt covers, each with a single shaded light above. There wasn't an empty seat around any of them. Chinese men were playing wagering games.

At one table there were five men playing poker. At another they were throwing craps and had placed an artificial backstop at one end of the table for the dice to bounce off. The noise was tremendous. As the money and chips flew, the voices and yells increased. They bet on card games, dice, and mahjong, and other games with chips and little sticks that Samuel couldn't identify. Judging from the excitement of the clients, he figured large sums of money must be changing hands in that clandestine casino. Excalibur began pulling on the lease, desperate to escape the smoke.

"Where is he?" asked Samuel.

The owner summoned with his index finger, indicating that Samuel should follow him to the back of the room to yet another door. He unlocked and opened it, revealing a flight of stairs going down to some sort of a dark basement. Halfway down, he turned on the light—a single bare bulb. Samuel couldn't see what was at the bottom, and he faced the owner with a questioning look.

"Way out," said the man. "Clients gamble. When have to leave, go through door, down stairs."

"Where does it lead?" asked Samuel.

"Chinatown."

"Did you build this?"

The man shook his head. "No, no. Many Chinese. More than hundred years old. You go down, look for man. Remember, no tell police," he said, as he muscled Samuel back to the landing at the top of the stairs. Excalibur, anxious to get away from the smoke, pulled on the leash, and both went down the stairs. The owner shut and locked the door behind them.

At the bottom they found themselves in a basement only dimly lit from the bulb in the stairwell. The floor was of stamped dirt and the walls were also made of uneven earth shored up by beams and bars like a mine tunnel. It smelled of humidity and excrement. Samuel trembled. What if the one-armed man hadn't left, and the owner had just locked them in this hole? No one would hear his cries; they were in the bowels of Chinatown. He imagined people and traffic above him.

He remembered that he'd read in a novel that Chinatown was built in the eighteen hundreds at the time of the gold rush and that all the illegal activities, from prostitution to gambling and murders, all took place underground. Just as the owner of the Won Ton Café said, these passageways were at least a hundred years old, and they continued to serve the same purposes.

He quickly adjusted to the dim lighting and saw a metal switch on a post in the tunnel. He supposed it was a switch. He pulled it and immediately some lights went on, all very dim, but they allowed him to figure out where he was. He couldn't believe his eyes. There were passageways leading in all directions. It was a real labyrinth. There were pieces of cardboard tacked on the walls, probably giving directions, but all the lettering was in Chinese. He couldn't decide which way to go, although it wouldn't have made any difference, because he didn't have a clue where the one-armed man had gone.

But Excalibur didn't have a language or a directional problem. He started pulling on the leash and ran in circles with his nose to the ground until he finally decided on one of the passages. He seemed to know whom they were following. Samuel followed him almost by feel in the semidarkness, careful not to fall into a hole or hit one of the pipes that crossed overhead.

Air seemed to be in short supply in that rancid atmosphere, and Samuel figured that the ventilation system, if that's what it was, was pretty primitive.

There were doors, some metal and some wood, marked in Chinese or with numbers that were barely distinguishable. He was sorry he didn't have matches or a lighter, which he always used to carry when he smoked. He saw a piece of cardboard with an arrow and supposed it was an exit, but Excalibur just kept following his nose, and Samuel thought it best to trust the dog's instinct.

They finally came to a bend in the passageway, and the

animal stopped in front of an iron ladder about six feet high, at the top of which was a door, also made of metal. He started sniffing frantically, whining and scratching the ground. Samuel tried to read what was written with splashes of white paint.

"I'll be dammed!" he exclaimed. The number was 838.

He lifted the dog in one arm and scurried up the ladder with one hand. He tried the door and was relieved that it was open. He let Excalibur into the cement basement of a building. He saw the pipes in the ceiling and could hear the sound of machines, possibly boilers. There were rows of doors with numbers on them, locked with padlocks. They looked like storage rooms for the inhabitants. He didn't have to search for an exit because the dog dragged him to some stairs. They climbed them and found themselves on a landing. He opened the only door and entered the lobby of 838 Grant Avenue.

The floor was black marble streaked with white, highly polished and reflecting the antique armoire that was up against one wall. A large mirror with a bamboo frame hung above it. There were expensive Chinese screens in two different locations, a sumptuous white sofa, and various plants to complete the decor. Next to an elevator was a glass case that held a list of tenants spelled out in brass letters. Samuel sighed, relieved there was no one at the guard desk, but he knew he didn't have much time because in a building like that, someone was usually guarding the entrance.

He examined the directory and saw that Mathew O'Hara was still listed as occupying the fifth floor. He had no doubt that's where Fu Fung Fat had ended up. Melba would be very proud when he told her of Excalibur's prowess. He headed for the exit, pulling the dog, who skated across the black marble.

\* \* \*

On his way back to Camelot, he went over what he'd learned and tried to figure out what to do next.

When he arrived, he handed Melba the leash and said, "I'll tell you what's going on in a minute. Right now I've got to make a phone call," and rushed toward the booth at the back of the bar.

He closed the door and the smell of rancid tobacco caught his nose. This time he didn't feel revulsion. As a matter of fact, he was dying for a cigarette. He dialed Charles's office and got him on the line.

"I've just followed Virginia's servant all the way from Mr. Song's to 838 Grant Avenue. That's O'Hara's penthouse."

"So what?" said Charles. "That's where the little shit lives."

"He got something at Mr. Song's, and he took it back there by way of a secret passage," said Samuel.

"A secret passage? What kind of secret passage?"

"One that goes under the streets of Chinatown," said Samuel.

"You're crazy," said Charles.

"No man, I swear."

"How did you discover it?" asked Charles, incredulous.

"I'll tell you later. Do you think you can get another search warrant? Maybe we can find some important evidence if we get to the apartment quickly. So far, no one knows that I've made the discovery."

"We searched every inch of that apartment already," said Charles. "I assure you there's nothing there that interests us."

You're a conceited asshole. I serve it up to you on a plate, and you don't even pay attention, thought Samuel. "Look, if the guy took something from a jar, a big package, it could be part of O'Hara's half million. It couldn't be all of it; there must be another jar with the rest. For that there has to be a key or a claim check. You never looked for those when you searched the apartment, did you?"

"Well, not exactly. We didn't know what we were looking for."

"Don't you think it's worth a try?"

"I'll get another warrant," Charles decided.

* * *

The team of U.S. marshals and Customs agents was back at the Grant Avenue apartment with Charles at seven thirty the next morning. Samuel agreed to wait at a café down the street, though he was dying of curiosity.

The feds brought an interpreter with them because they wanted to get answers from Fu Fung Fat. They questioned him for three hours, but they got absolutely no new information.

They also confronted Virginia Dimitri in a separate room. She was still in bed when they got there. They gave her time to get dressed, and she took almost an hour. She finally appeared, recently bathed and very stylishly dressed: a loop skirt, red blouse, sandals, and her hair in a bun. She announced that she needed a cup of coffee to start the morning, wasting another twenty minutes.

"We know you've a claim check from Mr. Song's, and this subpoena allows us to confiscate it. So hand it over."

"I have no idea what you're talking about. I have no connection with this person you call Mr. Song," she answered.

"How have you been supporting yourself since Mr. O'Hara was arrested?" asked Charles.

"I don't think my finances are any of your business."

Charles realized he wasn't going to intimidate that woman, and he'd lost enough time, so he gave the order to search the place from top to bottom and to destroy it if necessary in order to find what they were looking for: money, and probably a claim check and a key.

Virginia sat in the kitchen painting her fingernails and

drinking coffee, perfectly calm, while the men went through her apartment like a hurricane, emptying drawers, turning the furniture upside down, and emptying every container in the kitchen. The only thing they didn't do was take a look behind the ceiling panels.

The Customs agent who was interrogating Fu Fung Fat was pulling his hair out with frustration by the end.

"We're going to have to arrest this guy and threaten to deport him and his whole family back to Communist China, if he, in fact, has a family here. I've had a lot of them in my time, but he's the toughest nut I've ever interrogated," the agent told Charles.

Fu Fung Fat asked courteously if he could continue with his chores while they were destroying the apartment. He went into the kitchen and grabbed the garbage bag under the sink. It had already been examined, but one of the officer's, thinking that the servant was trying to whisk something out of the apartment, dumped its contents on the floor and went through it again, piece by piece, while the one-armed man smiled slyly. They found nothing. Four hours later they gave up.

"We know you're hiding something, Miss Dimitri," said Charles.

"Prove it."

"You can count on it. We'll be back."

"You'll have to, in order to put everything in its place and clean my house, if you don't want me to sue you for abuse of authority," she answered calmly.

"Try it, and let's see how far you get."

\* \* \*

Charles and the agents walked down the street to the place where Samuel had been waiting all morning. He'd already lost count of the number of cups of coffee he'd drunk.

# The Chinese Jars

"We didn't find a damn thing," announced Charles, in a bad mood.

"Clam down. We haven't lost anything," said Samuel.

"Nothing except my time!"

"You haven't lost it. Dimitri and her servant are scared and they will act soon. You didn't mention the passageway, right?"

"Of course not."

"For sure that's where she'll go next," smiled Samuel, rubbing his hands together in anticipation.

"How do we get access to that place?" asked Charles.

"I'll show you," said Samuel. "We have to sneak back into the building. Was the guard there when you left?"

"I think so. But that's not a problem. He knows we searched the floor. Agent Reiss, go and distract the guard," said Charles.

"How?" asked Reiss.

"However you please. Tell him you have to ask him some questions in private. Think of something, man, for chrissake."

"Did you bring flashlights?" asked Samuel.

"Flashlights? Of course not. No one goes around with flashlights in broad daylight," answered Charles.

"But I told you the passageways are dark!"

"You said there were light bulbs."

"I turned them on with a switch when I was there yesterday, but I can't guarantee there's light today.

"I'll go and buy flashlights," one of the agent's offered.

"No, I'd better go," replied Samuel, thinking that a fed over six feet tall in a suit, dark glasses, and a hat buying a half a dozen flashlights wouldn't go unnoticed.

While the rest waited, drinking coffee and smoking, he quickly went to one of the tourist stores in the area. In the middle of countless plastic dolls, reproductions of the Golden Gate Bridge, fans, erotic carvings in fake ivory, and suitcases, he found what he was looking for. Twenty minutes later he was back at the café.

Reiss left to deal with the guard while another man was stationed near the café to watch the front entrance to the building. Charles Perkins took a look outside to check if there were any strange goings-on, but Chinatown was involved in its own affairs, indifferent, as usual. Nobody gave a second look at the group of four men crossing the street as if they were marching off to war. Samuel hoped that Virginia and Fu Fung Fat were very busy and wouldn't think of getting close to a window and looking out to see them arrive.

They entered the lobby at 838 and went straight to the basement, where Samuel found the door that led to the passageway. After closing the door, they climbed down the metal ladder into the bowels of Chinatown.

"This is a shitty place to wait for something to happen, and I hate to waste my valuable time. Cross your fingers that you're right," said Charles, threatening him by pointing his finger, while he shined his flashlight on the assortment of overhead pipes covered with cobwebs filled with dead insects and at the wet ground splashed with puddles.

"Mr. Perkins, this place has rats," exclaimed one of the agents.

"What did you expect, flowers?" replied the attorney.

"We have to be patient. She feels trapped, and this is her avenue of escape. She'll show up," assured Samuel.

"Can we smoke?" asked one of the agents.

"I don't see why not. Too bad we didn't bring a picnic and sleeping bags," the attorney joked.

"Let's try and not draw anybody's attention," suggested Samuel.

"There's not a soul around here," exclaimed Charles.

"That's what you think," said Samuel.

\* \* \*

# The Chinese Jars

They crouched near the ladder, where it was totally dark. A short distance away they could see the passageway very poorly lit by the bulbs that hung from the ceiling. A lone Chinese man trotted by in a hurry without seeing them. After that three others went by them, including a woman with a baby on her back; if the passersby saw them, they didn't seem surprised. Samuel supposed that even a few Westerners used the labyrinth.

"This looks like the subterranean superhighway through Chinatown," whispered Charles.

"I would imagine that a lot of skullduggery goes on because of these passageways," answered Samuel, thinking of the gambling den in the back of the Won Ton Café and the dozens of others like it that no doubt existed all over the neighborhood.

Finally, more than an hour later, the basement door to 838 opened, and Fu Fung Fat came onto the platform at the top of the ladder and peered into the darkness, still holding the door open with his shoulder without an arm. The men hidden by the ladder froze. Fu Fung Fat, sure that no one saw or heard him, backed into the basement and closed the door.

"He's testing the terrain. He'll return soon," whispered Samuel.

Charles gave him a pat on the back. "The plan is bearing fruit," he said, obviously relieved. "At least there's some action."

Ten minutes later the door to the building opened again, and Fu Fung Fat reappeared dragging a large suitcase to the top of the landing. Behind him came Virginia Dimitri, dressed in black from head to toe, appropriate for discreet navigation of the underground highway, thought Samuel. She carried a suitcase, though it was half the size of the one her manservant was wrestling with.

Virginia tied a rope to the handle of the first suitcase, which seemed heavier, and she helped the servant let it down to the foot of the ladder, where it landed with a thud and stirred up dust. He then scurried down the ladder, with great agility considering he only had one arm. He untied the rope, and she pulled it up. She repeated the operation with the second suitcase, then they were both at the bottom with the baggage. They lingered a moment to let their eyes get accustomed to the darkness.

It was then that Charles made his presence known. "We've been expecting you, Miss Dimitri," he said, turning his flashlight on and shining it directly in her face. "Our subpoena is still effective, and we'd like to examine the contents of your suitcases."

Virginia was speechless. She stooped to set the small suitcase on the dirt floor, then straightened to her full height, folded her arms in front of her and confronting the attorney face-to-face. Her upper lip quivered slightly, but she seemed in perfect control of the situation.

"If you are going to invade my privacy, I have a right to an attorney. And get that light out of my eyes."

"All in due course. First we'll open the suitcases," answered Charles.

Two Customs agents corralled the manservant and patted him down to make sure he didn't have firearms.

"Let's do this in a more comfortable setting. Is that all right with you?" asked Charles, making fun of her.

Without giving her a chance to reply, they made the two suspects climb the ladder and brought up the suitcases. Once in the basement of the building, which was adequately lit with fluorescent lights, the agents handcuffed Fu Fung Fat's only wrist to a pipe. Virginia glanced fleetingly in all directions, as though she were looking for a place to run, but immediately realized the futility of such a course. She had a menacingly angry look in her eyes but didn't resist when her hands were cuffed behind her back.

# The Chinese Jars

The big suitcase was opened first. It was more than half full of packages of one-hundred-dollar bills, and the other half contained several outfits for the fashionable female.

"Well!" exclaimed Charles. "Are these your savings, Miss?"

Next they searched the smaller suitcase. It was full to the brim with more packages of one-hundred-dollar bills.

"This is a lot of money, but we're still missing about half of the half a million dollars we're looking for, and then there's the claim check and the key to the other jar at Mr. Song's. She has to have them somewhere. Search her," Samuel whispered to Charles, as he pulled him aside.

"It's not that easy," said Charles. "We have to have a reason."

Samuel heated up. "What the shit are you talking about? We find this woman in a secret passageway under the streets of Chinatown with a ton of dough, and that's not reason enough?"

By now, all the others were watching them.

"Okay, okay," said Charles, "quiet down. I'm in charge here." He adjusted his tie and straightened his shoulders. "Miss Dimitri, we know you have a claim check and a key for Mr. Song's Many Chinese Herbs in your possession, and we want you to turn them over to us now."

"You searched my house and you found nothing. Why don't you leave me in peace?" Virginia spit, livid with rage.

"You'll save yourself a lot of trouble if you cooperate."

"I don't have the slightest idea what you're talking about," she said defiantly.

"We'll have to search you. You leave us no option."

"If you lay one finger on me, you'll pay dearly. And if you don't release me immediately, I'll sue you and the government and I'll make sure you and that little bastard with you lose your jobs. Let me remind you I have connections in this town, in case you haven't figured that out already."

Samuel no longer had a job, so he considered the threat humorous.

"Well, then, Miss Dimitri, we'll take you into custody and we'll search your person. It won't be agreeable for you, I'll make sure of that," smirked Charles.

He called one of the Customs agents over and gave him instructions. "Take Miss Dimitri to the federal marshal's office and have her searched and then book her."

"What's the charge, Chief?" asked the Customs agent.

"Transporting stolen money," he said off the cuff.

Virginia laughed out loud. "You'll never make that stick, you son of a bitch. I'll be out in an hour and you'll pay the consequences."

"Not if I find what I'm looking for, you won't," said Charles. He gave the order that the manservant and the suitcases also be taken.

"Are there charges?"

"The same. Transporting stolen money," he answered. "This time we've got her. At least I hope so. There's thousands of dollars in those suitcases. Where did she get it and where was she taking it?"

"It's evident she planned to escape. That means she has the claim check and the key on her," said Samuel.

"If she has them on her, we'll find them."

* * *

The interrogation and search of Virginia Dimitri at the U.S. marshal's office was a raucous affair. She refused to answer any questions and demanded to consult with her attorney, who couldn't prevent the search. She had to be physically restrained by two matrons while she was stripped. Virginia threw the first tantrum of her life, which increased in intensity until she lost control. She broke free—scratching, biting and kicking. She screamed at the top of her lungs, "There, you see, nothing on me, you Lesbian bitches!" Another matron joined the fray, and Virginia was finally subdued and flattened against a table. The claim check and the key were found in a plastic bag inserted in her vagina.

The head matron winked at her, and said in a soothing voice, "It never fails, sugar. Those with the most to hide make the most noise."

They let her go and gave her a clean set of jailhouse garb, but Virginia was still foaming at the mouth and yelling expletives and pulling out her hair. They had to restrain her again. An hour later, she was still out of control and her voice was cracking. A doctor was called and she was sedated before she was locked up in the psychiatric ward.

\* \* \*

With the claim check and key in hand, Charles had a new subpoena issued, and he again appeared at Mr. Song's with two federal marshals, a Customs expert on fingerprints and, of course, Samuel, to whom he owed it all.

Mr. Song was his usual ceremonial self, bowing from behind the black lacquer counter, looking as strange as he did the first time they saw him.

He stroked his white wispy goatee as he examined the claim check and nodded affirmatively. He then looked up serenely at Samuel and Charles, placing both of his hands on the counter, as if weighing his options. Eventually he motioned to his assistant to get his niece. Fifteen long minutes elapsed. When Buckteeth finally showed up, she spent another ten minutes talking to her uncle. Then she got down to business. "Hello, Mr. Hamilton. How's your mood and your health?" she asked.

"Very well, thank you."

"I'm happy. You are welcome to come back. It will be cheaper now," she smiled, showing her charming rodent teeth.

Charles raised his eyebrows. "What's that all about? You haven't been dating this young girl, I hope."

"No, no, nothing like that. Mr. Song helped me stop smoking a while back. I'll tell you all about it later," explained Samuel, blushing.

"You tell your uncle that we have this claim check and key and this subpoena, just like last time," demanded Charles.

After she and her uncle talked for five minutes, she translated. "My honorable uncle says that you still haven't returned the jars you took the last time."

"As soon as the case is over, we'll return them, I promise. It's getting close now."

"When?"

"I can't tell you exactly. Right now I have to take another jar, the one that corresponds to this claim check."

"My honorable uncle repeats what he said the last time. The contents of the jar belong to you, but not the jar."

"We'll talk about that later. First I have to take a look at what's inside."

The assistant went up the ladder and brought down the jar in question. Samuel remembered that when Fu Fung Fat had been there previously, Mr. Song's assistant removed a smaller jar from the center of the wall, and there was now a gap where it had been.

Charles ordered the top of the jar be dusted for fingerprints before the contents were examined. Then they opened the jar and disgorged package after package of one-hundred-dollar bills, which he looked at closely in disbelief, before giving instructions that prints be lifted from them. "There's a lot of money here! Do you have any more jars that belong to Virginia Dimitri?" he asked Mr. Song.

"He only goes by the claim check number," she said. "He doesn't know a Virginia Dimitri."

"Ask him about the gap in the middle of the wall," said Samuel. "Whom did that belong to?"

"He says that person's business is finished. That's why that space is empty."

Samuel whispered to Charles, "Ask him where the jar is? That's the one that the manservant opened the other day."

"You need to bring us that jar," ordered Charles.

When Mr. Song understood what Charles wanted, he had his assistant go behind the bead curtain and get the medium-sized jar, which he put up on the counter.

"What was in this jar?" asked Charles.

Mr. Song waited for the translation.

"He has no idea," said the girl, and she burst out with contagious laughter. "And if my honorable uncle knew, he wouldn't tell you."

Charles ignored her. He also ordered that it be dusted for prints. He then counted the money. There was several hundred thousand dollars. They'd already recovered hundreds of thousands from Virginia Dimitri's suitcases. The total was more than half a million. The major part of the money, $500,000, probably belonged to Mathew O'Hara. The question was what was she going to do with it? The more important question was where did the rest come from and to whom did it belong?

Mr. Song followed them to the street, arguing in his language that he considered what they were doing robbery and an assault on his property, but he couldn't stop them from confiscating both jars.

Samuel, who now had a relationship with him and understood his frustrations, was the last to leave. He said goodbye with reverence to the albino, Buckteeth, and the assistant and promised them he'd personally see that the property was returned. "Tell your uncle I'm still not smoking," he said.

"Mr. Song says that is good. He also says he hopes you begin to understand how sinister this whole affair is, just as he told you."

"Yes, I believe I'm beginning to see that," said Samuel.

"My honorable uncle says to never bring your friends here again," the beaver translated.

\* \* \*

That weekend Melba and Samuel went to visit Mathew O'Hara, who by then had been in the hospital prison ward for two months. He'd lost almost forty pounds, and he looked twenty years older. They didn't know what to say, expecting to hear the worst, since it crossed their minds that he might be dying, but Mathew surprised them.

"I'm very happy to see you."

"We heard they couldn't save your leg," Melba blurted out.

"They amputated my leg. Imagine! After all I went though."

"You certainly have been through hell, Boss," Melba said, looking in anguish at the place where his leg should have been.

"Nothing compared to what Rafael's family's been through, I'm sure. I know you're close to them, Melba. Tell me how they're doing. I heard Rafael's wife had a healthy baby," said Mathew.

Melba had known him for many years. She remembered him as a man who was always in a hurry, restless, full of ambitious plans, and who never demonstrated the slightest interest in other people's problems. He didn't even remember his employees' names but never forgot those of people who could be of some use to him.

# The Chinese Jars

"Yes, he's a handsome boy. He looks like his father," Melba managed to answer.

"That's right," added Samuel. "They're an amazing family. Fortunately, they have each other."

"Melba, I want to do something for them, but I'm trapped in this bed and then I'll go to prison. Will you act as an intermediary?

"What d'ya want me to do?"

"I want you to pay them the monthly stipend of $500 from the bar that you usually pay to me.

"You mean that you are giving up your share of the bar, Boss?"

"The bar's in your name."

"Yeah, but we both know we're partners. How about if we put half in the name of Rafael's family, so if something happens to me there won't be a problem," she said.

"I didn't expect less from you," smiled Mathew.

"I know that you've lost much of your fortune, Mathew. This is very generous of you."

"I wouldn't be here today if it weren't for Rafael. I hope to meet his family one day. I'll never be able to pay that boy back for what he did for me. In truth, he gave me more than my life, he gave me a new life."

Samuel thought he was witnessing something he would always remember: the transformation of this man. Far from looking broken by the tragedy, Mathew seemed at peace and almost content.

"What about you, Mathew?" she asked. "What's in store?"

"My lawyer tells me I'll get out sooner now that all this has happened, but I need to go to a rehabilitation hospital and learn to walk with a prosthetic leg. I can't do that until my wounds heal and the swelling goes down. I still have a ways to go."

"I'm sorry," commented Samuel.

"Nothing to be sorry about, man. I've learned a great deal about myself, and that's what's really important. Look, I've got several years ahead, and I don't intend to waste them."

As they walked out, Samuel gave Melba his impression. "The pain has changed and elevated him as a person," he said emotionally.

"Yeah, we'll see," said Melba. "People don't change much, no matter what happens to 'em. I'm going to put the bar in the Garcias' name before he changes his mind."

* * *

A couple of days later, Samuel answered an urgent phone call from Melba and rushed to Camelot. Excalibur was wagging his tail with delirious enthusiasm.

"Okay, dog, calm down. I'll have to buy you another carrot for your fishbowl," he laughed, petting him.

Seated at the round table was a beefy man with the gray crew cut. It was Maurice Sandovich. He wasn't wearing his police uniform but was still recognizable. He was sipping a double or triple bourbon over the rocks and was talking earnestly with Melba.

"Hi, Samuel. Maurice has some news for you."

The last time he'd seen Sandovich was from behind a mirror during an interrogation. Sandovich had seen him only once.

"Hello, Maurice," he said. "It's nice to see you in a social environment instead of on official business."

"Nice to see ya, Counselor."

"No, you're mixing me up with Charles Perkins," said Samuel.

"Oh, yeah. You're the reporter guy."

Samuel blushed. In reality, he was an unemployed ad

salesman, but he accepted the compliment. "Do you want to talk to me?" he asked.

"I sure do. I was having a drink with my old friend Melba and telling her the latest gossip from the department, and your name came up. By the way, you wanna a drink?"

Samuel thought quickly. Should he trust this bastard? He was a pretty slippery customer at best, but maybe not as bad as Charles made him out to be. He remembered Melba's words: he was small potatoes. "Sure, I'll have a Scotch on the rocks."

Maurice whirled around in his seat and yelled at the bartender, "A Scotch on the rocks for my friend here, and another bourbon on the rocks for me. Make 'em doubles. On my tab."

"Yes, sir, coming right up," answered the bartender.

Melba gave Samuel a complicitous wink. They both knew that people like Sandovich never paid the bill.

"Anyway, your name came up when I told Melba that we arrested Dong Wong, a well-known fugitive in Chinatown. You remember, I was being questioned by the attorney guy and the Customs agent, and you were behind the mirror."

"How did you know it was me?"

"We cops know everything that goes on in front of us, my friend. But let's get back to Dong Wong. He was arrested last night. He was getting ready to leave town, and they got him at the airport."

"Wow! Does the U.S. attorney know about this?"

"Nope, just you and Melba outside of the department."

"You know how bad Charles wanted this guy, don't you?" said Samuel.

"Yeah, and he'll want him even more when I tell you what he said."

Samuel got his Scotch and drank it down in one long gulp.

"He spilled the beans."

"What? Did he confess?" exclaimed Samuel.

"It wasn't so simple. He figured we were trying to pin at least five Chinatown murders on him plus a bunch of other shit, so we asked what he had to offer in exchange for leniency. He told us plenty to try and save his ass from the gas chamber," explained Maurice.

"So what'd he say?" asked Samuel, taking mental note.

"He gave us the mastermind."

"You mean the mastermind behind all these crimes, including the murder of Rockwood and Louie?"

"Yes, sir, including the attempt on O'Hara. He gave us the one who organized the whole scheme. According to him, he was given orders to carry out the details, but the brain was someone else."

"Who?" asked Samuel.

"That Virginia Dimitri broad."

Samuel started hyperventilating. He couldn't believe what he had just heard. "Will you let me take notes on what you tell me for my newspaper?" he asked.

"Go right ahead, my friend."

He pulled his pad of paper and pencil out of his jacket pocket and for the next hour took notes from Maurice on how Dong Wong was paid by Virginia to kill Reginald after he'd collected the $50,000 from Xsing Ching. In other words, Reginald was the front man for Virginia for the blackmail, based on information she fed to him.

"She paid Dong Wong more money to have you and the attorney guy killed but there was a mix-up, and Chop Suey Louie got it instead," added Sandovich.

"What about the man who showed up to pay for his own obituary?" asked Samuel.

"Dong Wong hired an actor with black hair and a tuxedo to file it so the employee at the newspaper would remember it. Virginia wrote the obituary based on what Rockwell had told her about his life. It turned out to be false. He never belonged to the upper class, but she didn't know that.

"She also didn't think that Samuel would show up for his funeral service. That started to unravel everything," said Melba.

"Don't tell me. I bet she was also responsible for the death of Rafael Garcia and the attempt on Mathew O'Hara. But why?" asked Samuel.

"That's what I asked, why? Dong Wong said she also had a big pot of money she was hiding for O'Hara, and Wong thought she wanted him out of the way so she could keep it for herself. When she learned that half a million dollars would be in her hands to wire to Xsing Ching, she arranged it so that the feds would find out when the merchandise would be inspected and that's how they arrested Mathew O'Hara with his hands in the cookie jar. That was the best way to get him out of circulation, but she ran a big risk if he was alive. O'Hara isn't the kind of guy who just rolls over, so Virginia and Dong Wong planned to kill him in prison. The feds had traced the money in the San Quentin guard's account to some money she had in one of those jars at Mr. Songs."

"I wasn't told that," said Samuel and wondered how much more Charles was keeping from him. The deal was that he would be kept informed, but the attorney wasn't playing straight with him. He would have to find things out for himself. Sandovich was a treasure trove of information, a stroke of luck for which he had Melba to thank.

"Can I use your name as a source? This is hot stuff, and I can get it published tomorrow in the newspaper," he asked the cop.

"Not my name, for chrissake. You know how to do it. Unnamed sources in the police department, blah, blah, blah."

By now Samuel was puffed up and couldn't control his eagerness. He was thinking of how he needed to get this story to the night editor of the newspaper he used to work for, and how he needed to convince the man to publish it with his byline. If they didn't hire him as a reporter with this story, it meant there was no way out of his bad luck. He excused himself and rushed out the swinging door of Camelot, tightly griping his notebook.

\* \* \*

The next day Blanche burst into Melba's bedroom at an indecently early hour, waving the morning paper in front of her.

"What's wrong child for God's sakes? It's six thirty in the morning," mumbled Melba still half asleep.

"Look! They published him on the front page in enormous letters, and with his name: Samuel Hamilton, Reporter. Imagine!" exclaimed Blanche, and she read the headline:

DRAGON LADY IMPLICATED IN SEVERAL CHINATOWN MURDERS AND THE DOUBLE-CROSSING OF SAN FRANCISCO MILLIONAIRE MATHEW O'HARA.

"Don't you think it's stupendous? Samuel, a reporter!" she said enthusiastically.

"What does it say? Read it to me," grumbled Melba, feeling around the night table for her first cigarette.

# 18

## Samuel Holds Court

IT WASN'T a one-shot deal. Every day in the morning paper was another article by Samuel Hamilton expounding on "The Case of the Chinese Jars," as it was now popularly called. The crime stories competed with the space race between the United States and the Soviet Union, the construction of the Berlin Wall, and Jacqueline Kennedy, who'd become the world's fashion plate. He got credit for raising the circulation of the paper, and the local gossips worked overtime, giving him a reputation as an innovative reporter with a novelistic style. Whether it was true or not, he was assigned his own office, without a window but at least with a fan and his own typewriter—a black Underwood that weighed as much as a locomotive but with all the keys in good condition. He knew that the attention he was getting wouldn't last long, unless he could feed the insatiable morbidity of the readers with new stories. Fortunately, in San Francisco there was always a new scandal or crime.

Success changed him subtly. It was how he carried himself, how he dressed, and how he focused his energy. He felt like his old self, the one he'd been before his parents were murdered and he was forced to quit Stanford. The one he'd been before he had the car wreck that badly injured the girl, and the one he'd been before all those years selling ads out of the basement.

He knew he owed much to Melba. But because of work and the crazy hours he'd been keeping, he hadn't been to Camelot for a couple of weeks. Finally he made it there on a Sunday afternoon. Melba was sitting at the round table smoking a cigarette and drinking a beer with Excalibur at her side, his leash draped across her lap.

Samuel walked in the front door, and the dog almost suffered an attack of epilepsy. Jumping and barking, he put his front paws on the reporter's neatly pressed new khaki suit jacket and licked his outstretched hands. Samuel reached into his jacket pocket and gave him a treat, which Excalibur devoured in a second without chewing, then looked up in anticipation of more. Melba received him with less drama but with equal amounts of affection. He approached her with a broad smile on his blushing face and hugged her.

"What a difference a little success makes," she said, as she separated herself from him at arm's length and took measure of him from head to toe.

"Unbelievable, eh?" he said, as he enjoyed Melba's attention for a few seconds.

He looked around, searching for Blanche. When he spotted her behind the horseshoe bar, he excused himself and walked quickly to a stool opposite her, straddling it with both legs and with his feet planted in a pigeon-toed fashion on the lower rungs so he would be able to reach over the bar. She was happy to see him and watched as he took her hands and looked into her eyes, in a way in which he wouldn't have even thought of a few weeks before.

"Sorry I've been out of touch, Blanche. You won't believe how busy I've been."

# The Chinese Jars

"We know, Samuel. We read your articles in the newspaper every day."

"Really?" said Samuel, trying to look surprised, but instead acting full of self-importance. "You've been following the daily show, then?"

"Haven't missed an installment. I bet you have more to tell us, don't you?"

"Sure do. Come and sit with your mom and me at the table and I'll fill you in."

"Should I bring you a drink? Or are you still on soda?" she asked, with a certain malice.

"Once in a while I can have a drink."

"The usual?"

Samuel nodded, got down from the stool, and strutted back to the round table. He intended to sit down with an empty seat between him and Melba, but Excalibur anticipated where Samuel would go and tried to climb into the chair. Melba grabbed him by the collar.

"I knew you hadn't forgotten us," said Melba.

"Not a chance, Melba. You're the one who gave me most of the breaks on this story."

Blanche brought the Scotch on the rocks. She placed the drink in front of Samuel and sat down next to him. She looked young and fresh in her white sweats and her loose hair. "It's on the house," she said.

"Thank you. Thank you both for your support. Where do you want me to start?"

"You know I always thought that Reginald was a loser," said Melba. "So how did he get a good-looking tomato like Virginia to fall for him? She must have known what he was . What was her angle in all this?"

Samuel laughed. "The story is full of surprises," he said, as he stirred his drink with his index finger. "You remember me telling you there was a strange deposit in his checking account of $150 every month in addition to his paycheck, And we couldn't figure it out?"

"I remember that. I thought maybe he was stealing tips from the cocktail waitresses," she joked.

"Charles finally got to the bottom of it. It was from the Veterans Administration. He subpoenaed Reginald's file and found out that the poor bastard suffered from shellshock during the Korean War and was receiving a disability pension. But for sure he was weird before that."

"How'd he know where to look?" asked Blanche.

"The bank numbers told where the money came from," said Samuel. "From reading his medical records, it seems he was a real basket case, barely functional. He was so disturbed he never spent a cent. He converted practically all his earnings from the engraving shop into cash and deposited it in a jar at Mr. Song's. He slept in a closet, and he ate at the social functions he sneaked into. No wonder his liver was shot to shit, as the autopsy disclosed. He had severe mental problems and had even had several electric shock treatments at the V.A. hospital. He was also on heavy medication. I admit he fooled me, I believed all his stories."

"Do you think Virginia knew all that?" asked Blanche.

"She not only knew it but took advantage of it."

"How do you know that for sure?" asked Melba.

"Because in Chinatown all is known. There was a hole-in-the-wall Chinese teashop right down the street from Mathew's apartment on Grant Avenue. The owner, May Tan, told me that the two of them spent hours in her place over a period of about a year while all this was going on. Virginia always paid. Reginald just sat there drinking tea, smoking, and unloading his problems on Virginia, sometimes breaking down and sobbing. May said that Virginia was a good interrogator. The Chinese know these things. She figures he was putty in her hands."

# The Chinese Jars

"I still don't understand why he was killed," said Melba.

"According to Dong Wong," said Samuel, as he rolled his drink in his right hand and took a swig, crunching an ice cube with his teeth, "she got Reginald to do the dirty work of blackmailing Xsing Ching, the Chinese art dealer, and collecting the money. He turned it over to her when they were an item. But as always happens when there's that much at stake, he wanted more money to keep quiet."

"So he started blackmailing her," said Melba.

"Exactly. It's also possible that was just a story she made up. Maybe she planned it that way all along. We'll never know for sure, even if she writes her memoirs. At first she gave him three emeralds that she'd gotten from Colombia. We found them in Reginald's jar at Mr. Song's, along with $10,000 he'd saved, but it seems that Reginald also wanted half the $50,000 they'd taken from Xsing Ching. So Virginia told Dong Wong to get rid of Reginald. Dong and another Chinese thug pushed him in front of a trolley bus."

"Poor devil. I had no idea he was so disturbed," said Blanche.

"I want to ask a favor of you Melba," said Samuel.

"Whatever you want, son."

"The medical examiner changed the cause of death on Reginald's certificate. It doesn't read suicide anymore. Now it says it was at the hands of others. He'll turn the body over to me for burial, and the county will pay the cost. I'd like you to accompany me so we can give him a decent funeral."

"Of course, it's the least we can do," said Melba.

"You can count on me, too," added Blanche. "Is there more about the case you want to tell us?"

"I think you know the rest. It came out in the newspaper."

"Did you learn how to write like that at Stanford?" asked Melba, laughing.

Samuel wanted to ignore her comment, but couldn't help smiling.

"Did you know that all my columns were translated into Chinese and run in the local Chinatown paper?" said Samuel, standing up and stretching.

"I had no idea," said Melba, as she and Blanche stared at each other incredulously.

"You mentioned Mr. Song. Did he have anything to do with any of these crimes?" asked Blanche, who was paying very close attention. The sleeves of her sweatshirt were rolled up, her elbows rested on the round table, and her hands were firmly on her cheeks.

"No way. He's an honest broker. He watches out for people's money and possessions in Chinatown, and in some ways he's thought of as the ancient magistrate."

"What on earth do you mean by that?" asked Melba, scratching her blue-gray hair and squinting, while taking a puff on her Lucky Strike.

"Chinese people have a real fascination with detective stories, and this is from at least the sixth century on, from what I understand."

"You're pulling our leg," said Melba, smirking.

"No. Seriously. They love them, and they have a great reverence for honesty and impartial judgment."

"What's that got to do with Mr. Song?" asked Blanche.

"He's perceived in the community as a fair arbiter of justice. That's why people trust him with their money and no one tries to rob him. The first ancient magistrate was named Judge Dee, who supposedly existed in the sixth century. He was the prosecutor, the investigator, and the judge, all wrapped into one.

"A Dutch diplomat named Robert Van Gulik did a lot of research and recently published a series of Chinese mystery stories, based on this Judge Dee, in English, no less. He changed the setting to the sixteenth and seventeenth centuries, but we know that the judge existed long before that. The difference between their culture and ours was that Judge Dee solved the mysteries by divination."

"What does that mean?' asked Blanche.

"That means he used inductive or intuitive reasoning, like Melba does," said Samuel.

"You mean he guessed," laughed Melba.

"He used educated guesses."

"Was Song the real detective who solved this case?" asked Blanche.

"I wouldn't say that. But maybe the people in Chinatown believe it was him because, as I said, he's held in such high esteem in the community, and because those Chinese detective stories are part of their culture, he fits the bill."

"Maybe you should change your profession, Samuel, and start writing mysteries with Mr. Song as the detective who solves them." What do you think about that?" said Melba.

They all laughed. While Melba and Samuel clinked beer bottles and whiskey glass, Excalibur tried to jump onto Samuel's lap. He put his drink down and a serious look came over his face.

"No, never," he said, shaking his head and blushing, with his gaze fixed on Melba. "I've got my hands full just trying to report what happens without trying to invent it."

"Never say never," said Melba, winking.